SO THIS WAS HELEN O'MALLOCK. . .

She lay in an invalid's chair near the window. When Weldon came closer to meet her outstretched hand, he saw a pale face with shadows of weakness beneath the eyes. Hopelessly beautiful he thought her; more beautiful than any woman—except Francesca Laguarda. Laguarda was like a flaming light; and Helen O'Mallock something crystal through which light may shine, something pure and clear.

Weldon's heart ached a little. From both those girls, Helen, the invalid, and Francesca, the criminal, he had a touch of the same emotion. Both seemed beyond human help, but Weldon must try. . .

MAX BRAND

BORDER GUNS

WARNER PAPERBACK LIBRARY

A Warner Communications Company

WARNER PAPERBACK LIBRARY EDITION
First Printing: August, 1975

This Warner Paperback Library Edition is published by
arrangement with Dodd, Mead & Company, Inc.

Cover illustration by Carl Hantman

Warner Paperback Library is a division of Warner Books, Inc.,
75 Rockefeller Plaza, New York, N.Y. 10019.

W A Warner Communications Company

Printed in the United States of America

Not associated with Warner Press, Inc. of Anderson, Indiana

1. The Fire Eater

At five thirty Weldon opened his eyes and remained for a time on the flat of his back, arms luxuriously out-spread, while he studied the sagging ceiling above his head and breathed the warm, still air of the late afternoon. His thoughts were adrift. He could not for his life remember the nation, the State, or the town in which he found himself until he had heaved up his head and glanced out the window. The first thing that he saw was the brutal front of Bull Mountain.

He let his head sink back with a sigh of relief into the soft of the pillow. He was at San Trinidad, then, but little wonder that he needed to be reminded of the locality—so many places had flicked under his eyes of late, like cards under a thumb. Closing his eyes again, he let their names and their faces slip through his mind like water through a flume. And then he smiled. To lie with vacant mind, to think busily, passively to recollect, were all pleasant to Weldon. He could enjoy life for its own sake, unpointed, unmoralized, and all the functions of life were sweet to him. In digestion he could have rivaled a goat, in nerves, a fat-sided bull, calm lord of the pasture. To eat, to sleep, even to breathe, were delightful occupations for Weldon.

So he was in no haste now to rise. To another the heat in that little whitewashed chamber would have been as oppressive as a closed oven, but Weldon reveled in its very intensity, which relaxed muscles and brain.

But eventually hunger began to grow on him. He stretched out his hand to the door and drew it open.

"Food!" called Weldon, and the echo roared down the hall.

He closed his eyes again, and waited.

At length he heard the whispering of skirts. A Mexican chambermaid tapped at the open door—entered. Chambermaids are not bashful, as a rule, but he could feel the timidity of this one in her pausing steps as she came in.

"Señor?"

"No spik English?" invited Weldon.

"No, señor. *Il padre*—"

"Let your father be," said Weldon, in very fair Spanish.

He opened his eyes at last and looked up to her. She was almost unreasonably pretty!

The thought of food dropped from the mind of Weldon.

What would the señor have?

"One thing at a time!" said Weldon, and continued to survey her, not with rude inquiry—almost as he would look at a charming picture.

Then he sang softly, just above his breath:

"Eyes like the evening, and throat like the dawn!"

She blushed, and Weldon smiled kindly upon her.

Was the señor hungry? He was. What would he have? Anything in the house that was good. There were frijoles, then, of course. Equally of course, there were tortillas. In all Mexico there were no frijoles more excellent than the thin, white wafers which her mother patted out with her own authentic hands! There was some flesh of kid, ready for cooking. Cut small, and turned on many little spits, it could be roasted and ready in a few minutes. As for a bath, two strong *mozos* would carry up the water in buckets and he could have the whole of the tin tub in the adjoining room filled. It would be almost enough to swim in!

She left. The voice of Weldon pursued her gently:

"Eyes like the evening, and throat like the dawn!"

He heard her hesitate in the hall and then go on more slowly; so he sat up with a little chuckle.

"San Trinidad," murmured Weldon, "I like you fine!"

Afterwards he stood in the tin tub in the adjoining

room while the two admiring and awe-stricken *mozos* poured bucket after bucket of cold water over his great white shoulders, over his tides of quivering muscles.

When he had rubbed himself dry and dressed, he descended to the patio of the hotel, with his spurs clinking softly at every step. Golden spurs—how they flashed and glimmered as he crossed the open space into the sun!

It was a blasting, blazing heat. It turned the red roofs into red flame; it turned the white walls into white fire. But Weldon did not avoid it. He stood still in the center of the patio, and taking off his sombrero he allowed the hand of the sun to be laid upon him with all its force.

From the shadows of a vine-draped corner a little man with a thin, brown face said almost peevishly, in English: "Now, you'd better watch yourself, son. You'll be collecting sunstroke."

"Thanks," said Weldon. "But I need a sun bath."

He strolled over to one of the little tables that stood within the colonnade and there he lolled in a chair that creaked under his weight but managed to sustain it.

"It kills germs," said Weldon.

He had a way of doing that—completing a sentence or a speech in detached sections. He regarded the little man with his characteristic smile, genial, twinkling, a little stupid, as though he included every one among the good things of life.

Steaming frijoles wrapped in thin gray tortillas were brought to him. He began to eat, unhurryingly, vastly.

The little man with the thin, brown face behind his Mexican cigar raised his brows at this heap of disappearing food. Then he shifted a little in his chair, and he twitched the shoulder nearest to Weldon nervously.

The frijoles and the tortillas disappeared. Then came more tortillas and a great dish of roasted kid chopped into square chunks and toasted brown before an open fire. There was a dish of red sauce also. Into this, Weldon dipped each bit of meat. He was still unhurried, but the food began to disappear as though in a fire. He never crammed his mouth; it simply seemed capable of accommodating any given amount with ease.

The little man could not help but watch. Against his will his head was drawn over his shoulder to stare. He

7

kept snapping head and eyes to the front as though he were shaking off flies. He looked far off and drummed his thin finger tips rapidly on the top of the table, but still his eyes were drawn back to the meal which Weldon was making.

Weldon raised a special bit on the end of his knife. It was charred a trifle at the edges; the rest was thickly encrusted with brown; the red sauce dripped from it.

"Have some," invited Weldon.

The little man snapped around in his chair.

"Young man," he said, "am I old enough to tell you something?"

"Advice?" murmured Weldon. "The man that won't take free advice—he'll have to pay high for repentance."

"Well," began the other.

"Advice?" reiterated Weldon. "Advice is experience, done in shorthand."

"It is," said the other, "and therefore—"

The slow-speaking Weldon went on: "Good advice is better'n an eye in the hand."

"Of course it is, young man, and I want to tell you—"

"Him that won't be advised," went on Weldon in his soft and genial voice, "can't be helped."

"Go on, go on, go on!" said the other peevishly. "Finish up all that you've got to say on the subject. I can wait! I can wait!"

"I'd take advice from any man, as if he was my father," said Weldon. "Advice is better than whipping. And they say that the worst men may give the best advice!"

He smiled kindly upon the other.

"Are you gonna have some of this roast kid with me?"

The little man snapped his fingers. He was almost in a rage.

"No!" he cried. "I'm not going to have any of it! And another thing—that red sauce—you know what that is?"

Weldon hesitated, and then with his impervious good-nature he said: "Tastes like boiled down fire, partner. What might you think about it?"

The little man opened his eyes. He had a thin beard which gave a pointed, old-fashioned, almost sinister look to his face. The beard now quivered as he paused for words.

"Then why in heaven's name d'you eat it? It makes my tongue raw just to watch you!" he declared. "It makes the lining of my inwards curl up and shrivel off in chunks."

Weldon placed the debated morsel in his mouth. Yet he spoke around it, with no seeming difficulty:

"Does it, now?" said he. "Now, I'll tell you how it appears to me: Pretty near everything is good if you take it the right way—and if not—"

"Hello!" said the other. "Christian Science?"

"Why not?" suggested Weldon. "It's true that all of them that carry long knives ain't cooks. But you gotta teach a cook in his kitchen, not at the dinin' table. So I aim to take what I get."

The little man shuddered. He supported his head with both hands. His lips quivered around the cigar; rapid jets of smoke panted forth before his face, and through the smoke his eyes blinked at Weldon.

"When I think of what the inside of your stomach must be like!" sighed he.

"Never had a stomach ache in my life," said Weldon.

And he finished off both meat and sauce by rolling the last chunk of roasted flesh in the red liquid, covering it so thickly that he had to keep the morsel spinning on the way to his lips to retain the covering sauce.

The little man refused to see this dreadful concoction swallowed. He actually covered his eyes with both hands, but he could not help lowering those hands cautiously—just in time to see the act of swallowing performed.

He made a soft, choking sound, left his chair, took a few hurried paces back and forth, and then sat down again with a jar, and began to stare openly at Weldon.

2. A Free Man

The chambermaid—she seemed the servant of all work —stood before Weldon. She picked up the stack of empty dishes. But her wonder made her open-mouthed. She looked under the table; she glanced around the patio as though in search of a stray dog who could have had a portion of this huge meal; she even eyed the pockets of Weldon with some suspicion.

He turned them inside out.

At that, she put up her pretty hands and laughed.

"But no, señor. Only—it is wonderful!"

"There's something else to come," said Weldon.

"And that, señor?"

"You have beer?"

"Yes, señor."

"You keep it in your cellar?"

"Yes, señor."

"And is the cellar cool?"

"It drips with coolness! It is like ice. Even thinking about it makes one shiver!"

"Go down there and shiver a little for my sake," said Weldon. "Go down there and put your hands on the bottles until you find the one with the most chill in it. Bring that back to me, and bring three or four more bottles along with you."

She went away.

"Man, man," murmured the stranger, "aren't you burning up? Isn't there smoke in your throat and sparks in your eyes?"

Weldon looked upon him with perfect calm and rolled a cigarette with one hand. There was no haste in that gesture. And yet one twist of the fingers seemed to level the tobacco, fold in the paper edge, and complete the rolling. Weldon brushed the loose flap of the thin, brown paper across the tip of his tongue. He lighted a match, and it seemed to the stranger that half the length of the cigarette was drawn into those big lungs in a single breath. A raw, ugly stub of red cinders thrust itself out at the end of the cigarette, the paper curling back rapidly at its base.

"By heck," said the other, moistening his own dry lips and nervously tossing his cigar away, "I think you'll choke —and I almost hope that you do!"

"Friend," said Weldon—and as he began to speak the smoke commenced to issue from his lips in curls and wisps, and thin, blue-white puffs, and then in great, gushing torrents and clouds—"friend, I'm getting ready for a perfect minute. I'm putting the top on the mountain. Everything has got to be perfect. And then—and then—"

The girl appeared, loaded with bottles.

She set them on the table—six—side by side.

"Drink quickly," said the little stranger, fidgeting again in his chair. "I—I want to hear that beer hiss as it goes down."

"Patience, patience," murmured Weldon. "Patience makes perfect! Which is the coldest bottle, my dear?"

"This, señor. This, I think!"

"But we must know," said Weldon. "Otherwise, there'd be a perfect opportunity not perfectly used! That would be a shame, I'd say. How about you, partner. Do you drink with me?"

"Drink beer—that thin, bitter stuff," said the little man with violence. "I wouldn't taste it for thousands of dollars!"

"Wouldn't you now?" said Weldon. "Every man has got to ride his own trail. But when I think"—here he opened the bottle, pulling off the clamped metal cap with his unaided finger tips—"but when I think of what this bottle of beer is going to mean to me—"

"Oh, drink it, drink it, drink it, will you?" snapped the little stranger. "It gets on my nerves. Your throat will be

11

raw! It must be raw now! It's pickled as if it had been soaked in lye!"

"To you, my beautiful," said Weldon to the girl.

She clasped her hands and bowed to him.

"To you, to your eyes, to your lips, to your heart—"

He tipped the bottle.

Gurgling flowed the amber liquor.

The little man stared, stirred, half rose from his chair.

"Ah," said Weldon, and set down the empty bottle.

"My word!" said the little man.

"And now," said Weldon, "here's to make perfect, more perfect. Here's to the cook, bless her! And here's to the sauce that she served to me!"

The second bottle followed the first with equal speed. And when a single draught had emptied it, Weldon laid hold on a third.

"Man, man!" cried the little stranger in some uneasiness, "you'll burst yourself wide open!"

"You see my drink, but you don't see my thirst," answered Weldon mildly. "I had inside of me a desert of sand, under a sun at noon. Even the lizards were afraid to leave the shadows, and the cactus shriveled and began to smoke, and the buzzards staggered in the open air, and the bald-headed eagle put his head under his wing—"

"Oh, darn your desert!" snapped the other.

"But I've flooded the outer edges of that desert, and now there's only one dry place—right in the center, which I'm going to cover this time—if my aim is good! To you, beautiful, and the cook, and the motherland that bore the pair of you!"

The third bottle went down like the other two. Weldon leaned back in his chair and rolled another cigarette.

"And you ain't in any pain, I suppose?" snarled the other.

"No, Mr. Dickinson," said Weldon. "Not a mite. Will you smoke with me?"

Dickinson snapped his fingers, not once, but two or three times, like the rapid popping of crackers on the Fourth of July.

"You knew me all the time!" he said. "By heck, you knew me all the time!"

"Why, everybody knows you," smiled Weldon. "Everybody knows Jim Dickinson. Everybody admires him. Everybody wants to see him—"

"Aw, shut up, Weldon," said Mr. Dickinson.

He took out another cigar, lighted the wrong end of it, and struggled vainly to make it go. He was too excited to notice his mistake.

"How did you come?" asked Dickinson.

"All kinds of ways. Partly by horse, and partly by foot, and partly by train—"

"I don't believe it," said Dickinson. "I have had every train searched! Every train this side of—"

"Did you have your men look carefully at the engineers?" asked Weldon.

"Ha? What?" cried Dickinson. "Darnation! I don't believe it! What did you do with the man you displaced, then?"

"I put him to sleep in the tender."

Dickinson groaned.

"Well, well, well," he said. "And here you are! I don't believe it. I don't believe my eyes!"

"Why'd you come here, then, if you didn't expect me to get through?"

"I came on the odd chance. The thousandth chance I wasn't overlooking anything."

"Well," said Weldon, "so we meet at last—in Mexico!" The other writhed.

"When you have a chance," said Weldon, "look over to the entrance to the patio. There's a picture walking in. Spanish picture. Maybe Italian. Maybe a dash of French. Ain't she a sweetheart, Dickinson?"

"Why don't you talk English?" asked the other with irritation. "Why do you always use that hodgepodge of range slang and nonsense when you know better?"

"Talking, or walking," said Weldon, "I always aim to take the shortest cut."

He let his gaze drift past the other. At the patio entrance was a long, gray automobile, low of line, mighty of hood. The throbbing of the engine really could not be heard. There was a mere pulse in the air.

"That's a he-man's car," said Weldon. "And look what come out from under the wheel of it."

It was a girl, now slipping out of her duster and tossing it into the abandoned seat. She came across the court-yard with a light, rapid step, paused, glanced over the upper windows, and then entered the hotel.

"Eyes like the evening, and throat like the dawn!" sang Weldon gently, and then letting a great voice ring and boom like thunder, he repeated the line.

"You know her, do you?" asked Dickinson. "You're sending her a signal, are you? Mixed up in that business, too, eh?"

He nodded his head vigorously, and glared again at his younger companion.

"Know her?" said Weldon. "At least, I'll never forget her! Did you see her eyes?"

"I've seen her eyes," snarled Dickinson. "Like the evening? Like midnight, I'd say, with a murder thrown in for salt! You dunno her name?"

"No idea of it."

"That's Francesca Laguarda."

"Italian, eh?"

"*I* don't know. And I don't care. Only, how I'd like to jail her!"

"Is she crooked, Dickinson?"

"Crooked?" exclaimed Dickinson. "Crooked?"

He could only repeat the word; further definition choked him.

"I've seen them East," said Weldon, "and I've seen them West. But I never seen the mate of her."

"That's college grammar, I suppose?" suggested the irritable little man.

"It's post-graduate grammar," said Weldon, always with his smile.

"Well," snapped Dickinson, "I might as well tell you. They wired to me last night. Baxter is dead!"

"And now they'll want to hang me, of course?"

"They ought to, of course," said Dickinson with a grumble. "But that fool Baxter, just before he went out, confessed that it had been a frame to get you, that you'd simply fought your way out of it. And I suppose I gotta tell you that you're a free man to go where you please again!"

14

3. Where a Pretty Face Takes You

To this intelligence, Weldon responded by tilting up his head and watching for a long moment the swaying tendrils of the vine that hung like a suspended green shower before them.

"What a lucky thing," he said, "that Baxter didn't confess at once!"

"Lucky?" cried angry Mr. Dickinson. "Lucky?"

Suddenly his attitude changed. He slipped lower in his chair.

"Go on and explain that, Weldon."

"Why, man, then I never should have seen San Trinidad this trip! I never should have sat here and eaten roast kid and drunk beer and talked to the great Dickinson!"

He waved a big hand and smiled again, genially but a little blankly.

Dickinson stood up. All his movements were done with a jump. He leaned his shoulder against a thick, adobe pillar and looked at the other.

"How old are you, Weldon?"

"Just a few years younger than you think."

"By heck, young man, there's times when I think you're not out of swaddlin' clothes!"

Already the second cigarette was gone. The third was made and lighted.

"You'll ruin your lungs," said Dickinson.

Weldon blew to the ceiling a great cloud of white.

"Never bother me," he said.

The dyspeptic face of Dickinson wrinkled fiercely. He smoothed it with his hand again.

"I don't suppose so! I don't suppose so," said he. "A man of brass. Hammered brass! Hammered brass! Never a headache or a stomach ache or a chill or a fever in your life?"

"Never," nodded Weldon.

"Why do you do it?" asked Dickinson savagely. "Why? Why?"

"Drink beer?" asked Weldon.

"You know what I mean. Don't dodge around corners when I'm talking to you! Don't try any smart shifts and tricks with me, young man!"

Big Weldon submitted to this bullying with perfect calm. His eyes were like the eyes of a well-fed ox as they rested upon the face of his companion.

"For one thing, I hate work," he admitted.

"Just want to be a weight and a drain on society, eh?" asked Dickinson in the same savage manner.

He continued, expanding on his thought: "It's not right nor fair. We have enough trouble with the normal criminal classes. Half-wits, only shrewd to do wrong. Undernourished brains. Pathological cases that ought to be behind hospital walls, not behind bars; ignorant Latins and Orientals; dope fiends, drunkards, weak wits of all kinds. We have our share of trouble with those people. A criminal is crazy. I've always said so. I've always known so. But you're not crazy, Weldon. You have a good brain. That brain was well trained. Cost thousands to equip you mentally. What do you do with that equipment? Chuck it away!

"Worse than that! It's like using a fine battleship for petty, sneaking piracy! Why, if you're going to be a criminal, why don't you do something big? Why don't you smash the Bank of England, or rip the heart out of the United States mint, or burgle Wall Street—or something like that?"

"I never was inspired," said Weldon, his faint smile returning. "You're putting good ideas in my head!"

"Instead of that—why, you're like a bunch of tumbleweed, rolling where the wind blows you! Down to Mexico, up to Canada, a card game here, a gun fight there, knife battle yonder! And why? What do you gain? What do you put in the bank?"

"I live," said Weldon in a mild answer.

Dickinson pointed a trembling, bony forefinger at him.

"You've got no self-respect!" he declared.

"Because," said Weldon, "no one ever takes me seriously."

His glance wandered toward the upper range of windows that looked over the patio. A pair of shutters was being folded back. But afterwards, the window remained shut. Who should want to let in the light and not the air, at this time of day? For the sun was falling deeper to the west. The sting was lost from its rays. Rich, sleepy warmth exhaled from the ground, from the walls, and golden languor overspread the skies.

"And why don't people take you seriously?"

"There's my name," said Weldon.

"A good name. Why not? Used to be an honest name!" said Dickinson. "Until you began to roll it in the dust!"

He added with his usual snap: "Lorimer Everett Weldon. What can be wrong with the name?"

"Don't you see? The initials spell a word. Lew! Well, when a man is called Lew, you can't take him seriously. Can you?"

"Ah, nonsense! You have to get your smile out of everything. You begin with yourself and you never stop laughing!"

"Seriously."

"You're called other things than Lew."

"Yes. Big Boy. Blondy. The Big Kid. Serious names, Dickinson? I think not. The world takes me easily. I take the world easily. That's all."

"Well, well, well," said Dickinson. "And what do you want out of life?"

"The thing that lies around the corner."

"What lies around the corner?"

"I don't know," said Weldon.

"What?"

"If I knew, I wouldn't want it!"

Dickinson blew out a sharp whistle, of disgust, impatience—and of understanding also.

He sat down suddenly. The chair jarred and shook with his suddenness.

"I could use you," he said slowly. "I could use you, boy!"

"Hunting crooks?" asked Weldon.

"I could use you!" sighed Dickinson, and made no other answer.

"Who is the beautiful child with the big, gray car?" asked Weldon.

"What child?" snapped the other. "Child?"

"Francesca Laguarda, you called her."

"Child?" said Dickinson. "A cold-blooded hawk! Child? There's no child in her. Some women never are young. She was grown up when she was born."

"Like Athena," said Weldon.

"Like what?"

"Nothing. She's a lovely thing."

"All hell-cats are lovely."

The glance of Weldon strayed toward the recently unshuttered window. The glass of that window was of the worst quality, rolled unevenly, filled with waves, so that the high-lights were streaked across its surface irregularly. Nevertheless, behind the glass in the deep darkness of the chamber he saw a form. It looked like a daylight ghost.

"I've only seen her face. Perfect face! Perfect, perfect!" sighed Weldon.

"I've seen her hands, too," said Dickinson, "and I've seen her handiwork."

"Exquisite hands!" said Weldon, luxuriously closing his eyes and dreaming aloud. "Slender, pink-tipped fingers, soft and strong. Easily flowing lines, and a round, small wrist, with a blue vein shining through crystal—"

"Oh, shut up!" said Dickinson. "It makes me ache to hear you talk like that!"

"I was thinking aloud," said Weldon.

"That's why women are the worst criminals," said Dickinson. "They carry their shield with them. A man, honest or crooked, is a thing without a face or a feature. It's the heart and soul that makes a man. A woman's two thirds flesh and one third mind, and when that mind is bad, it still can dodge behind the body. Men prefer a woman to be a little bad. It's sauce to the dish. You, Weldon, you'd prefer 'em that way!"

"Yes," said Weldon thoughtfully. "A little sainted, or a little the reverse. No doubt you're right. But I never thought of it before. You cut at once to the quick of things, Dickinson!"

Like a fish rising through dark water, the form behind the window glimmered closer to the glass. Like a fish sinking again, it receded and was blotted out completely by the winking glass surface and the thick shadows inside.

Weldon stood up.

"Gonna take a walk," said he.

"Where? Where?" asked little Dickinson.

"I dunno. Come along?"

The two strolled across the patio. Rather, Weldon strolled, and Dickinson walked jerkily beside him, hurrying ahead, half turning and waiting for the other to catch up, like a child leading a great mastiff on a leash.

At the entrance to the patio, they paused beside the big, long, low gray car. It had four seats, fitted with armrests. A heavy luggage carrier was fastened on behind. The rear seats were set inside the rear axle, so that one could be sure of not too much lurch and pitch in taking a corner fast.

Weldon leaned thoughtfully on the front door.

"Eighty still," said he. "This baby was hot, a while ago. Eighty still, says the thermometer."

"She never cuts down below sixty," said Dickinson. "That's her idea of a slow pleasure spin. Ordinarily, she prefers something around ninety and a hundred."

"A hundred?" asked Weldon. "That's stepping!"

He opened the hood and looked at the engine.

"Nice, little, old straight eight," said he.

"No name of a maker, though," snapped Dickinson. "No name of a maker anywhere."

"It's Italian, old son," said Weldon. "And it's a special. No wonder she'll do a hundred! And then a little bit more, I make my guess! A little bit more! Does she need a hundred, Dickinson?"

"Does a bird need wings?" retorted the man of the law

19

bitterly. "And even a hundred ain't going to be enough for her, one day."

He knocked a small fist against his breast. His eyes were so fierce that Weldon had a sudden picture of the little man furnished with vast, condor wings, splitting the air at dazzling speed, and, far beneath, an automobile glistening and streaming along a winding road.

"You haven't told me what she does," said Weldon. "Do you mind telling?"

"If I knew," said the other, "I wouldn't mind telling. I'd even put it in the papers. If I knew! I only know a few of the footnotes about her. What would any woman or man want with a car like this on the border—unless he was a millionaire and a speed fool?"

"Smuggling?" said Weldon.

"Wonderful brain!" sneered Dickinson.

His bright eyes fastened on the face of Weldon and roved as he read.

"Guess I'll ramble along," said Weldon.

"Where, man? Where is there to walk in a town like this?"

"Oh, just around the corner."

"Oh—you be darned!" snapped Dickinson, and turned upon his heel.

There was a whisper in the air. The girl was coming back toward the car. "Good evening, Mr. Dickinson!" she said.

He made no pretense of cordiality. He glared back at her in hatred just pointed and sharpened by a touch of curiosity.

"Humph," said Dickinson.

It made no difference to her or to her smile.

Weldon, still lingering, opened the door for her, and she thanked him with the most direct, the most friendly of smiles.

She settled herself at the wheel, pressed a lever and pushed back the sliding seat an inch.

"You know cars?" she said to Weldon, still with that friendly smile.

He closed the door without a click—only a smooth, powerful pressure of his hand.

"Now and then I know them a little," said he.

"You'd like this."

"I would," said he.

To take his eyes from her was like taking his hand from a crown of rubies. He stepped back and raised his hat. The engine whirred, the big car whined in first, moved off, and then as the gears shifted without a jar into second it gathered momentum and swerved around the corner. Thereafter, he heard the faint, thrilling whisper of high speed and the pulse and throb of the great motor living in the air.

He replaced the hat.

Opposite him an old woman was squatted in her doorway, patting out wet tortillas for the evening meal. She did not look at her handiwork, but she grinned broadly at him.

He crossed the street and leaned a hand against the side of the house.

"You smile at me, mother?"

Her fat face wrinkled with silent laughter.

"Why not, señor?"

"Of course there's no reason."

She raised her hand, the palm of it glistening from the wet corn meal she had been working.

"Yesterday I was a beautiful young creature, too. I was a fool, though." She added: "But wise or foolish, this is where a pretty face takes you!"

She began to pat the tortillas again.

Weldon walked on around the corner.

4. On Top with the Danger

Around the corner he found Miguel Cabrero's. It was a twilight house. In the day, neither heat nor light could enter. In the night the small, unshaded, electric lights let one see the faces of the cards and the spots on the dice, and that was all. Only at the roulette wheels there were extra flares of illumination. But even there the light constantly altered, for the current was not stable, and the bulbs flared brilliant white or sank to dull yellow by turns, which gave the entire chamber an unreal appearance.

Nothing could be really cool in San Trinidad. Every opening of the street door let in a moist flood of warmth. But there were big electric fans purring like cats, here and there, casting forth gales as the fans swung slowly to and fro, with human hesitancies and resumptions of the rhythm.

For a long time, Weldon did not play. Every day, to him, had its own taste. Now he was tasting San Trinidad, slowly, carefully. And like a taster of wine, he did not attempt to gulp it down—on trust!

He had a glass of Mexican brandy before him—that pale fire which eats the brain! But to Weldon it was just right. Its odd, green taste finished off the picture his eyes beheld. It was not so much taste in his mouth as a flavor in his brain. He was stepping deeper and deeper into San Trinidad. He was walking around the corner!

A boy came by his corner table, showering wet bran and wood shavings upon the floor; others followed to sweep it up. They would keep up this work all the evening. It cooled the air, and that was its importance rather than an attempt at cleanliness.

Miguel Cabrero's gathered its crowd. It was not a very large crowd, but it was spending money. There is always money to spend in the Mexican towns near the American border. Most of those present were Mexicans of the middle class. There were not a few somber-faced peons, too. And there was a liberal sprinkling of Americans here, also. One could tell them by their voices. They were all well-behaved; they spoke very quietly, like men accustomed to win and lose money. But they spoke with a harsh monotony of sound, coming up from deep within and resounding through the nose. As for the Mexicans, there was a song in every throat.

They talked rapidly but sweetly. It was like the chatter of women at an afternoon tea, but more subdued, more somber.

So Weldon drank his brandy and the scene, and digested it, and was more and more pleased. He had seen such places before, many of them. But to Weldon every door of life opened upon a new room, and every moment was the crossing of a world. He never accused existence of dullness. He accused himself!

The roulette wheels were occupying most of the attention on this night. Every now and then the crowd around one of them would leave the wheel and flow back to the long bar which glimmered sedately at the rear of the room. Someone had made a big winning. Then the crowd flowed back. Bets were doubled. The wheel recouped its loss and grew fat again.

"You're Weldon. My name is Cunningham. May I sit down with you a moment?"

"Certainly," said Weldon.

The newcomer raised his hand. A waiter was conjured out of shadows.

"Beer, if you please."

The waiter vanished.

"I can't do that, you know," said Cunningham, pointing to the glass of brandy. "Not in this weather!"

He passed a handkerchief across his forehead. He was very hot. He wore a suit of linen. Where the coat bound his strong shoulders there were wet marks.

It was a fine forehead that he showed. A high-light gleamed on a knob above either eye; surely this man was not a fool. He was about thirty-five, with a brown, rugged, honest face and extremely steady eyes.

"You don't know me?"

"I don't," said Weldon. "Smoke?"

"I'll smoke my own."

He took out a small, silver box and rolled a cigarette with long-shredded tobacco. When he lighted it, the faint, sweet aroma of Turkish tobacco was in the air.

"I know about you, of course," said Cunningham.

Weldon waited. He was one of those rare men who can be comfortably silent. There was always that genial half-smile on his lips and in his kindly eyes, uncritical but observant.

"And so I'll ask you first if you're doing anything?"

"Not a thing."

"Do you want to work?"

"I never do."

"I understand, of course. Not really work."

"Well," said Weldon, "I love to be tempted, and I love to fall."

Cunningham smiled. He was a handsome fellow when he smiled in this fashion, and his appreciative eyes ran over Weldon—hands, shoulders, neck, and jaw.

"I run liquor, Chinamen, opium, and such stuff north across the river. I run cash, guns, ammunition, and a few luxuries like that south across the river. That's my business."

He spoke without any secretive lowering of his voice. The approaching waiter was almost sure to have heard the last part of the speech, Weldon thought.

"It's interesting work," said Cunningham, taking up his glass of beer, and surrounding its coldness with both hands. "I think you would like it."

"In part, perhaps," said Weldon.

"Of course," said Cunningham. "I wouldn't ask you to work on the opium and dope."

"Thanks," said Weldon.

"But the Chinamen and the liquor."

"Honest liquor—and honest Chinamen?" smiled Weldon.

"The liquor is honest," qualified Cunningham.

"I don't know," murmured Weldon.

Cunningham waited. After a moment, when there was no clearing of the thought in Weldon's eyes, he said:

"I'd like to have you understand that the money would be worth while. We pay different sorts of prices. Not very much to the rank and file. For the chiefs, who handle the greatest dangers, money is hardly any object."

Then he explained: "Of course, you would start at the top."

"With the dangers," smiled Weldon.

"Naturally, that's what you want! And that's why we want you, too!"

"Will you wait a few minutes?"

"A few hours—for you, Weldon!"

"I have fifteen hundred dollars. Are these games straight?"

"Cabrero is crooked. The games may be straight."

"Very well. Coming along?"

"I do my gambling in another way," smiled Cunningham, and Weldon left him at the table.

5. Fortune's Wheel

Weldon, going toward the nearest roulette table, passed one of the boys who constantly swept the floor of the gaming hall. He beckoned to the youngster and placed a broad-faced, silver peso in his grimy palm.

"There is still a man at my table. Americano. If he leaves that table, watch where he goes. Follow. Come back to tell me!"

The boy did not glance toward the table. There was simply a steely little glitter in his eyes, and he nodded, full of his work. Weldon went on toward the table. He watched only a moment, placed five hundred on the red, won, and put the doubled stake on the black. He won again. He placed the total on odd and once more he had doubled his stake. He had five thousand dollars in place of fifteen hundred, and this had been won in the course of a very few moments.

The other gamblers were watching him like hawks. They were preparing to follow his guidance, for a man whose luck is coming in is like a ship coming into port. It should be followed by all hungry birds of the air.

He began to play single numbers, thrice on the nine, thrice on the seven, thrice on the twenty-seven. The money was swallowed again by the machine, a hundred dollars at a time. The croupier, his face like yellow wax, emotionless as a mummy, watched and chanted in a droning voice. Those who followed the play of Weldon were already broke or discouraged by nine straight losses.

He lost four thousand dollars in a breath. He lost another thousand. Then the eighteen won for him. Thirty-five hundred back, on that stroke, and the croupier raised his dull, flameless eyes and looked at him steadily for half a second as the wheel spun once more.

A thousand on the red. Black won!

A thousand on the red. Black won.

A thousand on the black, and red won.

Another thousand on the black, and red won again.

There was a tug at Weldon's arm. He stepped back. The whisper of the boy whom he had hired as a spy barely reached his ear, and no other.

"A brake!" whispered the lad.

Weldon smiled kindly down to him.

"I thought so," said he. "And the gentleman?" For the table where he had sat was now empty.

"He was out at the side door into the alley. I followed. He stood in the gutter and smoked a cigarette. Very soon a señorita passed. She had a heavy mantilla over her head She said three words in English. The señor said three words in English, and she went in. Then he came back. Soon he will be at the table."

At that moment Cunningham reseated himself at the empty table. The boy disappeared in the crowd with an extra peso weighing down his pocket.

But Weldon put his last hundred on odd and smiled as he saw it win, and then doubled on the red. If there was a brake on this machine, they at least intended that he should keep a little money in his pocket.

Most of his thoughts were back at the table with Cunningham, or out yonder in the street, where the señorita in the heavy mantilla had passed by and spoken words of English.

There were many American men in this town; there were few or no American women. He would have given a great deal to have heard the voice of that woman, and he would have wagered more than he had lost at roulette that it was the same voice in which the girl at the wheel of the gray automobile had spoken to him that evening. A rich voice, rather deeply contralto, with the ring of a clear bell on it.

He put a hundred on number seventeen; it was lost.

He put another hundred on number seven. The wheel spun. The ball wavered back and forth from ten to four. Would it drop in seven? Suddenly the wheel slowed. The ball dropped in nine. With a soft hiss the wheel still revolved.

"Nine—black—"

"My friend!" said Weldon.

He had his proof now. There was a brake in that wheel, and the croupier had worked it a little awkwardly in this instance. A roulette wheel has the even movement of a planet. It dies softy, gradually; there is no sudden diminution in its pace, such as that alteration which his keen eye had noted.

"The señor speaks to me?" said the croupier.

He smiled on Weldon; a pretended pity softened his eyes.

"I speak to you. Step here with me."

"A thousand pities! I may not leave my place! It never is so in Cabrero's!"

The hand of Weldon made a little gesture, as of surrender, but coming close to the croupier, it fastened on

27

his shoulder. He was lifted from his little platform to the floor.

"Your wheel carries a brake, friend," said Weldon.

"Dios!" said the croupier.

It was as though a gun had been presented to his head. He writhed, and with his right hand he made an upward stroke at Weldon's body. It was a quick rather than a strong movement, but one does not need great strength to drive a pin-pointed dagger through a man's heart.

Weldon caught the armed hand in mid-air. He turned it with a jerk. There was the grinding sound of a bone breaking. The croupier cried out; the knife tingled on the floor like a musical, little silver bell.

Weldon stood on the platform where the croupier had been. The poor man was staggering toward the wall, one arm dangling, ruined, the other stretched before him, as though he fumbled his way through the dark.

"Friends—gentlemen—this machine is not honest," said Weldon. "There is a brake in it. I propose to examine it and see if I can find the brake. I hope to have your help—"

Help?

The crowd had scattered backwards from him as little waves roll away from a dropped stone in a pool. Voices began to shout. Nine tenths of the lights were snapped out. Only a dim twilight remained, and that dimness showed all the crowd of gamblers making for the doors.

Weldon took hold of the wheel and its stand and pulled upward. It was firm. He sagged his knees and pulled again. The wood parted like thick paper with a screeching sound, and he laid the machine and its pedestal upon one side.

Then he saw that while the crowd flowed outward like water, there were certain men who had not moved. They remained fixed while the torrent flowed around them. Outside in the street the noise of the panic crashed and roared, and voices shrilled with excitement and fear. But these men who had remained now began to converge on Weldon. There were six or seven of them, walking cautiously toward him, and every man was armed.

He dropped on his knees behind the table and opened the stem of the wheel as a boy opens an orange. It was a neat little contrivance, that brake. It would work as

28

delicately as the needle of a seamstress. A clumsy fellow, the croupier, to have put it on with such sudden violence. But perhaps he had grim orders, to lose no more money at that table. In truth, such things will happen at a gambling house!

Weldon picked out the important working parts of the brake and dropped them in his pocket.

Then he looked about him once more. The men were drawing to a rapid focus around him. He crossed his arms and swept his hands up. They came from beneath his armpits, each weighted with a long-barreled, old-fashioned, heavy Colt, single action, the sights and the triggers filed away, the hammers under his thumbs.

"I want no trouble," said Weldon clearly, in Spanish.

"Gringo beast!" said one of the men.

His voice had a sob of rage in it, and he fired point-blank.

Weldon felt a plucking at his shoulder, as though some-one had touched him there to draw his attention. He pitched face downward on the platform, beneath the next table.

"He is mine!" cried a wildly exultant voice.

But there lay Weldon, smiling happily, in the twilight, his guns extended, perfectly steady because of the butts being on the floor. He began to fire at the men's legs, between the knee and the hip. Unless a man is a real fighting hero, a .45-caliber slug placed in such a spot brings him down as though he were struck over the head with a club, and, having fallen, he forgets all about fighting. He feels that he is bleeding to death and shouts for help.

Such shouts rose now. Three men were down, one pitching back upon a dice table and involving it in the ruin of his fall. Footsteps sounded heavily on the floor—footsteps which retreated from Weldon. Then all the lights went out!

The place was pitch black. But in it, like three flashing lights, were the repeated voices of men calling in fear and agony.

Weldon rose to his knees and reloaded his weapons. Then he stood up and walked for the rear of the big room. As he stepped, the little golden spurs chinked and chimed sweetly on his heels, and yet he moved with as much certainty as though he were a stalking cat in the midst of that blackness.

The authorities would be there at once. It was only strange that they did not come sooner, unless they wanted to give the men of Cabrero an ample chance to finish this little business for themselves.

His hand touched the long, cold, smoothly polished bar. At the same time a faint glow, like fire, rang along it. The front door had been opened, and men with strong lights were entering. Weldon ran down the bar, leaped over it, and passed through the door beyond.

He ran through a dense crowd, also standing in darkness.

"The Americano?" someone asked him.

"The police will have him. He's wounded and can't run," said Weldon. He added: "Where is the room of Señor Cabrero? I know the name of this gringo. I want to tell him."

"Ah, it will warm his heart to know that! Come, come!"

One took him actually by the hand and led him through a dark passage. They reached a door, neatly rimmed around with light.

"Here!"

He tapped three times, paused, and tapped again.

"Enter!"

Weldon turned the knob, stepped through, and closed the door quickly behind him.

6. A Talented Man

Outside the door, however, willing to be known for his zealous service, the voice of a man was calling: "Señor, señor. I, Pedro, have brought you this man! He knows the name of the gringo!"

"That is well!" said Cabrero.

Weldon bowed to him.

Cabrero was patting the top of his desk with a fat hand which, when it was spread out flat, had little dimples over the top of each knuckle. Once he had been very small and delicately made, no doubt. As a boy, he must have been a beautiful creature, but he had begun to overflow. His cheeks were round and tight with fat. His eyes were so pouched by it that when he smiled, they disappeared.. Between each button of his waistcoat there was a bulge, and the upper sleeve of his coat was as tight as a sausage. He was so full of curves and his color was so high that he looked rather like a strangely shaped balloon which had just been blown up hard.

"You know this American? You yourself are an American?"

"Ah, yes," said Weldon. "The name of that man is Weldon."

"Why," said the head of the gaming house, smoothing one hand with another, "do you come to tell me about the name of this countryman of yours? Is he an enemy?"

There was much noise and shouting, dim in the distance, behind thick walls.

"Not publicly," said Weldon. "But privately—he has done me a great deal of harm."

31

Cabrero still smoothed his hand.

"I don't understand that," he said. "But I do understand that you want something done to this man?"

"Yes. I do."

"Then, if he escapes, where shall I find him?"

"But how can he escape from the whole police force of this city?"

"It has been done," said Cabrero. His eyes disappeared, but not with a smile. "I have very little time. I am very busy. Where shall I find this man?"

"Here," said Weldon.

"Still in my house?"

"Yes."

"Where in it?"

"Here," said Weldon.

Cabrero opened both his eyes. The lids had to struggle against the incumbent fat.

"*Dios!*" he said beneath his breath.

"I am Weldon," explained the American gently. "I won four thousand at your wheel—honestly. I lost the four thousand and another thousand on top of that. You have a safe behind you."

Cabrero turned gray.

He did not answer. A hand beat on the door: "Señor! Señor! The American, the pig-dog—he is gone!"

Weldon smiled.

"Be gone, fool!" cried Cabrero.

Footfalls retreated.

"Don't hesitate," said Weldon. "I told you what to do."

Steadily, his eyes as unblinking as those of a snake, the Mexican stared at him. There was no gun in the hands of Weldon, and yet Cabrero hesitated to reach for one of his own weapons. There was a button just behind his chair. He could press it by leaning back. There was another button under his foot. He could press that, also.

But both buttons simply brought armed men to his door. That was hardly enough! However, it was better to do what he could. He pressed the button on the floor. He leaned back against the wall. Like a whisper, a bell rang in the distance. He looked earnestly at Weldon. That gentleman's face did not alter.

"And now the safe?"

"Certainly!"

He turned, took a key from his pocket, twisted a knob in the face of the big safe, turned the key, and the door sagged open with the softest of hissing sounds.

"Five thousand," said Weldon gently, as one assisting the memory of a friend, without breaking too roughly upon the current of his thoughts.

"Five thousand, of course," said Cabrero pleasantly.

He counted out the money in crisp, fresh, hundred-dollar bills, American currency. He put the stack on the table and patted it with his hand.

"Will you count it now, my friend?"

"Thank you," said Weldon. "I counted them at the same time that you put them together. Now you may close the door of the safe again."

The color of Cabrero grew more clear and bright. He eagerly obeyed.

"And now, Señor Cabrero, a little note. It will run: 'I, Miguel Cabrero, having taken from Lorrimer Everett Weldon five thousand dollars by means of illegal gambling devices, and in particular by means of a brake on a roulette wheel, have returned the money to him on this day.' That will be all, señor, for the moment."

Cabrero looked down at the desk and folded his hands on top of it. Outside, in the hall, there was the faintest of sounds, a ghost of a noise. But he knew what it meant.

"Well—" he murmured.

He took out a paper and a fountain pen with a thick, flexible, stub point. With this he began to write. It was amazing to see the size of the letters which the little man wrote and the quantity of ink which went into every stroke. Though it flowed freely, he freshened the flow by shaking ink vigorously onto the floor, which already was thickly splattered. Then he took a sheet of fresh, white, blotting paper and passed it over the writing. He looked at the face of the blotter with curiosity. Every letter was well represented, and the writing on the paper had turned a pale blue.

"And that is all?"

"All of this step. Next, we go to look at your stable."

"Ah, well, you want a horse?"

"I think I should have one. Don't you?"

"As you please."

Weldon stepped backwards and opened the door halfway. He did not look out, but continued to gaze at the face of the Mexican, who saw in the hallway half a dozen crowded figures, naked guns in their hands. They had had to do work like this before. And a wave of cruel joy rushed over Miguel Cabrero and almost choked him.

Weldon was saying: "Tell your faithful friends to leave the hall. You are with an honest companion."

Mechanically the words fell from the lips of Cabrero. There was a soft tapping of heels. The hall was empty; a door clicked in the distance.

"So we can go on cheerfully to the stable," continued Weldon calmly. "You, my dear Cabrero, walking always in front, and I behind—to guard your back!"

Cabrero could not keep his upper lip from furling back across his white, glistening teeth. He was very angry indeed!

But he stood up and walked from the room, not in too much haste. He went down the hall. Fear was being born in him, and he was only anxious to see the last of this big demon, this American fiend!

They went from the corridor across an open yard. They entered a low shed. A dozen horses stood there. Weldon looked over them, noting their quarters only.

"Good!" said he. "And now your own horses?"

The lip of Cabrero furled back again, but again he made no sound. He began to tremble with fury greater than his fear, but he went on from the horse shed through a door at the end of it. Here there were six big box stalls; five of them were tenanted. There was an electric light burning over each one, and sauntering past them behind Cabrero, Weldon gave a long glance through each doorway.

Then he returned to a stall where was a tall chestnut, a horse of a weak, faded color.

"This one will do for me," said Weldon.

"*Dios!*" said the gambler through his teeth.

"And what did you pay for this excellent horse, my friend?"

"There stands fifteen hundred dollars in gold!"

"Tut! That is a price and a half! But the honest price?"

"Do you think it pays me to lie to you, you—"

Cabrero clipped down his fat lips and kept the last word from exploding. But his whole face and throat shuddered with his fury.

Weldon passed a hand into his pocket and fingered the recently received bills. Then he took out a sheaf of them and gave them to his companion. "For that price you throw in saddle and bridle, Cabrero?"

Cabrero turned purple as he looked at the money.

"An honest—man!" he said, breathing very hard.

"In spots," smiled the genial Weldon. "Will you saddle him?"

The gambler obeyed.

"Which is the best way out, Cabrero? You will be interested because you are going with me for a step or two."

Cabrero paused. Then it seemed better to take the chance.

"That door leads to an empty alley. You go down it and turn to the left. In five minutes you are out of town."

"Lead the way, then."

They left the shed. Outside, to be sure, there was a little alley, and Weldon sprang into the saddle. Cabrero whirled. He was looking into the muzzle of a .45-caliber Colt. Then he actually laughed aloud.

"'You, señor, are a talented man."

"One cannot live without learning a little," said the American.

Cabrero walked down to the head of the alley. There stretched a dimly winding way to the left, lost among the houses.

"This is the way, Cabrero?"

"Yes. Straight down this alley."

"I'll watch you go back, señor."

Cabrero bowed, turned, and walked without hurrying down the alley. When he had disappeared into the shed, Weldon sent the horse into the winding way, and then he heard from the distance behind him a thin whistle, rapidly repeated.

"He gives the signal!" smiled Weldon, and put the chestnut into a strong gallop.

7. Weldon Leaps

With the first stride, he knew that all was not well. The big horse lunged out his head like the thrust of a piston. Weldon drew hard on the reins—the chestnut merely shook his head and bored harder than before.

They began to fly down the alley. A pile of junk rose around a sharp bend. There was the dangerous glint of old, tin cans. But the chestnut flew by it.

"Good boy! Oh, good boy!" murmured Weldon.

Suddenly the chestnut braced himself. He slid twenty feet through thin, surface sand and brought up inches away from a tall, stone wall. It blocked the whole end of the alley, and Weldon could understand why it was that the gambler invited him to take this way.

He swung the chestnut around, for there might be time to get back across the throat of the passage leading out from the horse shed of Cabrero. But no, that chance was too small!

The wall was at least nine feet high. He cast his hand on it and lightened himself in the saddle, raising himself up. It was a broad wall, but a top stone stirred under his hand. A good, broad wall, at least a foot thick, and made of heavy stones. And yet that topmost one had stirred under his hand!

He laid hold of it; it gritted against its holding mortar and came away, falling with a deep thud on the sand beneath. He gripped the next stone below. It sagged. He pulled again with a force that made the gelding stagger.

But the stone came free. Powdered mortar showered down, and then the masonry on either side of the dislodged bit slipped loose.

Whoever built that wall had scorned the use of honest cement! Weldon laid hold upon it with mighty hands and it crumbled beneath him. A thick heap of stones fell; the chestnut danced uneasily, as his shins were barked by the impacts. But then all progress ended. The wall broadened to more than two feet and its rigid force belittled the might of Weldon. He understood, then. There had been this powerful wall, and the facing on top was merely a sort of palisade to heighten the effect.

There was well over five feet of that massive obstacle. Could the chestnut jump it?

Weldon whirled him away to a sufficient distance. There he sat motionless in the saddle. Behind him, distinctly, he heard a stifled grunt and curse, as of a man who stumbles as he runs. Then he pointed the chestnut, took him firmly in hand and sent him forward.

He knew by the first move that the fellow was a jumper. He went with short, springing bounds, like a rabbit spy-hopping when the hounds are an unknown distance behind. So the chestnut went at the fence.

But, after all, there is a gap between will and performance, and yonder was more than a five-foot wall, with the take-off reasonably slippery sand, littered, moreover, by big, rough-edged stones. As for the landing place on the farther side, it might be in a sheer ditch, for all he knew.

But there was a generous heart in that washed-out chestnut. In that convincing moment, Weldon knew why Cabrero had groaned when this mount was chosen. They shot under the wall; Weldon touched the tender flanks with the spurs and swayed his weight forward. Gallantly rose the chestnut, ears flattened, powerful quarters thrusting mightily. They soared high, and yet not high enough. Hanging in mid-leap, Weldon saw the splotched blackness of a garden beneath him—a soft landing, if ever they could make it!

But how would this fellow get his hind legs over? Then he felt the hitch of the loin muscles. He could see as though he were standing at one side the heels of the chestnut neatly tucked up under his belly, and they slid over with only a faint scraping of hoofs—shot down, and landed almost silently in garden loam.

Behind him, from the lane, voices suddenly boiled over with bewilderment and rage; footfalls came, running.

For that instant he was safe, but he was fenced around by that same lofty wall on three sides, and on the other was the awkward mass of the house. He turned in the saddle to watch the gap through which he had jumped the chestnut, and the smile of Weldon would not have been good to see, by daylight!

But, turning, something glinted in the side wall of the garden close—the handle of a door, perhaps!

He pushed the chestnut to it and leaned—a door indeed! But when he tried the handle, it was locked fast!

To make matters, if possible, worse, a shutter crashed open, and a man's voice called loudly: "Who is that?"

A good, ringing voice it was, as of a man of action, and, glancing up over his shoulder, there was enough starlight for Weldon to see the gleam of a long barrel.

Then an old maxim thrust into his mind: *He who rides must be ready for a fall!* He answered that maxim with his usual smile: "San Trinidad is not big enough to trip me!" Then he put the mouth of a revolver against the lock in the gate and fired. The gate was easily pushed wide. He dipped low in the saddle, and the chestnut carried him through, not into lane or street, but into open country, with the dim silver of the Rio Negro glimmering in the near distance. He had come through the edge of the town as through the wall of a fortress!

As he observed these things with his first glance, a gun barked with a short, hoarse cough and small shot rattled against the wall. But he was safe enough!

Yonder across the Rio Negro, he could see the blinking of a light or two and the sharp, upward thrust of a few roofs. That was the little town of Juniper on the American side, and he must make that place for safety.

He gave the chestnut his head again, but now the big fellow did not attempt to take charge as he had done in the alley. That barking of shins, that leap into darkness, that passage through the dark garden had, apparently, convinced him that this man was good enough to be his

38

master. He went smoothly, well in hand, and cantered down to the water's edge. There was not a sight or a sound behind; it was as though Miguel Cabrero wisely had made up his mind that bad luck must be accepted philosophically and the hands washed with at least an air of indifference!

So Weldon sat quietly by the river, for a moment, tasting life and this new moment with a placidly keen enjoyment. The river was as smooth as glass, except for a telltale, bubbling sound in the center. But one could not imagine that, not many moments before, this same water had been roaring through the black canyon, looking possessed of devils!

All was black from the side of San Trinidad, except at the bridgehead, where the customs people kept lights flaring as though to warn smugglers that there was no passing at that point! From the American shore, however, a scattering of rays made pale, yellow marks on the black of the water. And in the standing pools and backwater along the edges the stars revealed themselves. Weldon could have sat there in the saddle half the night, but after all, Cabrero was not as harmless as all that.

He went down to the widest place, which must necessarily be the shallowest. The chestnut walked carefully, his head pushed down, sniffing at the water as though he were asking after the secrets of its hidden depths. He plumped suddenly into a pool that soaked Weldon to the breast, swam a few struggling yards and found bottom again.

Dripping, cold, with the water crashing underfoot, they got up the farther shore, and Weldon rode calmly into the town. He found the hotel, gave the muddy, wet horse to the groom at the rear of the building, and stood by to watch the feeding of the good horse. In one hour he had become a friend, an intimate. He sniffed at Weldon affectionately, and Weldon stroked the lean, hard neck.

He said to the stable boy: "You shoot squirrels, son?"

"Sometimes. Why?"

"Where's your shotgun?"

"Right beside the door."

"Suppose you keep that gun with you, tonight, and you might sit in the manger, here."

The boy was silent, his face upturned.

Then Weldon explained frankly enough: "You know Miguel Cabrero?"

"Aw, sure."

"You know any good of him?"

"Aw, I don't!"

"I paid him fifteen hundred for that horse, but I think he'd like to get him back."

He put ten dollars into the hand of the youngster and that hand closed on the money so strongly that it crunched like a bone under the grip.

"One buck?" he asked hopefully.

"Ten bucks, son," said Weldon.

"Well," said the boy through his teeth, "there ain't enough greasers in the world to grab that hoss. You gwan in and go to sleep!"

Weldon took that advice. There was no charm about this hotel; there was no dignity about the proprietor. He was in his shirt sleeves, and clean sleeves they were not. He smoked the butt of a foul, black cigar as he showed Weldon to a room.

"Nothing better?" asked Weldon.

"It's good enough for me. Ain't it good enough for you?"

So Weldon took it with a little sigh. His fingers itched and his muscles quivered, but he let the proprietor depart in peace and settled down for the night.

He had not wakened until evening of that day; now it was not very late, but he was ready to sleep again. Sleep was the one servant always at his command. He locked the door and wedged a roll of matting beneath it. He put the chair sidewise beneath the window, and then he lay down, resolutely put out of his mind the smell of stale cookery which pervaded the room, and went to sleep.

Dreamless and pure as the sleep of a little child was this slumber of Weldon. Once a hand tried his door. He wakened and leveled a revolver. But the noise stopped. And Weldon slept again, and only wakened when the sun was high, casting a wave of brilliance and oven heat into the room. At the door a hand was beating. When he opened it, he found Cunningham on the outside.

8. Two Proposals

They breakfasted together in the dingy dining room and it was then that Weldon noticed a lump on the side of Cunningham's head.

"What's that?" he asked.

"I followed you a little too quickly," said Cunningham. "One of the Mexicans discouraged me in this way."

He changed the subject carelessly: "It was a grand little fight. But is it true that you called on Cabrero?"

"Yes. Cabrero showed me the way out."

Cunningham began to crumble the stiff, stale bread with his strong fingers.

"You say you really dropped in on Cabrero?"

"He's a polite fellow," said Weldon. "Gave me back what his crooked machine had taken from me."

Cunningham leaned back in his chair and sighed with pleasure.

"How I should have liked to see that! And then you took one of his horses?"

"Not at all! I bought one."

"What?"

"For fifteen hundred dollars. That's a fair price, isn't it?"

Cunningham shook with laughter, and then shook again. He wiped his eyes and steadied himself.

"I thought before that we would have to have you. Now I know it! You can write your own ticket, Weldon!"

"Are you the head of this work?" asked Weldon.

"I? By no means! I'm a sort of general of brigade, in contact with the enemy."

"May I ask some questions?"

"Not until you're in the organization."

"I'll try one. Who's the lovely child with the long, gray car?"

"She," said Cunningham, "is a darling."

"Yours?"

"Nobody's," said Cunningham, unaffronted by this calm bluntness. "She's all by herself. You like her?"

"Of course."

"There's no one like her," said Cunningham.

"Is she part of the show?"

Cunningham tapped the table thoughtfully.

"I can't tell you that," he decided.

"It might make a big difference," said Weldon.

Cunningham looked sharply at him.

"*That's* your weakness, is it?" said he.

"That's one of them."

"No matter what comes of this, let me tell you that Francesa is a fiend. Soberly, I tell you that!"

"Treacherous?"

"Dangerous!" said Cunningham. "There's no more heart in that beautiful body of hers than there is in that wooden post."

"Nonsense," smiled Weldon. "Everybody has a weakness."

"Hers is for danger."

"I have a special taste for hot things."

Cunningham shook his head gravely.

"Mind you—you're still on the outside. I'm talking out of school, now. But after your little game of last night I want to give you a fair chance from the start. Laguarda is a beauty. But look at her like a picture on the wall. Admire her all you please, but leave your heart out of it! You know, Weldon, there are two kinds. Those that go to perdition, and those that send others there. The first kind may be foolish but they're apt to be pathetic, too. The second kind are simply no good. You know Balzac?"

"I've tried him."

"There's one of the second kind in the 'Magic Skin.'"

42

Weldon observed the distant face of Bull Mountain, solid and formidable.

"Lovely voice," he observed. "Let's drop it!"

"Shall I talk terms?"

Weldon hesitated.

So far, he was inclined to like Cunningham in many ways. But he had not yet made up his mind, for that mind worked slowly, seeing many facets of an idea before it was fixed.

"I want some time," he said. "I may want even another look or two at La Trinidad."

"Riding Cabrero's horse?" asked Cunningham.

"Why not?" said Weldon.

Cunningham smiled, but his brow remained dark.

"You might get on with the Laguarda, after all. Whatever else she is, she's a daredevil!"

"Ah, but I'm not," protested Weldon. "Only, life can't be all beef and potatoes. Have to have a little pepper."

"You want to think things over," said Cunningham. "Good morning, Doctor!" He spoke to a bowed figure, coming slowly up the path. "I'll tell you this to begin with." He turned to Weldon again. "We'll offer a thousand a month. That's not final. Perhaps we could start you even higher. But a thousand per at least. I have authority to offer that. Afterwards—why, I know what you can do. Very soon you'd be cutting the big melons with us!"

"Suppose they can?" said Weldon.

"We have can-openers," smiled Cunningham.

"It's a very pleasant suggestion," said Weldon.

Then he waved the whole idea away.

"Let me have the thought for a while. The sun's hot enough here to incubate it!"

Cunningham nodded. And, when he had finished breakfast a little later, he left, with word that he would return in the evening, if possible.

Then Weldon went out on the veranda to smoke and dream. The stable boy came lounging around the corner and waited to be noticed.

"Sleep well?" asked Weldon.

The boy grinned.

"They come, all right," said he. "Two. I unhooded

the lantern when they got into the stall. You sure must've heard them screeching as they made their get-away. They seen the shotgun and thought it was a funeral."

Weldon gave him another ten dollars.

"That's to polish up your eyes," he smiled, and the boy disappeared.

There was no blacker scene in the world than the village street on which Weldon brooded. Across the river San Trinidad possessed a pungent charm. Mystery clung to the shadowy patios and the deep casements. But there was a street of frame shacks, such as the American throws up when he first lays his hand on a new land. Frame, or corrugated iron, or canvas, or anything cheap. Then he wrestles with the problems of the new country, and solves those problems. Afterwards, cities of brick and stone arise swiftly.

So Weldon understood this frontier, this staggering wreck of a village. The ground had been broken. It was not certain whether there ever would be a yield from the soil, but at least the investment had been small. Ten attempts—let one of them succeed and the return is richly worth while. So all across the continent the way was spotted with failures, little ruined villages which were soon rained back into the ground. But the tenth village always turned into a smoking city.

He thought of these things, dimly proud of his race, more than dimly aware that he was not a part of it. He was no portion of the current that flows, but a mere touch of unimportant foam upon the surface. He did not grow melancholy in this brooding. His thoughts were no more to him than pictures hung in a gallery, but he put himself on the wall along with other things and calmly regarded the ugly features.

A halting step came down the veranda and paused beside him.

"You're Mr. Weldon? I'm Doctor Henry Watts. May I sit down here?"

It was the bowed man who had come up the path.

He took the next chair, sitting down cautiously, lowering himself, as though he feared the strength of his legs might gave way. Then he mumbled for a moment, and

44

sighed. It seemed a great accomplishment that he had done so much as this!

He had in his hands a powerful, knotted stick on which he leaned, and seemed to regard the toes of his clumsy boots. Not riding boots. In every respect, Doctor Henry Watts was a pedestrian figure. He was a man who looked not more than fifty, but with the weakness of one at least ten years older. He had a long face, shrouded in part by a ragged, gray beard that grew up into scanty sideburns. His neck was thin, and two cords at the back of it thrusting out against his loose collar. It was a stiff, white collar. And the cuffs that showed beneath the bottom of his sleeves were clean and white, also. Very white they looked against the big, loose, blue veins that covered the backs of his hands.

Weldon, apparently dreaming over the sun-flooded street, was noting these details. He decided at once that Henry Watts was a gentleman and a man of education. The weakly sagging head seemed to be burdened with a weight of thought.

"Cunningham wants you, I see," said the doctor.

Weldon made no answer. He merely turned his pleasant, unintellectual smile upon the other.

"And, of course, he has good reason," went on Doctor Henry Watts, "after last night!"

Even Weldon's smile was not quite proof against this remark, and Henry Watts explained rather hastily, in his soft, deep voice: "Of course, everyone has heard about it. On the other side of the river, they chatter, you know. They talk a great deal. So we hear the reports on this side, too. There are wires that connect the two towns. Wires overground, wires underground!"

He lifted his weak head sidewise and smiled at Weldon, not with sharp, smart suggestion, but gently, like an old man amused at life and its odd ways.

"And when I heard what you had done," said he, "it occurred to me that perhaps you would let me talk to you seriously?"

"Of course you may," said Weldon, always gentle.

"I talked it over with my client," said Doctor Henry Watts. "She agreed with me that perhaps you were the man. We want you, also, Mr. Weldon, though we can't

45

offer you such high pay as Mr. Cunningham can offer. But we *can* offer you danger which is even greater, and the chance to do a beautiful and good deed, sir!"

9. A Lady in Distress

If a wayside beggar, raising himself, had been transformed into a shining emperor, it would not have been more wonderful to Weldon than to hear this quiet and sad-voiced old man so speak to him.

He replied with his usual gentleness: "You and a friend are in great trouble, Doctor Watts?"

"My friend is in great trouble, and I am worried because of her."

He looked wistfully at Weldon, as though he wanted most eagerly to find words for his thought, but found those words difficult and slow in coming to his tongue. But at last he said, seeing that the younger man waited with perfect courtesy and patience: "It is a little hard to talk so openly with a stranger. But suppose that I put the case to you nakedly, in outline. Then, if it interests you at all, we could go to the place and there you could make up your mind more definitely!"

Weldon hesitated. He would have been glad enough to come to the help of this good man and his friend, whoever she might be, but there was another matter which covered his mind as a great cloud will sometimes cover the sky.

There was Cunningham, shrewd, strong and brave; there was the wild work which lay at Cunningham's hand, ready to offer to him; there was the magnificent salary which went with that work—and upon how many things Weldon could spend money with pleasure!—and above all there was the fascinating figure of Francesca Laguarda, dangerous, beautiful, and strange. Though Cunningham would not admit that she was a part and portion of this illegal corporation of smugglers, he was reasonably sure that she was a member. Otherwise, Cunningham would not have been at such pains to warn him against her in the beginning before Weldon himself was included. However, he could not help listening to the doctor to the end. There was such eagerness and hope in the voice of Henry Watts that Weldon already felt like a cruel elder refusing money to a starving child.

So instead of speaking his mind he said simply: "There's no reason why I shouldn't hear you. I'd be happy to hear you, Doctor Watts."

"Thank you," said the old man. "Then, briefly, but as clearly as I can—as clearly as I can."

He locked his big, old, feeble hands together and nodded his head as the facts were summoned into his mind.

"I have a client—a patient, I should say. She lives yonder in the woods on the side of Las Altas. Do you see? If you look between those two chimneys and then just a little above them—there you see a raw, yellow gap on the side of the mountain. That is the canyon. Now, still lower and to the right the woods go up like shadows. Like shadows piled on one another! That is the place. And shadows there are piled there—shadows there are piled there! Danger, Heaven knows, and death, perhaps, for the purest and the dearest of women, Mr. Weldon!"

Now, Weldon was reasonably steadfast in his mind, and true to his first resolutions, but as the old doctor spoke, extending his uncertain hand, his dim eyes squinting at more than the physical facts of those mountains, and looking into a life of sorrow yonder among the pines, Weldon felt himself torn adrift from Cunningham and that first rich temptation. Even the splendid form of the Laguarda, as Cunningham was apt to call her, grew a little distant, and the sweet, low voice spoke far away in his mind.

He remained silent, but he sat a little forward in his chair and rested his elbows on his knees.

"She is Helen O'Mallock," said the doctor. "She lives there in the house which her father built. He was General O'Mallock. You may have heard of that name?"

"No, I haven't heard of it," said Weldon.

"When I first came West," said the doctor, "everyone knew about him. It seems wonderful to me that people forget so soon. He was one of the makers of the country. He was one of the strong-handed men who come first, and afterward the creepers like myself steal in. And when the strong men find a glorious empire, we find, perhaps, no more than peace—and pure air that cures disease!"

He shook his head, wondering mildly at these things. Weldon felt that another door had been opened for his comprehension of the good doctor; this was a confirmed invalid, and the weight of sickness was that which he still carried on his bowed shoulders.

The doctor went on, gathering his thoughts about him: "I don't want to trouble you about the general. He was a good and a great man. Should I say 'good'?"

He paused to decide that question more deliberately.

"Strong, at least," he qualified his words, "and good in the general effect. But like most strong men, he did not always keep his power confined to the best channels. He overflowed. He became at times a fierce flood that endangered those around him. He had many enemies. Some envied him. All feared him—except his daughter!"

At this word he came to another pause, for words seemed to bring into the mind of the old man such bright and powerful images that he had to halt in order to let them fade a little before he could put them into connected speech.

Then he said: "General O'Mallock fought Indians, rode a pony express, drove stages, did many things. He had no fear of any thing, or man, or mystery. When the flush of his youth was ended, then he turned his mind to other affairs than mere danger and fighting. Though, to the end, danger was his bright goddess, as she was to Harry Hotspur! Nevertheless, he found time to do other things. He bought cattle. They increased in numbers. He interested himself in mining. Wherever he put down his hand, there was gold when he removed it. He became wealthy. Ah, not overpoweringly rich as in these days of billionaires wealth is counted, but truly comfortable and more than comfortable. Now, as the years went by, he determined to marry. He was nearly fifty, then. He found a girl who loved his great, brave past, and who loved him because of it. As *Desdemona* loved *Othello*, Mr. Weldon. Quite that way!"

"This O'Mallock was a half-breed, then?" asked Weldon a little sharply.

"The purest, unmixed Irish," responded the doctor. "Oh, no, have no fear of that! He married. The unhappy wife died when her little girl was born—that beautiful Helen who lives there still in the old house! And as she grew up, the old general grew old. When she was ten, he was sixty. When she was twenty, he was seventy. Age brought a little stiffness upon his mind. He began to draw in from his greater activities. Little by little he sold off his properties, his cattle, his mines. You are bored, Mr. Weldon?"

"I? Oh, not a whit! Never more interested in my life, I think!"

"That makes me very happy. I cannot talk like Helen. But I can do my best! Now, then, when he had finished selling off his property, he died. His will simply left everything to his daughter. But now comes the strange touch! There was hardly anything to leave!"

He raised a long, gnarled forefinger as he spoke. His eyes widened with wonder and alarm beneath the bushy, gray brows.

"There was hardly a thing!" he repeated.

"He'd been playing the stock market on the side?" asked Weldon.

"Ah, perhaps, perhaps!"

"Everything swept clean away?"

"Ah, not everything! I should not say that. There is a small competence on which Helen O'Mallock lives. Up there in the old house. Poor child! Poor child! The grief caused by the death of her father brought on the greatest trouble of all, no doubt. Or perhaps the disease was there before. Strange, was it not, in this country of pure air, life-giving air? Consumption, Mr. Weldon!"

49

"Ah, that's bad!" said Weldon. "Poor girl!"

The old man looked tenderly upon him. "You have a gentle heart, sir," said he. Then he went on:

"But as she lay ill, weak, but still hopeful of life, she began to remember certain things. About the death of her father. The disappearance, so strangely, of his money. She began to fear that perhaps, after all, it had not been so natural—"

He paused; the dreadful thought had stopped his voice.

"And then, Mr. Weldon," he went on, breathless and hurrying in a whisper, "then, sir, lately she had felt certain that a man or men are trying to come to her in her house —for only one purpose— I beg your pardon. It is hard for me to go on."

He sank back in his chair. His hands were visibly quivering, though he had locked them together again.

"Do you mean—to do her harm?"

"I fear so. That is in her mind."

"Old enemies of her father?"

"Ah! That, perhaps!"

"Do you mean, Doctor Watts, that this girl lives yonder in fear of murder?"

"Yes, yes, yes! I mean that!"

Weldon set his teeth and his blue eyes blazed. "What people live in the house with her?" he asked.

"An old Negress. There is also a man of all work. He is old, too. And I live not very far away in the hills."

"An old man—a Negress—" said Weldon.

"And in this constant, dreadful fear, when she heard that you had done those extraordinary things in San Trinidad—because Señor Cabrero is a known man!" said the doctor confidentially—"she hoped against hope that perhaps she would be able to secure protection from you. Do you understand? She could not afford to give all that you could command from others, no doubt. But she would offer you a hundred dollars a month. And the life," the doctor hastened to add eagerly, "would be a very—er—simple one. There would be no onerous duties, no physical labor."

He paused; eagerly, almost pitifully, he waited. And Weldon saw with dreadful brightness the picture of this old man; the wasted girl lying in her bed; the frightened,

doddering Negress, and the unnamed peril which over-
hung that house. Far off, far off, now, sounded the voice of
Francesca Laguarda, like the chime of sheep bells,
drowned in the wind.

"Suppose we go up to see the house, and talk the whole
thing over?" said Weldon.

10. A House on a Hill

Weldon rode the tall chestnut up the hill. He was an
ugly beast with a great, long head that looked not the least
part of the good blood that was in him. However, he had
been tried and proved, and he went up the hill with a gait
as charming as his looks were ugly.

As for Doctor Watts, he had a little, inexpensive automobile which went with great roaring, and yet managed to
climb over the rough trail with a goatlike agility. It seemed
to Weldon that it went better uphill than on the level.

They had a full hour and a half of steady work before
them to the lower edge of the trees, and then there was
another stretch of even more difficult going, for the road-
bed was quite ruined, but at last they came on the site of
the house itself.

One expects inanimate things to share the emotions of
those near them. But if this was the house of misery, it had
not the slightest look of such a condition. It was a building
in the Spanish style, two stories high, and done in heavy
stone. The walls had a strange look, for the rocks had apparently been picked up just as they were found littering
the side of the mountain and worked haphazard into the
masonry, so that great points and jags often thrust out. Yet

even from a distance one could tell that the work was solidly done.

Over these heavy walls, strong enough to make a fortress, climbing vines wandered everywhere, springing from one roughness to another. One of the vines was in flower. It spilled white bloom down an entire side of the building.

It was not a big house. It was not a beautiful house. Its deep, rather narrow casements gave it a somewhat secluded, reflective appearance, and yet there was a vast air of contentment about it.

Weldon ventured to guess that the general was the sort of man who never had any doubts as to the value of what he was doing. That secure self-complacency showed in every nook of this structure, as Weldon saw it. Its ugly outline, for instance. The downhill wall was thrice the height of the upper. But he could see at least one good reason for placing the building at that spot. It was on a rounding of the mountain shoulder. West of north, one looked up the rough pass between Las Altas and Mount Cumberland; to the south the Rio Negro appeared, white with anger out of the muzzle of the Negro Canyon, and farther on one saw the river smooth itself to aproach dingy Juniper, and white San Trinidad on the farther bank. It was a sweeping view; it lifted one's heart to swing the eye across three parts of a circle in this fashion.

"He was a man with a will," observed Weldon.

He had dismounted from his horse, and the doctor had brought his old car to a halt and climbed out. He did not need to be told what was in Weldon's mind.

"The general was a man who *must* have his way," he answered. "Shall we go in?"

"Let's take our time," said Weldon. "We might as well look around."

There were not many outbuildings. The barn and stable was a smaller unit than one would have expected to find on the place of a rich man. There were a few sheds. Everything was made more substantially of the same rock-work out of which the house itself had been constructed. Between the stable and the rear of the house a sort of Spanish courtyard appeared. The house made one wall. There were rude stone parapets to make the other three quarters of the inclosure. The patio within was flagged with huge

52

stones, and in the center of it appeared the well, with a prodigious, black mouth.

"Cost a small fortune to dig that well, there," said the doctor. "But the general had started on that spot to find water, and he insisted on blasting his way down through the rock. He had to go deep, as you can see, before he came to the water!"

In fact, when Weldon leaned over the hole, he could not see water at all, at first. He had to shade his eyes and peer closely before he could see the gleam far beneath. A winding flight of stairs, streaked with green moss, went down the side of the well, circling in swift spirals which seemed to increase the apparent sense of depth.

This should have been a bleak enough patio, but on the contrary, in spite of its naked rock, it gave a most cheerful effect. There were some scant sprays of climbing vines growing here and there on the inclosing walls. The house wall itself was, like all the rest of that building, drenched in flowering greenery. And up the slope appeared first the sharply peaked roof of the barn, and then the tall and fragrant pines which mounted higher and higher in ranks that closed, very shortly, and became a solid mass of dark green.

"One could be pretty cheerful here," said Weldon.

"Ah, and the general was the happiest of men! He used to have his coffee here in the morning. He used to sit here on hot afternoons. He preferred this blind view to the sweeping one from the front, I think. That view was like himself. Huge and vital. And he liked contrasts. His wife was a delicate, clinging girl, for instance. Strong men are often like that!"

They entered the house, just as a shrill voice cried from the interior:

"You no-account rascal! You thief! I'm gunna jus' blast you one of these here days if I catch you in my house again, General!"

A black cat shot down the hall and darted between the legs of Weldon.

"That's the general, in this case," smiled the doctor. "General Sherman, Aunt Maggie calls him. Because he's a great plunderer of kitchen supplies."

"Is Maggie old enough to remember the Sherman days?"

"Not at all! But she was raised on the stories of them. She's a good soul!"

Aunt Maggie was seen waddling down the hall, a stout poker in her hand. When she saw them, she cleared the thunder from her brows and drew to one side with a pleasant smile.

"I've brought a friend to look the house over. He's interested in General O'Mallock!"

It seemed odd to Weldon that his presence should need to be explained in such detail to a Negress cook. As he went on, he made a point of stumbling over a small step, and that gave him a chance to glance back under his arm toward Aunt Maggie.

She had not moved from the place where she permitted them to pass her, and, looking after them, he thought that there was an expression of almost fierce suspicion on her face. However, cooks are apt to be odd people, and Negress cooks are no exception to that rule.

He went up the stairs, slowly. There was nothing on the first floor, as the doctor explained, except the kitchen, the storage rooms, and a few odd chambers for servants to occupy. Above were the important apartments.

He showed a dining room, a bedroom or two, with a bath across the hall. And Weldon was delighted with what he saw. Those deep, eyelike casements were even narrower from the inside than from the outside, for they were built funnel-shaped, though rectangular, of course. They gave an air of the most solid security to each room.

"Ah," said Weldon presently, "of course, the general was a veteran of the Indian days, and that's why these windows are really simply enlarged shot holes!"

"Exactly," smiled the doctor. "And the house is, as you see, built like a fort!"

He pointed to the thickness of the walls. The side wall was at least four feet through!

"You like it?" he asked Weldon eagerly.

"Of course I like it! There's no dog about this!"

"No, no pretense at all. The general was an honest man. You see the furniture. He could have had costly things carried here. But he preferred something more in keeping with the country. He had a sense of harmony. He never would have a piano brought here for his wife or his daughter.

" 'Go riding outdoors,' he would say. 'There's music enough when the wind gets into the pines!' He had a rough, determined way of speaking. He never was in doubt!"

"Of course he wasn't," murmured Weldon.

He was beginning to see the old general very clearly.

"Was he feeble in his last days?" he asked.

"Ah, no! Not a whit! He could jump into the saddle almost like a boy. And three days before he died, I saw him take one of those ponderous old Kentucky rifles and with it shoot a squirrel out of the top of a pine tree! No, no, his *body* was sound enough!"

At this inference of other and more terrible troubles than mere afflictions of the body, Weldon turned and glanced sharply at his companion, because it was a theme which readily could be expanded. But there was no enlargement of the thought. Doctor Watts had gone on to the door and opened it.

He closed it again and turned back, resting his shoulders against the door. His eyes were almost closed. There was pain in his lowered eyes.

"I am about to take you to see Helen O'Mallock," said he. He sighed, and then he went on: "As for her condition, I won't say that she is doomed, Mr. Weldon—"

"I hope not," said Weldon's grave voice.

"But I want you to understand that, for my part, I put her off the theory that what troubles her really is consumption. Even when her eyes are sunken and when there is fever in her cheeks, I try to make light of everything. I speak a little about persistent colds and a little about fevers—"

Just then, from the distance, Weldon heard a faint harsh cough, a dry, barking sound, rapidly repeated.

He took a long breath.

"Very well!" said he. "I'm to be cheerful. Is that it?"

"You understand exactly, my dear friend. I—I want you to just be a little warned before hand. She's a delicate creature. Her mother never was very strong. Helen, we

55

thought, would be quite robust. But—she seemed to melt
—she seemed to melt—"

Weldon hastily averted his eyes. His heart was very full
for this stricken, old man who, it was apparent, was pouring out his love upon this invalid girl! Then he passed on
before his guide.

11. Doctor and Patient

The doctor opened the door again. They passed into a
large bedroom, the bed itself in the corner to the right, a
large four-poster with a heavy canopy over it, so that it
looked like an echo of a dead century. It was, altogether,
one of the strangest chambers that Weldon ever had seen.
On the floor were the skins of a grizzly and a mountain
lion. On the walls hung masks of beasts of prey, and inter-
mixed among these were strange weapons of war, African
spears, with blades like leaves, razor sharp at the edge;
and long, slender bows, and delicate and deadly arrows.
There were Malay knives, with their terrible wavy edges.
There were deeply curved Arabian scimitars, and yonder
a pair of long, ancient muskets, their barrels richly ara-
besqued.

"This is the room of the general?" murmured Weldon.

"Yes. You are right. This is his room. Helen won't have
anything changed, though he's been dead more than a
year."

"He hunted in all those places?" said Weldon, indicating
a great rhinoceros horn on the one hand and the grim
mask of a tiger on the other.

"He was all over the world. He was a restless fellow before death made him quiet, at last!" said the doctor.

Suddenly a shudder passed through him, as though the memory of the old man had leaped up before his eyes and was not altogether comforting.

He went on to the next door.

"This is the room," he whispered, and his eyes softened as he spoke.

He drew the door open, and as it came ajar he said: "I have Mr. Weldon here, Helen. Shall I bring him in?"

A quiet voice answered. Weldon could not hear the words. The door was drawn wide, and he went in before the doctor.

She lay in an invalid's chair near the window. The sun fell strongly across the shawl which was wrapped around her feet. The dazzling brightness of that sun kept the rest of her in shadow, but when Weldon came closer to meet her outstretched hand, he saw a pale face with shadows of weakness beneath the eyes. Hopelessly beautiful he thought her; more beautiful than any woman he had seen in the wide course of his wanderings, except that girl of the day before, Francesca Laguarda. He reflected that the old saying has it that it never rains but always must pour. So he had found them almost together, dark-haired Francesca, golden-haired Helen. How different, too! The Laguarda like a flaming light; and Helen O'Mallock something crystal through which light may shine, something pure and clear.

She reminded him of something or of someone, but he told himself that it was because she lay there so weak, so ill. A cold hand touched his own. He looked down into mild eyes, without resistance, without a challenge in them. The great tragedy was upon her, said Weldon to himself, and by the death to which she was drawn she was made to resemble all who had died beautiful, and died young!

He stepped back a little, and stood where she could see him easily; he clasped his hands behind his back. It was as pleasant to look on her as it was to listen to music. But he would not regard her too fixedly.

"Dear Doctor Henry," said the girl, "you've talked to Mr. Weldon?"

Not like the bursting joy and the ring of the voice of the

Laguarda; it was a husky voice, rather, low and hushed by weakness, and yet with its own soft harmony. Weldon found himself drawing a long breath, and guarding that breath, lest it should be obvious that he was moved.

"I've talked to him," said Doctor Watts. "Very briefly, my dear girl. He wanted to come up to see the place and the situation."

Worry clouded her brow a little.

"It isn't a very jolly place," said she. "It's far away from town and a hard ride. You have to consider that, Mr. Weldon, if you'll even think about coming to us!"

Then, in order that he might have a chance to reflect on what she said, she murmured to the doctor: "And when shall *I* make that ride again, Doctor Henry?"

Doctor Watts stood beside her, holding her hand. His naturally bowed shoulders gave him the appearance of leaning above her.

"In a few days, no doubt. In a very few days, beyond a doubt, my dear, you'll be in the saddle again, blowing the roses back into your cheeks!"

"Really?" said she, and lifted slowly to him the great, dark eyes, with that faintest of smiles upon her lips.

But it seemed to Weldon that the doctor had spoken with a most clumsy pretense, and that she had looked straight through at the truth. What was that truth? That she would never walk from that house again, or leave it in any way, except when she was carried to her grave!

So thinking, Weldon could not help frowning a little.

The girl noticed and appeared to put a natural interpretation upon the look.

"Ah," she said, controlling her disappointment, "that is not all! That is not all against us! There would be no one to see and talk to, very much. Dear Doctor Henry comes to me almost every day. He would be about all. There's poor Dogget; he's not much good. And old Aunt Maggie will soon tire you. And I'm not very gay, you see!"

"You might paint the picture a little more cheerfully," broke in the doctor, almost with irritation. "There's no use in me bringing up a man all this distance, just to have you send him right-about-face, at once!"

Weldon could have cursed that complaining voice. The doctor was old, indeed, to exercise such small control.

The girl waited a little. She never spoke in haste, but always she seemed to consider for a moment what had last been said to her. So her gentle eyes now rested on the face of the doctor before she said: "But you see, I don't want him to come, lured by false pretenses, and then suddenly to find that it's such a drab, gray life. For if we had him here to protect us—oh, then it would be too sad to lose him again!"

"You've started to draw the portrait," said the doctor with inexcusably childish irritation. "Now you might as well finish the picture and tell him just why we want him. I only hinted at the facts."

She looked from Watts to Weldon.

She said simply: "We think that people are trying to enter the house and reach me."

Weldon could hardly speak. He managed to say: "To reach you?"

"The doctor saw someone in the hall the other day. The man didn't wait for questions. He went through a window! And then, a little before that, the lock of the rear door of the house was forced. But Maggie heard a noise and when she came out from her room, footsteps slipped away."

"They've come into the house for plunder, then," said Weldon, turning cold. "Of course, that's the reason!"

"There's nothing in my room worth stealing," said the girl. "You see!"

It was, in fact, very plainly furnished. A few prints were on the walls. There was a common rag rug on the floor. Certainly the general had not overburdened his daughter and only child with too rank a luxury.

"I have no jewels, except a couple of rings and a few beads, you know," said she. "Everyone knows that I haven't other things."

"But were these men trying to get at your room?"

"The man the doctor saw was at my door, working at it with a skeleton key, he thought. And when poor Maggie came down the other time, the footsteps she heard went away from near my door, also!"

Weldon swallowed hard.

He looked again at Helen O'Mallock and told himself that there were no men mean enough to wish to harm her.

59

And then he hesitated. There were men, however, to whom nothing could appeal, except money, however come at.

She was turning on her finger a ring which was set with a small, pale sapphire, a brilliant on either side.

"And it's a whole week ago," said the girl, "that—that —I think perhaps you had better tell him about that, Doctor Henry!"

Her head fell back on the cushion; her eyes almost closed.

Weldon cast a significant glance at the doctor and the latter nodded.

"We'd better go," he whispered. "We're going to leave you alone for a little, Helen. To talk things over between ourselves. There's nothing you want?"

"No. Nothing. You'll tell me the decision soon?"

"Yes."

They withdrew. In the room of the general they sat down close to the window and heard an outbreak of that same harsh, racking cough which Weldon had heard before.

"Why don't you do something?" he asked abruptly.

The doctor shrugged his shoulders.

"There's nothing to be done," he answered almost dryly. "Cough mixtures—they'd simply make her sick— and—I'm afraid—cough mixtures would never stop that cough!"

Weldon bit his lip and turned suddenly toward the window.

"Well, it's fatal, then?" he snapped across his shoulder.

"The consumption? I don't know! I don't know! One never can tell. There's the chance, always, of a turn for the better. But there's not much fighting spirit in her. No resistance in the mind, you know. I don't think that she much cares."

"She ought to be made to care!" said Weldon with resolution.

"Ah, my boy, and will you stay with her and prescribe, perhaps?"

"Stay here in the house? Man, man," said Weldon, "wild horses couldn't drag me away from it!"

12. Speaking of Poison

The doctor stopped further talk by raising his hand. He turned and hurried into the next room. It seemed to Weldon that there was something almost subtle and guilty in the manner of Henry Watts, as though he wished to announce this decision of Weldon's before the latter had any chance to change his mind.

From within the sick chamber—for the door had been left the slightest bit ajar—Weldon heard a low cry of joy. Then the cough again!

For some reason, it made him reach inside his coat and grip the handle of a Colt. But revolvers could do nothing against such an enemy as this.

The doctor came back, actually rubbing his hands together in his exultation. Weldon said to him sharply:

"You might consider, Doctor Watts, that this case isn't settled, even if we manage to keep the rats away from her! I think that girl is dying! And yet you can seem happy!"

It was rarely that Weldon was so outspoken. What he said seemed to depress the doctor very much, and he sat down, plucking at his beard.

"Of course, you're perhaps right," he said. "Only— one cannot help hoping, just as one cannot help praying, Mr. Weldon!"

The big man lost all animus. He sat down in turn.

"There was something else you were going to tell me," he said.

"And about what, pray?" said the doctor with absent mind. "I don't recall anything."

61

"The thing which was too much for the poor girl to tell me herself."

"Ah! That? Of course I must tell you. Shortly, too. That was seven or eight days ago, I think. There is always a glass of water at Helen's bedside, and when she drinks it, she usually puts a few drops of lemon in it. But that morning when she wakened she forgot the lemon, and when she tried the water it had an odd taste. It took her thirst away in one swallow, and therefore she put the glass aside.

"I came early that morning, by the grace of good fortune! She happened to speak of the odd taste of the water. I tried it myself. Afterward I analyzed it. I had other things to do. It was only yesterday that I finished the analysis."

From his coat he took a small vial and held it to the light. It appeared to contain a perfectly clear liquid, to Weldon. The doctor shook it. From the bottom there rose a faint film. Some sort of precipitate, perhaps, was there.

"Arsenic," said Doctor Henry Watts, his eyes thoughtful. "Arsenic," he repeated again.

Then he looked down with a benevolent smile to the younger man.

"They tried to poison her? It's hard to believe," said Weldon.

He rolled a cigarette and lighted it. He began to smoke in his own furious manner. He clouded the room almost instantly.

"Ah, yes, arsenic!" said the doctor, dwelling strangely on the word. "And a very neat solution of it, at that! There's enough of this, for instance, to kill a dog. Enough in this little vial!"

"And wasn't one swallow enough to almost kill that delicate girl?"

"You don't understand. This is not a common preparation. There is arsenic, and arsenic, you must remember. It's been called the fool's poison. Ah, not in the hands of an artist! Not at all! Not at all!"

The doctor actually laughed.

He seemed to enjoy the theme, and Weldon wrote him down as more than a little childish in some qualities of his mind.

"I thought that arsenic always left traces in the body?" He challenged the doctor's odd enthusiasm.

"Of course it does," admitted Henry Watts cheerfully. "But how many bodies are examined? And in these days of cremation, criminals may be sure that the evidence of their crimes will soon pass away in the fire that burns the victim. Oh, yes! Besides, there are kinds of compounds, as I was saying. One may give arsenic in such a way that the victim is nauseated. His head swims. It aches violently. He is afflicted with spasms. Well, those violent symptoms, of course, excite curiosity and there is usually a post-mortem. Believe me, my dear young friend, arsenic is a fool's poison only when it is in the hands of a fool!"

Weldon listened, as to an authoritative voice. A scientific earnestness and surety appeared in the bowed, time-weakened doctor.

"This poison, for instance, would not have operated for several days. And then, when the drink of strange-tasting lemonade was quite forgotten, Helen would have fallen into a quiet sleep and never opened her eyes again. Poor child! Poor child!"

"But," objected Weldon, "you didn't know it was arsenic until yesterday?"

"I didn't know. But I suspected as soon as I had tasted that water myself. First I tasted it without lemon, and there was a faint taste. Only perceptible, say, to a very fine palate like Helen's, or to a man with professional understanding of such things. Add even two drops of lemon juice and all the taste disappears at once!"

Weldon nodded. He was beginning to admire this old man. And he was rather amused to note the manner in which Henry Watts lost his almost crushed humility and spread his elbows at the board, once he dipped into a scientific theme.

"Of course I gave antidotes at once. Gradually. From day to day. And now Helen will feel not even a trace of the poison."

"Interesting. Most interesting," said Weldon. "And you haven't an idea about the persons who tried to do this trick?"

"Ah, the same ones who twice were caught in the house. No doubt of that!"

"Ones? One man, I think you found each time."

"Yes. But not the maker of the poison, or he who administered it."

"You're sure of that?"

"Certainly! As sure as I am that there still is lightning somewhere in heaven!"

"Will you tell me why?"

"At once! Those were rude bunglers. They betrayed themselves by the noise they made, but this other—this man"—he shook the little phial and smiled upon it with the most singular appearance of affection—"this man is as secret as death itself! He steps without sound. He passes more softly than a shadow. A wise, talented, gentle spirit, no doubt!"

Weldon withheld comment.

"No doubt," said the doctor thoughtfully, "as he leaned above that beautiful girl, he blessed her loveliness. He rejoiced, let us say, that he was sending her out of this world before time had stained her ever so little!"

"Ah?" said Weldon politely.

"But afterward, when the poison did not take effect, he would not willingly run the risk of entering the house a second time in person, and he dispatched to the place a hired man, who failed. And another hired man, who likewise failed. But, sooner or later, this original genius will come again! Perhaps you will see him, Mr. Weldon!"

"I hope so," said Weldon grimly.

"If you can lay hands upon him, treat him gently, for my sake!"

"Enlarge that idea a little, Doctor, if you please!"

"Because before he dies, I should like to talk to him, dip into his cultivated mind—taste the beauty of his soul. I am growing poetic," chuckled the doctor.

"A little," admitted Weldon.

"To a scientific inquirer," said the doctor in rather a changed tone, as though taking more heed of his audience, "even the most hideous germ is a splendid spectacle. But this poison intrigues me. Arsenic! The fools' poison! What fools they are to call it so!"

He turned a little and confronted Weldon more squarely.

"Do you know that once there were more brands of

arsenic poison than there are brands of wine in modern France?"

Weldon did not reply. There was no need. The old fellow was off in the midst of an enthusiastic lecture.

"In the great Italian days," said Doctor Watts, "when men lived a lifetime in half a dozen years and when lives, as you may say, were therefore trebly worth taking, they understood how to compound these poisons. Arsenic thrice refined! They would poison cattle, and draw from the dead body a frightfully potent serum, and this again produced death, and death fortified death mysteriously. The secret has been lost. We only in a general way know the results. We know that men challenged to a duel suddenly dropped dead—fear and excitement, said the spectators, and buried him. They did not think that the excitement combining with the poison was indeed fatal—but only with that assistance. Or again, a man drank wine in the evening, and died the instant he tasted food the next day. Poisoned food? It is examined, what is left of it, and found perfectly innocent. The hand of God, say the medical men!

"They were like that, those old criminals. They imitated the hand of God, its mystery, its silence, its strength. But I've spoken of only crude and rude effects. They could proceed with wonderful delicacy. You dine in my palace. On the morrow you travel from Rome to Florence. And when that dinner is days and days forgotten, suddenly you sicken. 'Fever!' says one physician. 'The heart!' says another. You die.

"Very well. There were other kinds. Sometimes when the victim was close at hand, with the utmost delicacy the potions were graduated. From month to month the poor sufferer sickened. He passed into a decline. A change of air was prescribed. He departed for a journey. In France or Egypt his strength left him and he died in his bed! Poison? It was never dreamed of!

"But show me the modern touch that can equal these old things! Show me the aconite, the prussic acid, so handled that it produces such artistic results!"

Weldon nodded. He was vastly interested. He began to feel that there were infinitely more pages to the nature of the doctor than at first he had dreamed. But then, it is always true of the withdrawn scholar that his enthusiasms are strange and unlike those of the ordinary man in the street.

"And this unknown man, this fiend who tried to poison Helen O'Mallock—you think he had that lost art, eh?"

"He? Not altogether. Oh, no, for this is not any great triumph of the art. However, it is something out of the ordinary. And there is enough to this compound to make me believe that something more than walls and bars and a decrepit Negress and a doddering, old, serving man are necessary to keep the life in the body of beautiful Helen. Would you not agree to that?"

"With all my heart," said Weldon. Then he added: "I don't know what you people know of me. I'm afraid that you're taking me a little too much for granted. I take it that I'm not one of the world's blackest scoundrels, but at the same time I've lived more on the wrong than on the right side of the fence. I have more training in getting away from trouble with the law than in helping to trace out a clever crime."

"My dear, dear friend—" said the smiling doctor.

"Let me finish. The other night I had a bit of an adventure in San Trinidad. That may have made me seem very clever in your eyes. I'm not. Frankly, I'm not. I have an extraordinarily strong pair of hands. My nerves are fairly steady. And I shoot a bit closer to the center than a good man. But, Doctor, I've never succeeded in accomplishing any really extraordinary thing in my life; and if we're matched here against some unusual criminal, I give you my word that I advise you with all my heart to call in a talented worker. I'll assist him if he wants assistance. Or I'll stay here and play watchdog. That's what I earnestly suggest that you do!"

The doctor, his brows puckering up a little, regarded Weldon long and calmly. It was an odd characteristic of Henry Watts that, though he generally kept his eyes upon the ground, when he raised them, those eyes were able to look straight into the heart of another. So he seemed to be looking at Weldon now, as at the page of a book, reading busily.

He was not able to conceal that he was rather alarmed

and worried by what he saw. He began to shake his head ever so little.

"I see that you're an honest man, Weldon," he said. "Don't protest that you're not. But for the time being, we have you and we want you. If—I beg your pardon—but *if* we should decide that after all we must try to get someone else—that is to say—ah—"

Weldon smiled.

"The moment you make up your mind as to that," said he, "of course I'm ready to go."

The doctor sighed and smiled.

He stretched out his hand and shook that of Weldon with a good deal of heartiness.

"We're going to get on, we're going to get on," said he. "I haven't the least doubt that you're the man for us! Not the least doubt in the world. Now we'll go and fix you in your room! But first, you'll want a drink of something. We have some old wine in the cellars. If you—"

"Thank you," answered Weldon, "I've stopped drinking. I'll have nothing whatever while I'm here."

The doctor turned on him with a vague astonishment. He seemed about to protest, but then shook his head and led the way.

13. Bolts and Bars

It was a comfortable room, plainly furnished, like all the chambers in the house, in which there appeared nothing eccentric, except the apartment of the general himself. On one side of it opened the library. On the other side was the room of Helen O'Mallock, from which the old servant Dogget, with the assistance of Weldon himself, soon rigged a bell rope communicating with a little brazen bell at the head of Weldon's bed. One touch of the bell rope, therefore, would bring him to her aid. Her door was locked, to be sure, but he was furnished with a key, so that he could enter in the case of a desperate call for help.

This appeared to Weldon not at all an ample security. He suggested, accordingly, that the other door from her room—that is to say, the one into the chamber of her father should be secured firmly and at once, and that heavy bars be placed across her two windows. To this the doctor seemed about to agree, when he recollected himself.

"I'll have her in a state of nervous collapse before the slightest danger of an attack being made on her," said the doctor.

"No," said Weldon, "that girl has stronger nerves than you think. It's physical weakness that bothers her—not her nerves! I have an idea that she has her share of

... seemed greatly surprised at this statement. ... seem highly pleased with Weldon or the ... and it was very much as though he felt ... courage to his patient was equivalent to ... ine. However, Weldon was firm. As he ... were four means of ingress into that ... one was through his door. Besides ... windows to which one might climb ... or, without one, by means of the ... rooted in the wall, or by holding ... ns of the wall itself. And, in addi- ... from the general's room to that of ... was it to guard the one door if ... d with bolts and locks?

... d. There happened by good ... cement—though rather old— ... There was plenty of iron junk, and plenty, also, of stout planks.

The doctor took Helen O'Mallock in her invalid chair to another room where she could sit in the sun. Then Dogget, the man of all work, came to help Weldon at the labor of sealing the room. It was not a great task. The planks were spiked in place across the general's room—from Helen O'Mallock's side. A curtain hung over these planks by Aunt Maggie concealed them well enough.

She went darkly about this work, glowering at Weldon from time to time. Old Dogget was far more willing. He was a cheerful, simple-minded fellow who had been at sea for many years until a fall from aloft on the main yard had nearly knocked the life out of his body and left him with a crooked back. He could no longer run up the rigging, so he had begun work ashore, and, as he said, had found life on dry land all doldrums or Cape Stiff weather, until at last he made harbor with the general and came to anchor, as he hoped, for the rest of his days. He was a gentle fellow, of sixty or so, but very fond of referring to wilder and grander days, when many a time he had been the first man aloft to the topgallant yards. He had tasted life on the Hooghly, on the China coast, in the gay ports of old Australia, and now his pleasure was chiefly in stuffing his pipe with sliced-up plug tobacco and smoking it slowly, comfortable in the reek and the stench of it, while he remembered the great days of sail and the adventures under canvas. Like all sailors, he was a handy man, and therefore he was quite at home working with Weldon on the window bars. Holes had to be chiseled deep into the rock. Little physical labor had come the way of Weldon, but he had done some mining, and experience with a jack and a drill now helped him quickly to sink deep pits. Then the iron bars, previously sawed off from bits of varying sizes in the junk heap, were inserted, and the cement worked all around to secure the grip. When this was done with both the windows, the day was growing old, and Weldon freely admitted to Dogget and the doctor also that what had been accomplished was really not enough to keep the room from being entered. But he was equally sure that no one could drag down those bars without making such a noise that the soundest sleeper would be wakened and given ample time for raising an alarm.

This rough work was then covered with a coat of gray paint, and Weldon sat down with a sore hand and a more placid conscience. He felt that at least he had interposed one hurdle between Helen O'Mallock and danger.

She was put to bed by Aunt Maggie at sunset each day.

And this evening she asked to see Weldon. He found her looking pale even against the white of her pillow. The golden light of her curls at one shoulder made the contrast the greater, and her eyes were wonderfully large and dark.

She seemed too feeble to make much of a move to greet him. So he came close to the bed and leaned a little above her. Then she said in that soft voice, with the telltale trace of huskiness in it: "Days and days and days I've wanted something across those windows—and I didn't even know it until you put the bars up, Mr. Weldon! I'm going to sleep to-night—the first time in so long, so long!"

Weldon went out of the room with a full heart, and found his supper waiting for him in the library—for that adjoined, as has been said, his own room, and the sound of the bell was clearly audible there.

The doctor, who had remained all the day, came in for a last moment of talk. He begged Weldon under no circumstances to make any noise. Miss O'Mallock might sleep as sound as exhaustion could devise a slumber; or again, she might be awakened instantly by the faintest scratch.

"She'll never complain," said the doctor. "As long as you're here, you'll never hear an unkind word from her, or a complaining one. You'll have to consult yourself, therefore. Move like a cat, Mr. Weldon, after the sun goes down. Never disturb her or tap at her door, no matter what you have to say. Wait until the next day for that!"

Weldon agreed, willingly enough.

Then the doctor took his hand in both of his.

"Heaven bless you, dear boy," said he, "for your goodness and your kindness to us! I know that Roger Cunningham would give you many and many a thousand dollars to work for him. But stay here—follow your conscience—and perhaps Heaven will make up the difference!"

The good doctor was so moved with the sterling worth of Weldon that there were even tears in his eyes as he spoke. Then he left the room, and went down the hallway with a faltering step.

14. A Man in the House

It was with Weldon as with a skipper who sees the last of the stevedores tumbled over the side of the ship, and the pilot cast off, and the owners' last message ended. With the closing of the front door which announced the departure of the doctor from the house, Weldon was alone in command. He had for crew a dour-faced old Negress and a crippled sailor. His cargo was the life or death of lovely Helen O'Mallock, and the very certainty that death would not be long delayed from her, at any rate, made the keeping of her from foul play all the more important to him. As for the voyage he was to steer, he had no doubt that dangers would come rushing upon him fast enough.

He sat down to his supper, but presently he was aware that both the library windows looked straight in upon him. He got up from the table and went to them. The wall was stiff and straight beneath him, but the green vines swept up it like clinging spray, and there was the same rough masonry by which a man might climb.

He lingered there a moment. The sun was well down, only the horizon was softly banded with color, and the stars were beginning to shine, thin and weak, except where Venus hung, a ball of golden fire. Up from the vines the sweetness of their blossoms rose to him, and Weldon dreamed a little, and let his thoughts fly south to the lights of San Trinidad. Even at that distance he could see their long, pale hands upon the surface of the river. He could not help but think of Francesca Laguarda. Where was she now, or where was she bound, wild as a bird of prey, as

71

keen, as swift, as beautiful? The heart of Weldon ached a little. From both those girls, the invalid and the criminal, he had a touch of the same emotion. For both were lost beyond human help, it seemed, but one of them was eternally lost as well.

Aye, and he could not say that he wanted to be with her in order to save her from herself!

He went slowly back to the table and was about to sit down, when the bell jangled. He hastened, his heart in his throat, to the door of Helen O'Mallock's room.

It was not unlikely that there would be an attempt at this very moment. A cleverly chosen moment, before the new guard had settled to his vigil!

He wrenched the key around in the lock—but the door was fast. There was no further ringing of the bell! Desperately he gave the door his shoulder. An iron bolt tore with a screech from its fastening and he flung himself into the room, revolver in hand.

He saw the pale glow of the bedside lamp, and the paler face of Helen O'Mallock beside it. Nothing else, at the first sweep of his eyes.

"What is it?" said Weldon savagely. "What has happened? What frightened you?"

He was beside her, not looking at her; but one mighty hand hovered above her, as though instinctively to ward off a blow directed at her fragility, and in the other hand his revolver was ready. With his eyes he searched the corners of the room, the fluttering curtain, the deep hollows of the windows.

"What have I done! What have I done!" murmured the girl. "There was nothing—only—only—"

Weldon jerked himself erect and turned to her.

"Forgive me!" said he. "Of course you simply wanted me to do something for you. But I thought—at first—I—"

She completed the thought for him bravely and steadily.

"You thought someone was here? Of course you thought that! And you came—like a lion! It would have been a dreadful thing if another man had been here. I—I don't think you would have stopped to ask questions!"

He allowed himself one deep, deep breath.

"I'm not usually like this," he said. "But then, I'm not

accustomed to such a thing as this. As soon as I get more settled into the thought that men really could try to harm you—well, in the meantime, I'm sorry I came like such a fool! But—why was the door bolted as well as locked?"

"Poor Aunt Maggie!" said the girl. "That was she, no doubt. Just old custom made her do it."

"There's nothing I can do for you?"

"No."

He was withdrawing, but as he reached the door she said in that faint voice—it barely reached him: "I haven't told you why I rang. I'll be more careful another time. But a moment ago I thought—it was a sort of wild, foolish, giddy feeling—that you had gone—that you had left the house, Mr. Weldon, and that I was alone in it again with Aunt Maggie, and old Dogget."

When he was back at his cooling supper, he sat down with a scowl on his brow. His heart was still racing from the shock of that summons, but it was not that which kept the thoughtful frown on his forehead. She had felt that he had left her the moment before. Was it not at that very moment that his thoughts had been flying south to San Trinidad and Francesca Laguarda?

Well, there is such a thing as mental transference, he argued with himself, only this was a strange and quick proof of it! And it gave Weldon a melancholy pleasure to think that so quickly there had been established between him and that poor girl a sympathy so profound and so sensitive. If only he could step into her mind as she had stepped into his, it would be hard indeed if the machinations of even the most subtle poisoner could reach her life!

Aunt Maggie came wheezing to the library door just as he finished dragging the table to a place where the windows did not command it so easily.

"Did I hear something up here? Wasn't there some kind of a screechin' and a screamin' up here?" gasped Aunt Maggie.

She had a hand pressed close against her flowing skirt, but Weldon had a glimpse of a cleaver weighty enough for the felling of a bullock.

He was pleased at the sight of it, more pleased than he had been before with her black, sour face. But he raised a finger and pointed at her.

"You bolted the door of Miss O'Mallock—the door that opens onto my room."

"What door is there left to bolt?" asked the cook fiercely. "Besides, I didn't bolt it. How could I? How could I leave the room after boltin' a door like that? Could I go reachin' in through that door and shove the bolt home? What for are you talkin' to me like that, Mr. Weldon?"

"The door was bolted. I had to break it open," said he.

"If that door was bolted, you *couldn't* bust it open," she declared confidently. "I know what them bolts is fastened with, white man!"

He looked calmly at her, more calmly than he felt. After all, she was right in the first place. The door could not have been bolted from the inside—unless Helen O'Mallock left her bed to do it! And that, of course, was unthinkable. Who, then, had slipped the bolt?

The answer was simple. No one at all had slipped that bolt, but being made to work easily, being constantly used before, the jar of closing the door when the Negress left the room had been sufficient to engage the tip of the bolt with its lodging place.

"The door had to be broken open," he said dryly, to get rid of the Negress.

Aunt Maggie was not to be so discarded.

"What you find to break it open with?" she asked.

"My shoulder."

"You—your shoulder!" said she. From disdain and scorn her voice altered swiftly.

"Most like it ain't fat that you got on them shoulders of yours, then," said Aunt Maggie.

She waddled a few steps into the room. The enormous breadth of her grin was sufficient to warm the heart of Weldon. It made up for her accustomed sulkiness.

"Ah'm just gunna go back to the kitchen and thank the Lawd that we got a man in the house, after all, these days," said Aunt Maggie. "But how'd the table come there?"

"I put it there," said Weldon.

She glanced at the windows with sudden understanding.

"Well, sir, Mr. Weldon," said she, "Ah'm a mighty proud woman to be cookin' for you, sir!"

And she waddled off into the dimness of the hallway, her cleaver silver-bright in her hand as she went. There was no fear in that heart of hers!

Weldon smiled after her.

He finished his supper and then turned his attention to the library. It was a collection of books after his taste—not fiction, but memoirs, odd bits of history, old bound magazine files, volumes of letters, biographies, and among the latter he found a fat tome which was the history of the O'Mallocks.

He sat down to that, greedily.

Half the night he spent over it, while Aunt Maggie first removed his supper tray with a husky "good night," and then left the house to him and that pulsing, whispering silence which pervades old places.

It was an old family, that of O'Mallock. It dawned upon Occidental history writers about the same time that Henry II began to send warriors to Celtic Ireland from Norman England, and thereafter the O'Mallocks were in the midst of all the Irish struggles for freedom. In the days of Elizabeth, an O'Mallock had even been honored with execution in proud London itself!

After that the details became more full. The O'Mallocks were becoming a shade more civilized. They were leaving letters and memoirs from which the family history could be built up in detail. And what detail it was!

They had done everything. They had been everywhere! Soldiering chiefly!

One had been a captain of the host at Perugia in the golden age of the fierce Baglioni, and had fought against a brother commanding a section of wild riders for Florence. And another had followed Constable Bourbon with a detail of Swiss pikemen. And another had marched under Gustavus, while his own cousin followed Wallenstein. One had led a column of steady English at Fontenoy, and another had charged with those soldiers of the Irish brigade to beat them back.

It seemed ever that way. The family was not large. But there were always enough of them to maintain the old nest in Ireland from which went out a sufficient supply of fighters to strike on both sides with truly beautiful Irish logic! There was always a Protestant O'Mallock to irritate his Catholic brothers. There was always an O'Mallock in Spain to cross swords with an O'Mallock in France.

They had sailed the sea, and in every imaginable service there also.

In short, the blood of the O'Mallocks had been so rich and so wild that it was not strange to Weldon that the old general himself had been such a firebrand. There was nothing about him in this book. It had been written during his life, but his exploits were not detailed. Indeed, there was no need of that. For the O'Mallocks were always the same steel. Not a one of them but loved fighting for its own sake. Not a one of them but was rich in invention and usually poor in pounds. They were desperate enemies; they were desperate friends. They were cavaliers of high adventure.

In addition, there was something to be said on a darker side. It was no wonder if the general had many enemies, if he were like the rest of his clan. Their wit, sometimes, was akin to dangerous cunning. And there was a sort of cruel craft about most of them.

But the general was dead, and all that was left of the fire, the blood, the brain, the fury of the O'Mallocks was locked up in the body of that poor girl, now set about with enmities not of her making.

The fire was burning low; it would soon be out. And the jewel of all the clan would be lost forever!

15. Empty!

When Weldon at last laid aside the book it was past midnight. The air was cold and dead in the room, so he unshuttered a window and leaned into the purer air of the night. He was not tired. He was not sleepy. For nature had given him the gift of accumulating rest as a camel accumulates fat, ready to be expended on long efforts of any kind. It was well, of course, to be within sound of the bell in the girl's room, but from what the doctor had said, he was more than reasonably sure that she would not call him. Like a good watchman, this was the time to make rounds.

So he locked the library door and that of his own room as well, and took the keys with him. He had on a pair of canvas shoes with rubber soles which made soundless walking an easy thing even for a man of his weight. He had, in addition, an excellent bull's-eye lantern, small but throwing a strong ray of light which he very well knew how to manipulate.

The hall itself was not a pleasant place for shaken nerves. There were two curtains breaking up its length, and these curtains stirred and shifted in an uncanny manner as little drafts worked at them. He would suggest to the doctor the next morning that they do away with these draperies. This house must be looked upon as a ship made ready for battle, and the decks must be cleared for action!

There were two stairways; one from the middle of the hall, a broad flight of steps, turning in a really noble curve as it descended, and the other at the southern end of the hall, a narrow servants' stairs.

He went down the smaller—if for no other purpose, to familiarize himself with all the passages of the house during the night. In the lower floor, at last, he began to explore from room to room. Most of the doors were locked. On the others he practiced the silence of his hand in turning the knobs and then gradually pushing the door open. For this can be done so that even the rustiest hinges in the world will give forth not a sound. A door open, he would probe at the darkness inside, using the lantern so that a mere needle of light escaped. With that needle he dotted the chamber skillfully, here and there, and in an amazingly short time he knew what was in it.

He had nothing particular to gain by this, except that he wanted to refresh himself in every lesson of stealth and subtle quiet that ever he had learned before. He was going into training, as it were, for the prosecution of this work, just as a man will go into training for a prize fight. And if he could bring mind and nerve and body to the proper pitch, he promised a keen struggle to those shadowy enemies of the girl.

Stepping back from the door of the storeroom, and closing it behind him, he had finished examining everything on the lower floor of the house. There remained a cellar of unknown size. A battered door opened upon it at the end of the corridor.

On this he worked with equal care, and finally he was able to open it soundlessly, as he thought. A steep, damp flight of steps pitched down before his eyes. It was evidently well below the level of water, for streaks of moisture appeared on the walls, and on the stone steps were traces of moisture; even little flat pools in the hollows of the stones, with the single ray of the lantern dripping across them.

Felt slippers, he observed to himself, would be better for this sort of work of exploration than the rubber soles, which would be sure to slip on wet stones.

However, he was firm on proceeding with this exploration. He kept close to the outer wall—because it gave him an easier way of getting slowly and carefully around every corner of the winding steps—and so he went down as though ten tigerish foes were crouching for him on the way!

He was very happy. What the fiery, red sauce of San Trinidad was to his appetite, such was a touch of danger to his somewhat phlegmatic nature.

He reached the first turning of the stairs and was about to continue, when he decided to fling another ray from the lantern before him.

No larger than a thread was that little point of light which he cast before him—and it fell straight upon a man's face coming up the stairs from below! Instantly his thumb flicked the shutter wide open, and the stairs were filled with a shaft of light, and through that light Weldon aimed his revolver—at Doctor Henry Watts!

The poor doctor clung to the side of the stairs with a hand thrown up before his face, and distinctly Weldon heard him murmur: "Heaven receive my soul!" Plainly the doctor thought that his last moment had come.

"It's I," said Weldon.

The doctor did not seem to understand. His brain was numbed with horror until Weldon descended to him and touched his shoulder. Then he shuddered violently and seemed to waken.

"I thought—I thought—" he began. "Weldon! Weldon!" he said then, and fumbled at the arm of the younger man as though to reassure himself of his actual presence. "But you are up in your room beside poor Helen, listening for the sound of her bell! How can you be down here, Weldon?"

"Suppose I ask you why *you* are here?" returned Weldon, his smile not at all pleasant to see. "Did you leave something behind you?"

"I had a thought," explained the doctor in his earnest manner, "that the reason they searched in the cellar of the house might be that they hoped—"

He paused and ran a hand over his mouth and down through his straggling beard, as though amazed that he should have spoken such words.

"I don't want any secrets that are unnecessary," said Weldon. "I don't want to force you to talk, Doctor Watts!"

The doctor hesitated and then shrugged his shoulders.

"Helen wanted to tell you everything from the first. She was right. There was no use bringing you here unless we were to tell you whatever we know. Come down here with me!"

Weldon followed him. They had reached a lower corridor, apparently directly under the main hall of the house. This passage had been worked in solid rock. Soft rock it was. Exactly what its nature, Weldon could not tell, but the surface, at least, was very dark, and there were marks of pick strokes more than a foot long. They had broken out this ground as though it were little harder than earth!

He saw doors on each side. One of these, the doctor opened, and Weldon saw before him an irregularly shaped room. The rays of his lantern refused to penetrate to the farthest corners. Deep, deep into the mountain side it extended, with high racks everywhere. The majority of them were empty, but there were quantities of dust-covered bottles.

"The general made wine an extravagance," said the doctor. "You see how thoroughly he did it!"

He closed the door and went straight down to the end of the corridor.

"Now you'll see what Helen wanted to show you at once. While I—forgive me—thought it would be better to wait until we knew you a little better!"

"I understand that," replied Weldon.

The doctor leaned. At the sheer face of the rock he fumbled for a moment and then stepped hastily aside. Weldon saw a mass of stone a foot across lean slowly and then fall suddenly with a clink. It opened out like a folding shelf. Inside, there was a little cavity.

"Now you see!" said the doctor.

Weldon, on his knees, was pouring light into the interior of the hole. He stood up and dusted his knees.

"When the general died," said Doctor Watts, "he should have left a big fortune to Helen. But there was almost nothing, as I told you. Now, sir, we have proofs that he converted large sums into cash. And this was a hiding place for his wealth. As he grew older, he came to distrust banks!"

The doctor said with real emotion: "I have no doubt that in this house the old general had secreted hundreds of thousands of dollars before the end came upon him!"

"And how was this found?" asked Weldon curiously.

"In a strange way! It was two months after the death of the general. The tomb he wanted cut into the face of the mountain had been completed and his body was placed in it, when a heavy earthquake shook the house. Going down to see if the foundations had been injured in any manner, we found that this shelf of rock had opened. Inside, there was this cavity—empty as you see it now! But when Helen came down to see it, she said at once she was sure that after the death of the general someone had opened this place and stolen the contents. It seemed likely!"

"You didn't have any suspicions?"

"Suspicions? Yes. But that's hardly the point at present."

"I don't know a more important point," said Weldon dryly.

"I mean to say, I can tell you about them afterward. We took it for granted that the entire fortune had disappeared from this hiding place. But still attempts continued to be made upon the house, beginning a short time ago. Why? Because there is still more money hidden away somewhere, and that money the thieves are after!"

"Do they expect to find it in the room of Helen O'Mallock?"

"Ah, but you see the point in this: If they kill her, the house is then closed for a time, at least. It's not likely that many purchasers would be found for a lonely building such as this, lost in the mountains and the pines. Let the house once be closed, and then the scoundrels will come to pillage it. They know that they cannot lay their hands on it at once, but they want freedom for a long search!"

The anger of the doctor and his scorn and rage against these villains made his voice rise higher. There was even a sort of fire in his eyes as he spoke. Then he went on: "Tonight I had a sudden thought. The general was apt to do things symmetrically. Might he not have put a similar treasure chest at the farther end of the hall? We had sounded the walls all over, but I thought that I remembered a little, rough projection."

He closed the stone shelf over the aperture and took Weldon to the farther end of the hall. There was, to be sure, a slight swelling out of the wall, and this the old man tapped.

"You see, I have the place blueprinted in my mind. But I was wrong here. Sound the wall for yourself, and there's nothing, and under a glass you see nothing more, either!"

Weldon tried for himself. Around the empty hiding place there was a very thin line visible, but then it had been opened many times; while the other hiding place, if another there were, had never been opened since the day when the general first sealed it, and carefully covered up the marks of the chisel!

He stood up again and turned to the doctor.

"You're a man with a sound mind, Doctor Watts," said

he. "D'you seriously believe that there is money hidden away in this house?"

"No," said the doctor gravely, "but there are three possibilities. The general may have squandered a great part of his money in unknown ways. Or he may have put it all away in the other crypt, yonder. Or, failing either of the first two possibilities, there may indeed be another portion of money—twice as great as the first, even!—hidden somewhere in the walls or the cellar of the house, or perhaps in the caves of the mountain!"

"Then," said Weldon, "why not tear down this house to the foundations and search every stone?"

"Are you and I to do the work alone?" asked the doctor, smiling. "And if we don't, how are we to find other men whom we could trust in such a search?"

He added: "Besides, to dig down through these foundations of solid rock and open up all the wall surface would cost a hundred thousand dollars, and even then, the money might not be found—might not be here."

Weldon was silenced. He suggested that the doctor come up with him to his room, and Henry Watts agreed willingly.

16. A Light Touch

When they came into his room, Weldon lighted the wood in the fireplace. The doctor, in the meantime, paced up and down the chamber. And as the smoke first rolled out and then the flame began to catch and sing, Weldon looked at the old fellow with increasing respect. Only the body of the doctor was feeble; his brains were lively enough. He was no hero, and yet he had courage enough to leave his own cottage in the middle of the night and come here for the purpose of examining the damp, cold, dark cellar of a house where, as he knew, there might be untold dangers!

Now, however, the doctor was not thinking of buried treasure and its possible hiding places. For he presently stopped in his pacing and said to Weldon: "There she lies, wide awake, listening to the night noises, praying for the daylight to come—and yet never uttering a single complaint!"

"Doesn't she sleep well at night?" asked Weldon anxiously.

"You will see! She sleeps hours in the day. At night I'm sure that she hardly closes her eyes. I try to make her confess, but she will smile and say that the night passed off very well. However, I have ways of telling!"

He nodded his old head with a frown.

"What ways of telling, Doctor Watts?"

"The books she reads, and the number of them that she gets through," said the doctor. "You can't read big, solid volumes in a moment between sleeping and waking."

"Then why don't we see if she's sleeping now?" asked Weldon. "It's a frightful thing for even a strong man to lie awake night after night! It would fray the nerves of Hercules thin, not to mention the nerves of a sick girl. There should be someone to talk to her—amuse her in some way."

He stepped toward the door, but the doctor threw up his hand in haste.

"Wrong, wrong!" said he. "It must not be done, my dear Weldon! You must understand that though I'm not a Christian Scientist, I'm a great believer in the power the mind holds over the body. Oh, a great believer in that! What is it that keeps strength in her now? Simply the thought that she is not seriously ill! We talk cheerfully together. We plan the trips and the rides which we soon will be able to take together. It is always just a few days —and then she will be up! I talk to her seriously of her good progress."

"How long has she been in bed?"

"A few weeks now."

"And still she expects to be well almost any day?"

"And yet she's not a fool, you would say," interpreted the doctor. "Of course she's not! But hope is a blinding bandage across the eyes. Believe me, it is an opiate which puts the mind to sleep. She is filled with hope. That is why I never question her too closely about her sleepless nights. All is done with a light touch. I smile. I am very gay when I am with her. So we carry on the battle!

"But," he went on in a graver voice, "if I begin to make midnight visits to her, she will grow suspicious, distressed. She will be concerned for you and me, keeping vigils for her sake. Then her nerves will begin to give way in real earnest. Believe me, my dear young man, when I tell you that we are dealing with a creature as delicate as gossamer, a soul as fragile as petals of flowers."

"I do believe you," said Weldon, "and I'll offer no more advice."

For he was touched by this speech, though he could not help smiling at the thought of the old doctor being gay! Mirth for Henry Watts would be like a song from an owl!

"I would like to know," said Weldon, "just how the general died. Was it a long illness?"

The doctor shook his head. His face was sad.

"Young man," he said a little impatiently, "if it had been a long illness, he would have been able to tell us where he had put away his property, I take it?"

Weldon nodded. "A sudden death, then?"

"In the middle of the afternoon, in his chair in the library. You've noticed the big leather chair?"

"With a foot rest before it?"

"That's it!"

"And he died there?"

"He'd spoken a word about a bad headache the day before. That morning he remained in bed late. Ah, if I had had a chance to talk with him about his symptoms! But, as a matter of fact, it irritated the general to have any one suspect that he could be sick. He used to say that he had not spent ten hours in bed between sunrise and sunset since he was a child. He never was sick. He refused to be!"

He sighed and then went on: "These men of iron, Mr. Weldon! I take it that you're one of the same cast yourself, in a way!"

"Not at all," answered Weldon; "next to being perfectly well there's nothing better than a fever, say. Clouds floating across your mind. The world made into another place. Voices sound like waves breaking in a cave. No, I have enjoyed a good many sicknesses, and the best part is the convalescence—lying weak as water, your body shrunk, and an enormous appetite beginning to gnaw at the insides like a wolf!"

He chuckled. "You see I'm the very opposite of the general!"

The doctor looked at him for a moment from beneath shaggy brows.

"You're a strange young man," said he.

"And the general's death?"

"No doubt he'd been weakening for months. But forcing himself on. Keeping the iron mask before our eyes. You see, he was over seventy——"

"But very fit, you said."

"No one is fit at seventy," answered the doctor with a touch of dryness, "and the fool who tries to be a young man at that age kills himself with the effort!"

Weldon was a little startled, but there were these flashes of unexpected bluntness in the doctor.

"He did spend several hours after sunrise in his bed on that last day," went on Henry Watts. "At lunch I noticed that he wasn't eating much."

"You were living here, then?"

"I used to come here for a shameless lot of meals. When I called the general's attention to the fact that he was not eating with appetite he was angry, and forced a large meal down his throat. You see the foolish pride of the man! Then, after lunch, when he should have lain down to rest —I suggested that he should—he snapped at me, and went into the library instead. No quiet reading for him. He picked up a history of the O'Mallocks. A very stirring thing. Well, age, bad digestion, much too heavy a meal, weakness which had been increasing lately, and then the shock of the stirring narratives in that book—all those combined to strike him suddenly. He died in his chair! We found his head fallen on his chest.

" 'He's sleeping!' whispered Helen to me. 'Dear dad! How we'll tease him about this!'

" 'We will,' said I.

"But after we were out of the room, I managed to slip back into it. I was not so sure about that sleep. There was something odd about the manner in which one hand was gripped and the other relaxed.

"I found him dead, and the body cold!"

"The heart?" asked Weldon.

"No doubt about that. The heart cannot stand the strain of all the foolish things that people will insist on doing to it. The heart must break at last. Fray the strongest cable for seventy years and at last even a small strain will make it burst. And yet it seemed impossible. I looked down at the bowed, dead head of the general. I could not believe that he was really gone from us. Even though I knew that his heart had stopped beating, I expected him to start up at any moment and laugh in my face. 'Death? Do you think I would surrender to death? Only for a moment—to show it that I despise it!'

"I really expected the dead body to spring up. You who did not know him cannot imagine his vitality!"

In fact, the doctor was so thoroughly overcome by the memory of that tragic moment that he placed a hand before his face and steadied himself by resting the other hand on the back of a chair.

"And you're sure," asked Weldon, "that there was no foul play?"

"Foul play?" gasped the doctor, dropping his screening hand.

"Poison, say?" suggested Weldon.

The doctor merely gaped.

"Of course, I know nothing about such things. I merely make the suggestion."

"Good heavens!" whispered the doctor.

He sank into the chair. He was so overcome by the horrible idea that he shook violently, and his lips parted and twitched.

"You see," explained Weldon, sorry for the shock which he had given Doctor Watts, "it seemed to me that it would be possible. And there would be a reason. Kill the general, so that the criminals would be left more free to search the house for the treasure they thought was in it. Then escape with the money which they found in that secret compartment you just have shown me. Afterward they come back again. By Heaven!" exclaimed Weldon, as the thought struck home to him. "There was the case of the poisoned water for Helen O'Mallock! You see how it fits in with the rest? They poisoned the general first. Now they return to see if they can't get some more spoil, and they're using the same methods in order to get rid of the poor girl!"

"Are you right?" said the doctor hollowly. "Can you be right? Ah, Weldon, right or wrong, you put a terrible burden on my soul! Suppose that crime was committed— and I in the house? Under my very eyes—and I with professional skill thrown away!"

He struck his hands heavily together and stared at the fire.

Then Weldon stood up from his chair and said quietly:

"We've got to get Helen O'Mallock away from this house."

"Ha?"

"We've got to have her moved. Let them rob the place! But let's keep her life. That's the main work."

"You'd kill her in ten minutes," said the doctor, "by even suggesting such a thing!"

"She's not as fragile as that, I hope," answered Weldon.

"You!" cried the doctor.

His excitement was growing great.

"I tell you," said Weldon, "this gloomy old place, and the memory of her father constantly coming back to her mind while she's in it, are enough to throw a strong man off balance, let alone a girl like her. She's got to have a change of place and a change of air!"

"Good heavens!" breathed the doctor. "Do you mean that you'd argue the point with her?"

"Would? I mean that I will!"

"I tell you," said Doctor Watts, "I forbid such a mad attempt! My dear Helen—my poor child—to be torn away from the house, taken I don't know where—the fatigue of the journey would kill her. Or, if not, to miss the things she has grown up with—to be placed in some sanitarium —horrible, horrible! Weldon, I know you mean well. But I repeat to you! As a doctor, with all my professional weight, I forbid such a thing!"

Weldon looked earnestly at him. No doubt Watts meant

the best in the world for Helen O'Mallock. But suddenly it struck Weldon that it would be very odd if this man, so long divorced from active practice, should still retain any great ability as a physician. There was a great deal of talk constantly on his lips about nerves, tenderness, shock, and other outmoded catch phrases. In that moment, Weldon resolved that he would see to it that other medical advice should be called in.

17. "Come Fast!"

He determined that at least there was nothing to be gained by antagonizing the good doctor. He saw that worthy man from the house and said good night to him. The doctor was very much troubled. He held Weldon's hand for a moment in both his.

"I have angered you, Weldon!" he said anxiously. "I've upset you. You feel that I'm tyrannical. That I perhaps am making great mistakes. Perhaps! I pray that I am not. Only, I must do what conscience and my professional experience tell me is best!"

Weldon said very heartily: "Doctor, I assure you I have every faith in your conscience."

He did not say "in your skill," but the doctor seemed relieved and went off with his rather rapid, fumbling stride. Weldon, watching him disappear, felt a touch of pity. He never saw the back of the old doctor, in fact, without a touch of that same emotion.

For his own part, he softly went around the house again. He did not try those dark, cold, reeking lower passages, but he toured around on the outside. He could not help feeling that it would be impossible to spy out the approach of skulkers toward the house. They had ample cover from the trees, and where the trees left off, outjutting rocks commenced. He himself would have guaranteed reaching the place even if a hundred eyes constantly scanned all the ground about the house.

He went on carefully through the dark, completed the tour, and came to the rear of the patio wall just as a thin sickle of moon sailed out from among the clouds and floated for a moment in the mysterious black sea of heaven. At the same time, something glistened on the side of the mountain above him.

He jerked himself about to face it, and saw—merely the glinting of some smoothly polished columns under the pale moonshine! He was surprised at that. He had not noticed such a structure before, when he came to the house in the sunlight. But, at that time, he had been directing all his attention to the house and the patio itself.

He went up the hill to the gleaming columns.

There were four of them, plain Doric affairs of granite; and their transporting to this place must have cost a bit of money. They held up a roof, or a pseudo roof. As a matter of fact, except for the columns, the place consisted of the dark rock of the mountain of Las Altas itself. This had been cut away, and when Weldon turned his bull's-eye into the place he saw at once what it was. A deep hollow had been chiseled into the face of the mountain, the columns inserted for the sake of supporting the entrance—or merely for ornament—and behind the columns there was a rather pretty scroll work of partially gilded iron to keep intruders—man or beast— from the interior. That interior contained a plain stone sarcophagus, undecorated except for a roll at either end. It was the tomb of the general, of course.

It looked so fresh and newly done that Weldon felt as though the old man must have been closed within that ponderous lid hardly the day before.

Then he turned back to the house, entered, and went softly up the stairs to his room.

It was three o'clock, and the rest of that night he spent in the library reading. It was not a pleasant session, at the best, with the wind occasionally stooping from the cold heart of the sky and crying out about the building. And his eyes grew heavy from following the print. At last he lay back and fastened his mind on the problem, for though he had no idea of trying to solve the thing by sheer inspiration, he wanted the facts to be ordered in his mind.

For this reason he restated everything and came to the odd conclusion that Francesca Laguarda was responsible for his presence in the O'Mallock house at that moment!

But then, his train of reasoning was not entirely absurd.

It was her dark and lovely face, her musical voice, which had started his heart beating at an unusual rate; and that in turn had made him look about for diversion— diversion which he found in heavy gambling in Cabrero's place; and the exploits at Cabrero's place, in turn, brought him to the notice of the good doctor, and the doctor brought him up the hill to the new adventure. So he reverted to Francesca Laguarda and wondered if he would ever see her again. He felt an odd surety that he would. No doubt she lived in the midst of dangers of the gun and the law, to say nothing of reckless automobile driving, and yet he was oddly sure their trails would cross again.

"In jail, perhaps!" smiled Weldon to himself.

In the meantime, he had much to try to learn here. He wanted to push, if he could, the inquiry as to the manner in which the general had died. There was one fairly sure way of finding out. They could exhume the body. He remembered gruesome tales of bodies dead for ten years in which the presence of poison had been detected. Arsenic poisoning in every case, he thought it had been!

Suppose he could prevail upon the doctor to have the body ordered out of the grave? The thing might be managed without letting Helen O'Mallock learn of it. He nodded grimly to himself as he arrived at that step in his plans. In the second place, he could only hope that he would be able to entrap the next visitors to the house of O'Mallock!

With this in mind, he found that the dawn had come. It made a rich picture from the window as he turned the shutters back. The Rio Negro quite belied its dark name and became a river of fire. The windows of the two towns blinked at him like crimson lightning again and again, and gradually the rose faded from the sky and the strong sun sailed up the height.

Aunt Maggie came not long afterward.

She paused, with her broadest grin, on her way to the room of Helen O'Mallock.

"You ain't no sleeper, sir," said she.

Weldon retired to a bathroom to bathe and shave. When that was finished, he found breakfast waiting, and he ate it with a grand appetite. Matters seemed better to him this morning. The sun lifts the veil from our minds and carries away despondency. He finished his coffee, smoked his cigarette, and hailed Aunt Maggie on her way back from the sickroom. She herself would take a letter for him when she went down to the market with her mule and cart.

So he sat at the library table and wrote the message.

Dear Ben: Come up to see me at once at the O'Mallock house. You will find out in San Trinidad or Juniper where the place is. Bring along your medical kit, please, if you have one with you. If not, buy a new one. I mean, stethoscope, thermometer, and your apparatus for taking blood pressure. I have a patient here for you. Come fast!

He sealed the envelope and wrote on the outside "Doctor Benjamin Wilbur" and put down the name of the hotel in San Trinidad. He was reasonably sure that Wilbur would be at the place by this time. They had appointed a tryst for which Wilbur had been overdue even the day before.

He was a rare fellow, this Wilbur, doubtless as complete a scoundrel as any man that ever walked in shoes, and with a criminal ability that ranged from cracking safes to picking pockets. But he was a pleasant companion, always amusing, usually walking on the heels of some rare adventure; and when Weldon was in his chronic state of hunger for excitement, he was apt to call on Wilbur, as he had not long before and asked for this appointment. But, in addition to his other qualities, Wilbur was a remarkable physician. Weldon himself had seen operations performed by him in the wilderness—delicate operations, when Wilbur had no more than a hunting knife and a pair of wire tweezers and a common needle and thread. He knew the human body and the frailties of the human mind, this educated crook, and this was a place where he could show his talents.

Weldon felt that he was stepping a little behind the back of Watts in sending off this letter, but he was willing to overstep the bounds of politeness far more than this if he could do good to the sick girl.

Then his bell rang, and he went in to see her.

She was in her chair beside the window, her hands and the page of her book in dazzling sun, her face half lost in the upturned collar of a bed jacket.

Had he slept well? Yes, very well. And she? She had had a good night, thanks to him—knowing that he was so near and that no harm could come to her! Had she been upset because of the way in which he broke down the door of her chamber? No, on the contrary, that was what had made her feel so secure. And her eyes looked at his hands, and then, slowly, turned up to his face, and she smiled at him like a child, with trust.

But as he left the room again, he heard a softly stifled yawn and knew that she had done what the doctor predicted—lain awake all night; and now she would sleep if she could, in the warm comfort of the sun!

18. What Had He Seen?

A little after midday, Wilbur arrived. Weldon, drowsing after luncheon, wakened at the sound of the man's step in the hall. He thought at first it was the old doctor, who had not made his appearance as yet. But, after a moment, he knew that Doctor Watts never could have moved with such a cadence.

Aunt Maggie brought the stranger to the library door and stood aside with the look of a watchdog until she saw Weldon take the newcomer's hand. Wilbur was drawn in, the door closed. They sat down beside a window and examined each other with faint smiles. They had been through much together. They were not really friends; but theirs was a mutual respect, and behind them lay much history which each had shared with the other.

"Is this game worth while, Lew?" asked the doctor.

"Ben, my boy," said Weldon, "this isn't a game. It's a three-ringed circus."

"You have to watch the three rings all at once, eh?"

"I have to if I can. But this show is all in the dark, and I'm straining my eyes to find out what's happening."

"Do I step in?"

"You stay out," said Weldon with decision. "There's no real need of your talents here, my boy."

"But this?"

Wilbur touched with his hand the little morocco case which he carried.

"Two rooms from this there's a girl ill with consumption," said Weldon. "You're to see her for me. Mind you, you're simply here to pay me a friendly visit. I hope that you will be allowed to examine her. You understand? She's a delicate thing."

"How delicate?" asked Wilbur.

"In every way. The brave kind, my boy!"

"Beautiful, of course?" said the doctor, showing a fine, white set of teeth as he smiled.

He would have been remarkably handsome except for the extreme height of his forehead, which made his entire face seem rather elongated.

"I've only seen one woman more beautiful," said Weldon.

"Then she can't be so delicate as all that," replied Wilbur. "Beauty is a light, Lew; it doesn't shine from burned-out lamps!"

Weldon brushed this idea quickly to one side.

"You're going to revise your ideas of women when you meet her."

"Is this a rich marriage, Lew?" asked the other, calmly turning his head and noting the contents of the room.

"She is going to die!" said Weldon, leaning a bit forward.

The doctor nodded, unmoved.

"I mean to say," explained Weldon, "the old fellow who's taking care of her believes that she'll never get out of this decline. A grand old man he is. But probably half a century behind the times in his medical ideas. Wilbur, if you save her I—"

He paused.

"As much as all that?" said Wilbur with his cynical smile.

"More, more!" said Weldon.

The other nodded with a brightening eye. "I'll do my best for her," said he. "As a matter of fact, I wouldn't miss a chance of doing you a serious good turn. It is bound to come back to me later on. I'm a gold digger, you know!"

He waved an airy hand, but Weldon knew that, in fact, it was a confession of faith.

"And have I been brought down here for this, Lew?"

"You have, for this job only. I'm sorry."

"Tush! It's nothing. Go ahead and prepare my way."

So Weldon went to the sickroom and tapped on the door. A sleepy voice told him to enter. He apologized for disturbing Miss O'Mallock, but it had happened by a rare chance that an old friend of his had come to visit him—a truly great doctor. Would she let the physician see her?

She opened her eyes and looked up as though she were greatly frightened.

"Do you think I need any doctor other than dear Doctor Henry, Mr. Weldon?"

"Of course, Doctor Watts will cure you. But here's a fellow who might show you a short cut. And, after all, don't you owe it to yourself to take every chance?"

She closed her eyes to think.

"You're kind," said she. "If Doctor Watts could be asked about it first?"

Weldon bit his lip. It was exactly the thing which he had feared.

"Very well," he said. "But Wilbur is staying only a short time——"

"Won't you introduce him to me, at least? Then afterward—if Doctor Watts——"

Weldon went back to his friend.

"You're to be allowed to sit in her presence for a little while," said he. "But the old fossil has to be consulted before you examine her. Come with me and be agreeable, Wilbur. Wipe the sneer off your face and off your mind. Will you try to do that?"

He took Wilbur into the sickroom. Helen O'Mallock lay in peace and smiled at the new medical man with perfect trust, while Wilbur led off smoothly and pleasantly with talk about Las Altas and the southern mountains, and weird burro trails which he had followed among them. Weldon thought that he managed it very well and he was surprised and disappointed when, at the end of a half hour, Wilbur announced that he must not tire the patient.

He promptly retreated to Weldon's room, where the latter said grimly: "You were just beginning to win her confidence, man! What do you mean by breaking off the talk like that before you had a chance to——"

Wilbur raised his hand.

"I was there long enough to find out all that I wanted to find out."

"You were!"

"I was."

"You know what's wrong with her, then? Do you really know, Wilbur?"

Instead of answering at once, Wilbur looked long at his companion.

"And *you* don't know?" he asked sharply at length.

"I? I'm not a doctor. How *should* I know?"

Wilbur dropped into silence again, walking rapidly up and down the room.

"It's serious—of course," suggested Weldon, following the other with gloomy eyes.

Wilbur shrugged his shoulders.

"It's fatal, man?" went on Weldon.

The doctor spun about, dropped his hands into his coat pockets, and stared again at Weldon.

"*I'm* not the patient," said Weldon. "Don't act as though you were studying a disease in me."

"Come clean with me," said the doctor. "You're in love with this girl?"

"I? No."

He answered slowly, looking carefully into his mind.

"I see," said Wilbur, and began to pace the room again.

"You see what?" snarled Weldon.

"But you're serious about this?"

"Entirely! Don't be so mysterious! Tell me at once: Can anything be done for this poor girl?"

Wilbur considered again, but once more he shook his head.

"Not by me," he said. "I couldn't help her."

"Does that mean that nobody could help her?"

"No, it doesn't mean that."

"Benjamin, I'm within an ace of chucking you through that window!" cried Weldon. He added: "Will you talk out to me?"

He was astonished to hear the other say calmly: "No, I won't talk out to you. I've said every word that I intend to say about her and her case."

"Will you tell me why?"

"I am not a Sir Galahad or a King Arthur," said Wilbur. "However, I'm a doctor, and there is such a thing as professional etiquette."

He shut his teeth together with a snap and Weldon, angry and confused, realized that there was no more to be had from him on that subject.

He turned suddenly to another theme.

"Very well, then. We'll let that drop. But tell me another thing. Is it difficult to discover if a man has died of poison?"

"It depends on the kind. And how long the man has been dead."

"Say arsenic—and dead one year."

"Perfectly simple," said the other.

"You're sure?"

"Yes."

"Then go back to Juniper," said Weldon, "and return

here after dark. Come as silently as a thief. Will you do that?"

"To make an autopsy, man?"

"Yes."

"Wait a moment, Lew. Do you mean to open a grave?"

"I mean just that."

"It's a horrible business," said Wilbur slowly.

"Listen to me," said Weldon. "If it's horrible for you, do you think it's not ten times more horrible for me?"

"True," nodded the other.

"You'll come, then?"

"I can't refuse you anything, Lew. But I would like to ask—"

"Ask nothing. Not a word."

"Very well."

"I'll expect you an hour or so after sunset. No, make it eleven o'clock."

Doctor Wilbur sighed.

"Friends," said he at last, "are expensive luxuries. Good-by!"

He left at once to ride back to Juniper, and Weldon watched him away. He was almost inclined to call back Wilbur at the last moment, for he was committing them to a course of action which might ruin them both. However, he finally snapped his fingers and turned away. Every nerve in his body was jumping.

For what had Wilbur, in fifteen minutes, seen in Helen O'Mallock? What was the thing which professional courtesy kept him from mentioning?

19. Someone Before Them!

When Doctor Watts arrived later that afternoon, Weldon told him at once of the coming of his friend, Wilbur, and the old man listened earnestly.

"Heaven forgive me," said he, "if I should not see that everything possible is done for Helen! Send for the doctor again."

But Weldon excused himself. It was improbable, he said, that he could get Wilbur out to the house again.

"Did he see Helen while he was here?" asked Watts.

"He did—for a few minutes."

"And what did he make of her?" asked Watts, looking fixedly at Weldon.

"Nothing," said Weldon. "Of course, he simply sat and chatted."

"Sat and chatted," said Watts, muttering. "Sat and chatted! And he made nothing of the case? Tell me, Weldon, is that fellow really a good doctor?"

"A wonderful doctor," said Weldon with conviction.

"He made nothing of her—he made nothing of her," said Doctor Henry Watts half to himself. "Ah!"

He kept on nodding for a moment, as though this were a most extraordinary thing. It increased the bewilderment of Weldon almost to the point of expression. But he resolutely kept silence. There was about Helen O'Mallock something extraordinary which to the professional eye of a doctor revealed information of the greatest importance. In fact, Wilbur had thought it strange, apparently, that

Weldon himself had not detected it, even with an unprofessional eye.

What could it be? He strained his mind at the problem. Watts went on to see his patient and Weldon followed him to the door of the room, in time to see the greeting, in time to hear her asking eagerly if he thought it a good thing that she should be seen by the new doctor.

"By all means! By all means!" said Watts. "If Weldon can get him up here again. Ah, my dear, you should have let him look you over even while I was away! Because two heads are better than one, eh? There are short cuts to a complete cure, at times."

Weldon, having heard enough, went back to doze in his chair in the library. He was much relieved when he discovered that Watts was not so narrow-minded as to wish to keep the care of the patient entirely to himself.

But what was it that struck Wilbur so forcibly? The beauty of the girl, of course. Her pathos, too. Her shadowed, wearied eyes, as well. But what beyond, so much that Wilbur had not credited that Weldon himself had not seen the thing? He determined that if Wilbur did come that night, he would tax him more closely and try to get at the meaning of his odd remarks and his still more odd attitude.

But, when the meeting actually took place, other things drove that question from Weldon's mind. Well before the appointed time he was waiting, walking impatiently up and down. The faint sound of crunching pine needles halted him, expectant.

From beneath the trees, the tall form of Wilbur stepped. He looked calmly about him, even as he came forward.

"What nights you have up here!" said the doctor. "What nights, eh, for a man in love?"

"We'll take our poetry a little later," said Weldon. "Have you everything?"

"I hope so."

He showed his case of instruments.

"I need a strong light, Lew."

"I have one here. It will throw strong light for an hour."

"That's time enough. Are you ready?"

"Ready as can be!"

He led the way up the hill toward the dimly revealed

99

columns of the tomb of the general. At the gate he paused and fell to work on the lock with several long, strangely formed keys.

"How much danger of being watched at this game, old fellow?" asked Wilbur cheerfully.

"About two chances out of three of being caught."

The doctor whistled.

"That's cheerful," said he. "However—how's the tomb arranged?"

"I found out today from the cook. There's a top slab of stone. Under that is a plain pine coffin of thin sheets of granite, and the body is inside that, wrapped in lead."

"No metal clamps to hold down the outer cover?"

"It makes no difference. I have a saw here that will go through them as though they were butter and not iron at all!"

"Sing ho!" smiled Wilbur. "You always were a clever fellow, Weldon."

The door presently gave way under the manipulations of Weldon, and he pushed it wide with a careful touch.

"Good silent hinges even on a grave," said Wilbur, "and that I call the height of luxury! Let me have that light a moment, will you?"

Weldon passed it to his companion, who sent a ray of the light on one of the hinges, touched it, and rubbed his fingertips together.

"Quite so! Quite so!" said the doctor. "They've been oiling this hinge, old fellow. By gad, they make things convenient for ghosts here! Or ghouls, should I say?"

Weldon snatched the light and stared at the hinge in turn. The oil had been put on with care. Only by closely looking could one see a faint gleam, and then it rubbed off as grease on his fingertips.

"Black, too," observed the doctor. "So careful to keep everything right that they've even gone the length of blackening the oil so that it would look like a stain on the iron. Who takes care of these gates?"

Silently, Weldon went ahead. He passed under the canopy of the tomb. He stood beside the long, ponderous sarcophagus.

"Hold the light," he said briefly, and then laid hold of one end of the topmost slab.

It was a ponderous weight, but it yielded at once to his strength of arm. The lantern was held ready by his companion, and as the stone moved, he darted a ray inside.

"Empty!" said he. "Quite hollow, old boy!"

Weldon replaced the lid. He turned slowly away, and without a word they left the grave and returned to the dark shadow of the trees.

"Someone went before us," murmured Wilbur cheerfully. "Oiled the gate to keep it from screeching, and having cut through the iron clamps that held the upper slab in place, they took out the body—and where are we, Lew? Can you tell me?"

"Was it done recently or long ago?" asked Weldon.

"Recently, of course. That oil hasn't been there more than twenty-four hours. It hasn't had a chance to thicken up yet."

"Recently!" murmured Weldon. "Then someone has guessed that I might come out here. Somebody has been here before me, and the place has been rifled so that I won't have a chance to find out the secret of the general's death!"

"It looks very much like it."

"Darn your smooth, smug way!" yawned Weldon.

He stretched himself and yawned.

"I like it better and better," said he.

"You do? I confess if I were in your boots, I'd like it less and less. Someone's watching you and reading your mind, old-timer. And if he can read your mind, he's clever enough to make all manner of trouble for you."

"Of course he is," said Weldon. "But suppose I play my game in my own way—let the fellow catch me if he can! That's what I propose."

"Cold steel in the hollow of your back, Lew. Think it over! Is it worth while? Would ten like her be worth the price?"

"Don't read my mind," Weldon protested dryly. "Leave that for the man who opened this grave today. By Jove, it must have been today!"

"Of course it was! And that means, this evening."

Weldon muttered softly.

"I'm going back."

"To the tomb?"

"Yes."

"Tell me. Do you need me any longer?"

"Not a bit. Can I let you have money? Are you short?"

"Your money would do me no good. There's not enough of it. So long, Lew!"

"How long are you here?"

"Until I hear from you."

"That may be never."

"Ah, well," said the cheerful doctor, "a man has to take the chances as they come to him. So long again!"

20. "I'll Tell Everything!"

Wilbur went lightly down the hill, and Weldon, instead of going at once to the grave, as he had announced that he would, slipped softly through the trees behind the tall doctor. He had had a definite reason in wishing to send Wilbur away. It was no formed and solid thought, but a suspicion, which he wished to follow out.

It was a fair night overhead, the moon was not yet up, but the bright multitude of stars gave a faint light. The wind did not stir. But the fragrance of the pines floated down in silent rain, drenching the air. Weldon took heed of all this as he slipped along behind his friend. For his mind could not be so preoccupied that his senses failed to perceive all that was around him.

The doctor, with a good deal of cunning, had lodged his horse below the house and to the left of it in a thick growth of trees. To this place Weldon softly followed him, and saw him untether and mount the animal.

Nothing stirred around him. Weldon himself crouched low in the shadow of the brush and he watched keenly, seeing that the doctor was safely getting away. Well mounted, he left the trees. The soft sound of the footfalls of the horse, taking off at a walk, was quickly out of the ears of the listener—and then a form slipped from the brush just opposite him and started up the slope in the direction of the house.

Joy shot through the heart of Weldon, and for the first time he felt that he had his hand on some thread of the quiet mystery that lay in the atmosphere of the place. The form drew closer in passing—a woman!

He stepped like a panther after her and took her from behind by the elbows.

It was like putting hands on a wildcat. Twice she almost had writhed herself free. Twice he tightened his grip. At last she stood still.

"You're breaking my arms," said she quietly.

It was the first sound she had made. Afterward she was quiet again, panting a little. Her hair had fallen down. It rushed in a great wave over her shoulders, and the ray of a star glistened on it. Weldon did not relax his grip, but waited a moment, thinking.

"Who are you?" he asked.

She was silent.

He had a sailor's habit of carrying knife and twine, without which a man is hardly a man aboard a ship. So first he worked his hold down to her wrists, slender, round, strong. He shifted both wrists into one hand, and he cautioned her gravely: "If you try to tear free now, I'll snap the bones like pipestems. I mean that, my dear."

Whatever she thought of the threat, she stood still, while he worked the strong twine round and round the wrists, binding them inextricably together. Then he freed her.

"Face me," said Weldon.

She turned toward him.

"Will you tell me now who you are?"

He hardly waited for the answer which he knew he would not get, and sent a flash from the bull's-eye across her face.

Francesca Laguarda!

Even those iron nerves of Weldon were a little unstrung. And then horror stiffened him.

"Who else is here with you?" he asked her.

"No one."

"You've sent them away then, have you?"

She did not answer.

"Before we go into the house," said he, "I'm going to ask you what brought you here?"

Again she was silent.

"Of course, it's a good game," said Weldon—"dumb when the questions come. It's the right game, as a rule. But I'm not a common dick. I knew you were crooked, my dear, the first moment I saw you. I've heard bits about you since, and they all point the same way. But until this moment I didn't guess what a pure breed of wildcat you are. Is that right, Francesca? Is there any streak of good in you?"

He chuckled at the thought that she might answer such a question.

Then he said gravely: "As a matter of fact, Francesca, there is something to be gained if you'll confess to me. I'm not ordinarily a stone so far as a pretty girl is concerned. I take a good deal of interest in pretty girls. A *great* deal of interest in them, as a matter of fact. And you're beautiful enough, my dear, to open my heart. I can't help wanting to go easily with you. I don't want to throw you into jail. I don't want to fit a rope around that soft little throat of yours."

He paused to let these ideas become planted in her mind, and then he continued more harshly: "But, my dear, it is very true that unless you give me information—a ton of it, Francesca—I'm going to do all those things. I'm going to take you down to the jail; and I'm going to sit in front of your door to see that you don't get away; and I'm going to see that justice is done on you—unless you'll give me a chance to do justice on your friends!"

He waited. Still there was no answer from Francesca Laguarda.

Anger began to rise in Weldon. He stepped a little closer to her so that the fragrance of her was in his nostrils, mixed with the pure sweetness of the pines. He

104

snapped on the bull's-eye and sent a strong shaft flooding upward across his face and hers.

She was so close that they were almost touching, but there was no real fear in those shining black eyes of hers. Instead, busy thought was filling them. Actively her keen young brain was turning and twisting for a way of escape, just as her body had been turning and twisting a moment before in his grip.

"Look at me, beauty," said he. "Do I have the look of meaning what I say? Do I have the look of a fellow who will be able to push himself through to the finish of a deal? Can I be cruel? Could I harden my heart against Helen of Troy, even? Look at me, my dear, and then tell me what you think?"

Long and straight was the glance with which she probed his eyes, his mind, even. And then her eyes closed. It was answer enough, and he snapped out the light with a harsh little laugh.

"You're right, Francesca," said he. "I'm a brute and a bully, and I'll treat you exactly like a man unless you choose to talk to me."

He heard her draw a breath and knew that she was weakening.

"About what must I talk?" she asked him faintly.

"One moment and I'll show you. Come with me."

He kept two fingers on her arm. It was true that she could not run away from him, and her tied hands could do nothing against him, but still he felt much safer when he was actually in touch with her.

He guided her beneath the face of the house, and through the trees, and toward the tomb upon the hillside. He expected that she would hold back, but she did not attempt to resist.

Straight up to the gate of the tomb he led her, and then said sternly:

"Francesca, what I do with you depends entirely on your frankness with me. Tell me from the shoulder! Who was it that helped you to open that gate, and cut the irons that held the upper slab, and steal the body out of the grave?"

She had been steady as a rock up to that moment. Now she gasped quickly and reeled a little. He supported her, looking down keenly in the starlight, for he was reasonably sure that she was merely shamming. But there was something about her quick gasping for breath that convinced him. She was disturbed in all truth now!

"Good!" said Weldon. "A hard young woman you are, Francesca! When I first met you, I thought that you were simply a clever thief, a grand smuggler, a daredevil at the wheel of a car, and a very successful worker of men. But when I found out that murder and the rest were on your list as well—why, it dampened my spirits a little, Francesca. But now I begin to think that you may almost have a streak of conscience in you. Is that right, my dear? And if it is right, will you talk out and tell papa all about this grave robbing?"

She said faintly: "I'll tell you everything. I'll talk— I'll tell you everything. But will you give me—a little moment—to—to—"

"Steady, steady!" said he. "All the time in the world. No hurry, Francesca. Just walk up and down with me. Then we'll begin to open up the subject."

21. In a Vital Point

The moon came up suddenly as he walked her back and forth on the little level stretch before the tomb, so he led her back into the woods. Here, in a long, narrow clearing, they passed back and forth, into deepest shadow, and then again into the pale shining of the moon, by which he could see her face, doubly pale, and her eyes, doubly large and dark.

106

He talked to her carelessly of herself while he waited for her to grow calmer.

"I feel as if I know you very well, Francesca," said he. "I feel as though we'd walked this same ground before. Sentimentally walked back and forth and admired the moon, and the trees, and other things. I feel that we've been very fond of one another. I feel as if I've seen your face many times. But that's true of all the beauties. They open the heart and give one something important to think about. They connect one with great thoughts. Great crimes; great follies; great tragedies; great mercies; nothing small should come from a woman with a face like yours. So that I'm glad, my dear, that you're in harmony; a soul as big as the soul of a man, inside, and the beauty of an angel, outside. It makes the picture good. How many things could ruin you! A voice like the voices of chorus girls. A foolish laugh. A loose tongue. Contemptible vices. But you have none of those things. Tush! You're all made of one piece. You are, in fact, a grand girl, Francesca! Sweet, sweet Francesca; sweet poison! How much better to have you even the demon that you are, than to have you an innocuous little fool? In fact, my dear, clearly as I begin to see behind the scenes, into the darkness that might be called Francesca's soul, I could be in love with you. Mad with love; drunk with love! I could build pyramids—or wreck jails—for Francesca! However, I know of a flower that I hold up before my eyes, and it makes me safe from you. It makes me free of care, completely. She that lies in the house, yonder! Do you know her, Francesca? Answer me, because I'm curious."

"I know her," said Francesca faintly.

"Are you feeling better now?"

"Yes."

"But before we begin the other thing, tell me if you ever saw her face to face?"

"Yes. I've seen her face to face."

"And she saw you?"

"No. Not exactly."

"Are you being honest?"

"Yes, I think I am. She was going past me, absent-minded. But I was watching for her like a hawk."

107

"Good!" said Weldon. "Like a hawk! Of course, you're always like a hawk. Always really fierce. Do you ever soften, Francesca? Does anything ever cause you to open your heart?"

"Why do you ask me?" said the girl.

"Isn't it a fair question?"

She was silent, but she raised her head a little and he knew that she was staring angrily at him.

"A moment ago," said he, "I thought that even Francesca, even terrible and grim Francesca might be touched if she were to meet that dying girl in the house, yonder! But now I see that I was wrong! She could melt steel. But she couldn't melt Francesca."

The girl broke in sharply: "You're talking a great deal of nonsense. If you have something to get out of me, will you come to the point?"

"Thank you," said he. "I needed a touch of the whip. Now I'll try to keep the running fast and straight. In the first place, since we're working on the task of finding out all about these matters from the beginning—you had a hand in the killing of the general?"

"No, no!" said the girl.

Weldon listened, amazed. There was a burst of real emotion, real horror and disgust, in that soft cry. He did not dream of doubting her!

"You had no hand in the actual killing of the general, then?"

"No," she repeated with a shudder.

"But afterward you came into this job?"

"Yes."

"When you first saw the girl and she first saw you— that was when you entered?"

"Yes."

"You had been looking about for her, so as to see what you could do with her?"

"Yes."

"Now go on from that point, please. Who asked you to start on this business?"

"No one," said the girl.

"By Heaven," cried Weldon, "how can that be possible? The general was killed—you had no hand in it— but afterward you came into the case all by yourself?"

"Yes," she said.

"You admit that he was killed with poison?"

He heard the slight catch of her breath, and he went on: "But though you had nothing to do with that, you helped the murderers to steal the body away from the grave tonight? You knew that I suspected the murder, and that I intended to have a private autopsy performed. You knew that?"

"No."

"Come, come!" said Weldon. "Then why were you out here tonight?"

"It's useless for me to tell you. You are sure not to believe what I say."

"Try me, try me, my dear girl. I will stretch every point in your favor, if you like!"

"I've been interested in this old house for a long time," said Francesca.

"Good!" he commented dryly. "Artistic interest? Or did you want a quiet place for your old age?"

"Very well," said the girl. "If you intend to scoff at everything I say from the beginning, you may go on with the scoffing. But I'll not go on with the talking."

"You're right," he confessed. "I know you're right. Will you strike ahead then, Francesca? Tell your own story, straight out and uninterrupted; but if I find you lying, I'll start you for real misery on earth—because that's what prison life would be for you!"

"No," said the girl, "you never could keep me in prison."

"You're the clever lass who would melt your way out, is that it?"

"My life is always my own," said she.

And though she said it quietly, he knew that she meant it. It gave him a little touch of awe and respect for her. He even bowed to his prisoner.

"Francesca," he said, "I salute you. Continue!"

"I told you that I was interested in this house, in the beginning. The reason was that I wanted a place where we could arrange easy deposits of loads brought over the frontier. In the old cellars up here we could dump shipments and they'd never be found. And a couple of safe men could guard them here. Then we could work from this side, distributing. This could be our shipment headquarters for goods going into Mexico, too."

"That's neat and probable," he said.

"There was no one in the house except the girl," said Francesca. "I wondered how I could get her out of the place."

"And then you had a clever thought—slow poison, eh?"

She started, but instantly she laughed, and the sound was quiet music under the trees.

"I *am* all evil to you," said she.

He was rather taken aback by her calm. She had regained entire possession of herself.

"Go on," he directed, rather ashamed of his suggestion.

"I didn't want to harm her. First I wondered if the place could be bought, but she's a fool. She put a sentimental value on the house and wouldn't take money for it."

"Poor girl!"

"Well, I wanted to play fair with her, Lew."

"You know that name of mine?"

"Yes. I know all about you."

She said it shortly, as though the information were not of much importance. "But since I couldn't have the house by fair means I made up my mind that I'd frighten her away. Ghosts—strange appearances—that sort of thing."

"Ah!"

"So I sent up some of the boys to just let themselves be seen drifting about in the interior—to do something weird, if they could manage it."

"And that poor girl an invalid! Go on!"

"They were both spotted. *Dio mio! Dio mio!* What young fools they were!"

"Are you Italian?" asked Weldon.

"When they had both failed," went on Francesca Laguarda, leaving that last question unanswered, "I thought it would be a good idea if I tried my own hand. There are little tricks of making oneself up."

"You were going to show yourself to her, were you?"

"That was my idea. I came up the hill, and on the way I heard someone coming. I slipped behind some brush. It was a man who got on a horse and rode away. After he had gone, I started on for the house, and I hadn't made ten steps before you had me."

"That's the full truth?"

"Yes."

"And what was your make-up to be?"

"There's a little metal box in the pocket of my jacket."

He found it, opened it, and the cold light of phosphorus was seen.

"Done up in this stuff, you would have killed her," said Weldon. "Go on!"

His anger was coming back.

"That's all there is to tell."

"How would you have got to her?"

"Not through your barred windows."

"You know about them?"

"Of course. While you were in the library, I intended to open the door of your room, get to the girl's, and slip in. After that—"

"When she screamed?"

"Sounds won't carry from her room to the library."

"You simply would have slipped out again?"

"I would have tried to."

"How would you have opened my door?"

"I have a key."

"Where?"

"In the same pocket."

He found it and flashed the light on it. His careful eye could remember the pattern; and it was identical with his door key. Certainly her story was hanging together.

"What spies did you use to learn all this?"

"No spy at all."

"Be careful, Francesca!"

"I am careful. I'm telling the truth. The Negress can't keep from talking. When she goes down to market she lets everything out about what's going on in the house."

Weldon bit his lip. Certainly it was very possible.

"You had nothing to do with the removal of the body of old O'Mallock tonight?"

"Not a thing."

"Francesca, I'm sorry to tell you that you're a clever, calm, and quiet liar, but a liar nevertheless."

She made no protest.

"I wonder what would be the best first step!" murmured Weldon. "She's seen you before? I'm going to take you into the house, Francesca, and there I'm going to introduce you to Mis O'Mallock by name, and see what she can make of you!"

He knew by the electric start of Francesca that he had touched her in a vital point.

22. The Slamming of a Door

He was rather cruelly pleased when he saw that she feared this step, for her calm before this time had irritated him. She was totally in his power, but she had refused to show any signs of funk. Now she said, steadily enough: "What do you gain by that, Lew?"

"I'm not quite sure," said he. "But if it upsets you, my dear, I know that it's a good idea."

And taking her by the arm, he urged her forward. She did not actually press back against him, but she went with slow steps, and he thought that he felt a tremor run through her. They had almost reached the door when she paused.

"What can I do to change your mind?" she asked him. "You have me at your mercy!"

He would have guessed that that speech had never been on her lips before.

"You could begin by telling me why you dread facing Helen O'Mallock so terribly."

"Is that enough?"

"I don't know. You might try. A good, logical story, Francesca, is all that I ask from you."

"It's as simple as could be," said the girl. "This is the way of it. I was sent to the States for my education, and I went to the same school that Helen O'Mallock attended."

It was, in fact, a simple explanation. He pondered it for a moment.

"Why not tell her that same story that you told me? She's as mild as milk, Francesca."

"And then stand by and hear you tell her how I planned to frighten her out of her father's house?"

"That's a point," nodded Weldon. "But—tell me—you were a great friend of Helen O'Mallock's at school. Is that it?"

"I was her best friend."

"And that, in the first place, was what made you know how she could be played up?"

"Yes."

"Rather an unfair advantage to take of her, wasn't it?"

She was silent, but he saw her head droop a little, and it seemed wonderfully strange to him that she should be so troubled by what, in her wild life, must seem a small affair.

"Tell me one more thing. Had she ever harmed you in any way?"

"Never."

"Something that irritated you, Francesca. I mean to say: You were rather fond of some youngster who preferred a blond beauty to a dark one like you."

"Helen? She never looked at the men!"

She said it with careless certainty, and he bit his lip.

"No excuse for you, then? You see, I'm trying to talk on your side of the fence," said Weldon. "I don't want to think that you're not only a crook but a cold-hearted crook, too. But you had no reason. Helen O'Mallock had something that you wanted. You set yourself to get it. You knew she was ill?"

"No," said Francesca.

But her answer was neither easy nor quick, and he shook his head.

"It won't do," said he. "You have to come with me, Francesca. Right up the stairs and into Helen's room, and then I'll watch you meet her."

He put his hand on her arm to urge her forward, but

at that, it seemed as though the strength melted from her. She shuddered and then sank on her knees with something that was half groan and half sob.

It was a cruel thing to do, but Weldon was not bent on mercy just then. He was thinking of that pale and helpless girl who lay upstairs in her chamber, bravely fighting against despair, smiling gently on the death that lay before her. The bull's-eye flashed in his hand and shone dazzling on the face of Francesca. He saw it white and strained with fear and with grief, as well, and hopelessness stared up at him from her eyes.

He snapped the light out again, rather staggered. Even Cunningham, master of men that he was, had spoken of this girl as a grand spirit, a leader and a conqueror, as it were; and here she was on her knees. No matter how beautifully she might be able to play a part, this total dissolution of her will power was not what he had expected. He was pinched for a moment with remorse.

"Francesca," he said, "there's no good funking it this way. Stand up, will you?"

He put his hands beneath her arms and drew her erect, but still she swayed a little, quite helpless in all seeming. She had begun to sob. She seemed to fight against that weakness, but the hollow sound still rose and broke in her throat.

"It's no good," he said again. "I don't like to push this thing through, but I have to do it."

She leaned against him; he supported her almost like a lover in his arms, the violence of her weeping sending a faint tremor through him.

"Lew!" she whispered brokenly. "I know about you. I know that you're fair and straight. Be fair and straight now. No matter what you think, I swear that you'll do no good by this thing. It will kill me as surely as bullets or poison—and it won't do Helen a whit of good!"

"It will kill you?" said Weldon. "How will it kill you? Is Helen a basilisk?"

She did not answer.

He shook her gently but impatiently.

"Francesca, if you want your second chance with me,

114

you'll have to talk out. How will it kill you if you come before Helen O'Mallock?"

She stammered. The words were not clear to him.

"I didn't understand," said he. "Is it because she would know enough and, seeing you, she would be able to put certain things together? Would she know enough to put a hangman's rope around your neck, Francesca? Is that it?"

"Heaven help me!" was all that she said in answer, and her sobbing grew heavier than ever.

"Mind you," said Weldon, "I don't like the business. But I have to go through with it. Can you walk? No? Then I'll carry you!"

He picked her up in his arms and bore her rapidly toward the house. She did not attempt to resist. She did not plead any more, but turned her face to his shoulder and shook with grief and misery and helplessness until Weldon's teeth were hard set. He felt an overwhelming wonder that he had found the way to strike down this young tigress and unnerve her. He had not the slightest idea what made her so dread facing Helen O'Mallock; and he was burning with curiosity to find out. He knew then with a sudden and vast certainty that when those two stood face to face, all this mystery would be solved at a stroke —yes, even the death of the general, even the removal of the long-buried body! And yet he pitied Francesca Laguarda.

As he carried her into the shaft of yellow light that streamed through the open rear door of the house, he paused a moment. She was beautiful even now, with her masses of black hair streaming over her shoulders. Her face was covered, but he could see the throat, and that curve of the cheek which Italian painters of the golden age had known how to paint.

In that moment of pause, he had time to wonder greatly at himself. He knew that she was a criminal, that there was little good to be said of her. He knew that he was carrying her to a room where a pale, sweet-faced girl would strip Francesca of her mask and show her ugly, naked soul. And yet in the same instant, he knew that he loved her. The wonder and the sweet pain of love were in his heart.

Yet he went on quickly and entered the hall.

Aunt Maggie came out on him, carrying an armful of clothes which she dropped as she saw Weldon and his burden.

"Lord, Lord!" she said. "What you all got there, Mr. Weldon?"

"I've got an answer to several questions," said Weldon. "Come along behind me. I may need you!"

He went up the steps, the Negress following with grunts of surprise, and he even heard her cry out with a sort of sudden amazement.

He carried her into the library. He was glad that Aunt Maggie had kept up a fire in that room; it gave it a welcome and familiar touch of comfort. He laid Francesca Laguarda on the couch. She turned her face again, until it was half covered by the upholstered back of the couch. She was not weeping, but she was trembling violently from head to foot.

It would not do to take her in this condition and show her to Helen O'Mallock. This wild, disheveled, storm-tossed form was enough to unsteady stronger nerves than those of that delicate child.

"Aunt Maggie," he said to the Negress, "do you know how to pull this girl together?"

She stood beside him with her arms folded on her ample bosom, a scowl on her forehead, her lips compressed.

"What you gunna do with her?" she asked sharply.

"I'm going to try to make her presentable—with your help. And then I'm going to take her into Miss O'Mallock's room."

The cook started, with a gasp. Her black eyes glittered with emotion as she stared at Weldon. But she made no comment.

"You're right," said Weldon in quiet explanation. "It would not do to show her to your mistress in this condition. She has to be made presentable. What can we do?"

"She's gunna faint," said Aunt Maggie slowly. "I know by the tremblin' of her. A whiff of ammonia would do her a power of good."

"Where is the ammonia?"

"I'll get it. On the kitchen table, beside the door."

"Stay here with her. Watch her like a hawk. Her hands

are well tied, and if she tries to get to her feet, throw your weight on her!"

Aunt Maggie looked down at the big, amber palms of her hands with a grim nod, and Weldon hurried from the room. He wanted to save time, and he wanted to get his eyes away from Francesca Laguarda for a few moments, for her beauty was like an opiate, stealing his senses.

He had reached the kitchen and picked up the ammonia bottle when he heard distinctly from above a loud, harsh cry, and then the heavy slamming of a door.

23. Aunt Maggie Out

No greyhound on a course ever ran more swiftly than Weldon. The ammonia bottle crashed on the floor. Gun in hand, he bounded up the stairs and reached the library door to find it shut. He tried it—the key was turned. But he had his own way with doors in a time of emergency. He drew back and hurled his weight against it, using the bunched muscles of his right shoulder as a sort of pad against the shock. The door groaned under the impact and gave a little. He flung himself forward again, like a charging bull, and lurched through the wreckage of the door into the chamber, half stunned, but with his gun ready and swinging to find a victim.

There was no victim in sight. Only Aunt Maggie half knelt, half lay in the corner against the window, and the same glance showed Weldon a little tangle of twine on the hearth.

Mysteriously, Francesca had managed to free herself

of the twine, had attacked the old Negress, then slammed and locked this door, and then—

The window, perhaps!

If she was tigress enough to manage the other two feats, she was tigress enough to manage this one!

He gained that window with a bound and leaned far out. The moon rode high and clear. All that face of the building was naked, except for the climbing vine, whose leaves shivered and winked like pale silver in the moonlight. He scanned the ground beneath the wall.

It seemed impossible that she could have managed to climb down the face of the wall so rapidly. Certainly, in the time since that door was slammed and locked, she could not possibly have got down the hall to escape in another manner.

His own room, perhaps?

He went for it on the run—but though it was a woman for whom he searched, he had his teeth set, and his gun ready. Beautiful she might be, and his heart full of her, but she was as dangerous as fire!

He gained his room. Both closets he jerked open in turn, and then he even glanced under the bed.

She was not there!

He stood still in the middle of the room and, drawing a long breath, he tried to make his brain clear, and yet it would not.

How could she, in the first place, have freed her wrists? He knew something about securing hands in case of need, and he never had made a more careful job than he had with the small, soft hands of Francesca. Granted that her hands were free, with what did she attack the Negress?

He strode back into the library and found Aunt Maggie standing swaying, her hands pressed to her head.

"She freed herself from the twine and got at you, Aunt Maggie?" he asked quickly.

"She done that!" groaned the cook.

"How did you manage to get her away?"

"You cain't catch a lightning flash with your bare hands!" declared Aunt Maggie.

"Of course you can't. And then?"

Aunt Maggie pointed to a stick of firewood which lay in the middle of the hearth.

"That!" nodded Weldon. "She went past you like a flash, got her hand on that, then dropped you with it. And which way did she run?"

"The lights was turned off," said Aunt Maggie. "I couldn't see nothin'."

"Badly stunned, eh?"

"If you got that ammonia, Mr. Weldon, I sure could use a sniff of it!"

"Sit down here," he directed. "The little fiend! I hardly see how she— But forget about her, Aunt Maggie!"

"I will," said the Negress, "as soon as the bell stops death-tollin' in my head. My head ain't iron, Mr. Weldon!"

He, stepping back from her, picked up the fallen twine and passed it restlessly through his fingers, he saw that the ends were not frayed or rubbed through, but concisely cut.

How could she have managed that, lying helplessly on her back on the sofa?

"Aunt Maggie," he said, "can you talk now?"

"I don't want to talk," said she. "I want to go to bed and try to sleep off this here headache, Mr. Weldon! She raised a lump like an egg here."

"Let me see," said Weldon.

"Ain't you never seen a bump on the head before?" asked Aunt Maggie, scowling.

"It might be a fracture. You'd better let me see the place."

"I ain't gunna," said she stubbornly.

To Weldon it was almost more bewildering than all else which he had seen and heard on this strange evening. That Aunt Maggie, or any other Negro, male or female, should fail to make the most of such an injury, received in such a way, fairly clouded his brain.

However, he did not push that inquiry further, merely saying: "How did it happen, Aunt Maggie? What did she do? Did you let her sit up on the couch?"

"What would I be letting her do that for?" asked Aunt Maggie, with a darker scowl than ever.

"I'm only asking questions," said Weldon.

"Then answer 'em yourself," said Aunt Maggie. "I'm pretty tired and I'm pretty sick in the head. It was you that brought that young woman right here into this room. What kind of questions could *you* answer about her, I'd like pretty much to know?"

She marched for the door, and Weldon let her go until, reaching it, she case a sidewise glance at him.

"Aunt Maggie!" he called suddenly.

She turned on him with a jump.

"What right you got yellin' at a woman like that?" asked Aunt Maggie.

"Come back here by the fire!" said Weldon.

"I ain't gunna," said Aunt Maggie. "I'm tired. I'm gunna go to bed and try to—"

"Dream about what she paid you for setting her free?"

"Paid?" gasped Aunt Maggie.

But her dark face turned a peculiar ashen color, strange to see.

He raised a threatening forefinger and shook it at her.

"Very well, Aunt Maggie, if you won't talk, I'll tell you what happened!"

She started again. It seemed to Weldon that if ever guilt appeared in a human face it appeared in hers now.

"The moment I left the room," said Weldon slowly, "she turned on the couch and looked up at you, and let you see the most beautiful face that ever told lies, eh? Was that what happened first?"

"I ain't talkin' and I ain't listenin'," said Aunt Maggie. "What do I care about pretty faces?"

She turned away, but only partly. A peculiar fascination kept her half facing him, and her eyes glittered like the eyes of a wild animal as she watched and waited.

"Then she offered you something of a good deal of importance, Aunt Maggie. Money from her purse, or maybe the purse itself, or even a ring from her finger!"

"She didn't have no rings on her fingers," said Aunt Maggie fiercely.

"Money then—and a promise of a heap more of it if you would cut the string that tied her hands together. And you did it!"

"I did not!" cried Aunt Maggie.

"Then you pretended to be stunned," said he in quiet continuation. "And the proof that you've been lying is that there is no lump at all on your head!"

She winced. Then: "White man," she said, "I ain't heard no more fool talk than this since I was a mite of a baby!"

She started for the door with a rush, but Weldon sprang before her.

"You've done that part of it!" said he. "But now tell me what that woman—or spirit—or whatever she is—did afterward. Which way did she go? Into my room? Through this window? Or—did she fade into the wall?"

He swept it, as he spoke, with a suspicious eye, remembering its four feet and more of thickness. After all, the general was exactly the sort of odd old chap who might well have arranged some such secret device in the walls of his house.

Aunt Maggie had turned sullen. She struck at the hand which held her fat arm, but when that blow failed to dislodge his hold, she made no further effort, simply refusing to speak, and staring at him sullenly.

"Maggie," he said to her, with all the solemnity which he could muster, "I want you to know that that young girl who was here—pretty as she was, graceful, and all that—is the very person who may be the death of your mistress. Do you hear me?"

She looked him straight in the eye and deigned no reply. And suddenly he knew that there was nothing which he could say. There was nothing he could do with her. He had his own suspicions, which he felt to be founded upon a very Gibraltar of certainty, but those suspicions were of no use to him in any court of law.

He loosed her arm and stepped away from her.

"Go back to your room, then, and pack up your things, and get out of this house. Because I more than suspect that you're a member of the filthy crew that is haunting the old place, and if I have another day to work on you, it may be hanging business. Do you hear me? Believe what I say, because I mean it!"

She gave him a murderous side glance and then walked slowly past him and through the doorway.

He, thoroughly dissatisfied with himself, began to pace up and down the floor. He never should have left that girl alone with a slow-handed fool like Aunt Maggie. Once she was gone, he should have raced downstairs and tried

121

to find trace of her near the house. And as a result of this whole evening's work he simply knew that Francesca the beautiful was connected with the fiendish work that went on at the O'Mallock house, and that even the cook, Aunt Maggie, might have a part in it.

Then, gloomily, he settled himself for his night's vigil.

24. Aunt Maggie In

In the morning he was amazed to see Aunt Maggie enter the library with his breakfast tray. He was amazed; he was angered, too.

"You're going to try to stay on and bluff it out?" said he. "Aunt Maggie, it will be a black day for you, I promise you!"

She turned on him in sudden heat.

"Mr. Weldon," said she, "right from now on, I don't want no more words with you. You're nothing but a barkin' dog, and I don't fear your bite none whatever!"

With that she swept almost majestically from the room, leaving him more angered, more bewildered than ever. More bewildered, because he had not expected such calm self-assurance from the cook; angered, because it was the clearest proof of his impotence that the only way he could strike at her was to talk frankly with the one person to whom he wished to reveal not a thing.

He held his own counsel until mid-morning, when Doctor Henry Watts came to the house; and then he greeted the doctor with an almost sardonic courtesy.

"You look a little pinched, my dear boy," said the doctor gently, and he patted the heavy shoulder of Weldon almost affectionately. "Now, you must turn in and really sleep today. I'll take charge of my dear Helen. Is there any news?"

Weldon looked vaguely at him. "News?" he said, "Oh, nothing of much importance."

"Good," said the doctor, "I was right from the first moment. I knew that once a formidable person like you had come to the house, the others would not dare to come near it! They're afraid of you, Weldon. They know about you, and they're wonderfully afraid of you!"

"In fact," said Weldon, "they're not paying any particular attention to me or to any other living man. They're more interested in the dead!"

"Dead?" said the doctor, falling back a pace.

"The dead!" said Weldon.

The doctor moved back close toward the door, his lips parted, and his frightened eyes were fixed upon Weldon.

"You need rest," he said in a voice that was very uncertain. "You've been going without sleep too long, Weldon. I insist that you turn in now and sleep the clock around. I'll take care of everything here!"

He made a fine, large gesture, and Weldon smiled a little.

"I mean the general when I speak about the dead," said Weldon.

"Ah? Ah?" said the other.

"The general, lying out there dead in his grave. Is that clear?"

"Clear and horrible! Horrible and clear!" said Henry Watts. "Good heavens, Weldon, what do you mean?"

"That they've taken the body of the general out of its grave and spirited it away!"

The doctor clasped his old, heavily veined hands together.

"Taken—the—dead—body—away!" he echoed. "But, Weldon, Weldon, who are they?"

"I wish I knew!" said Weldon through his teeth. "Ah, I wish with all my heart that I knew! Because if I did, I'd go on their trail, and I'd be on that trail for the sake of the fight that I could get out of it. I'm growing a little excited, Doctor. You're right when you say that, and I intend to use a gun freely. I'm going to sprinkle this case with lead the way a man sprinkles fresh meat with salt, before I'm through!"

"The general's body!" said the doctor, his slow, old brain reverting to that fact. "But how could they?"

"By cutting the irons that hold down the slab of stone," said Weldon shortly, "and then by lifting the body out and carting it off. That's how it could be done!"

"And the grave lies open!" gasped the doctor.

"The grave is closed as neatly as ever," said Weldon. "There was more than half a chance that we never would notice what had happened."

"Ah, Weldon, and how did you chance to notice what had happened?"

"Because I went there to do the same thing."

"The same thing?"

"I went there to have an autopsy performed on that body, because I have a very good idea that the general died of poison, Doctor Watts!"

The doctor turned white and dropped into a chair.

"Good Heaven!" he breathed in the most helpless voice.

"There's no Heaven in it," said Weldon. "The fiend is running the affairs of this house! Doctor, go in and give Miss O'Mallock a stimulant that will give her strength for an hour or so."

"What do you mean?" said the doctor, still white, and now trembling violently, as these ideas overwhelmed him.

"Because I have some things to tell her that may almost shake the soul out of her body."

"Weldon," cried the doctor, "I can't permit it! Heavens, what is happening! The world is gone mad! My brain spins! And now you want to subject my poor dear Helen to such a shock as this?"

Weldon said simply: "You've been in charge here for some time. I don't want to hurt your feelings, but you've made a mess of things. Now you're going to do as I tell you. Go to her at once and give her something to steady her, and then let me know when I can come in."

"Very well," said Henry Watts and, standing up, he went meekly toward the room of Helen O'Mallock.

Weldon heard the knock, heard the old fellow enter the room, and the soft click as the door was closed. Then he sat down and waited for almost half an hour before Aunt Maggie swept through—evidently summoned by the bell.

She gave Weldon a look not of hostility, he thought, but rather of curiosity and interest, as though she wondered what he might be able to do next, and his color rose a little. It was very odd! Certainly he must have fallen off from the man he used to be if he was unable to strike a little awe into the heart of an old Negress, no matter how deep in crime she might be.

Aunt Maggie went and came again, hooking her thumb over her shoulder, while she jerked her head at Weldon and said briefly:

"She can see you now, white man!"

He gave her a scowl, rather childish in his pettishness, and went on toward the room of Helen O'Mallock.

The door was ajar. As he came closer, he heard her voice, always a little husky and low-pitched, but now speaking cheerfully with Doctor Watts; and when he opened the door he found her sitting in the full flash of the morning sun, a great straw hat with a huge, flapping brim drawn down on her head. It left her face quite in shadow, but the golden hair shone like metal in this radiance.

She smiled her good morning to Weldon. The doctor rose and hovered around her with a sort of maternal anxiety.

"You want to talk to Helen?" he said to Weldon. "I don't suppose you mind if I stay with her?"

"Oh, of course not," said Helen gently, smiling up to him.

"I have to talk to you alone," said Weldon. "I'll see you later," he added to Watts.

And the doctor, still hesitant, went to the door, fumbled at the handle of it, and then left in jerky haste, as though he were driving himself.

Weldon waited until the latch had clicked. Then he sat down in the chair opposite the girl. Her hands were folded in her lap. In spite of himself, he could not raise his eyes at once to her face, but dwelt on the crystal pallor of those slender fingers, through which the sun seemed shining with a rosy glow.

At last he forced himself to terseness.

"I've come to talk seriously and in a way that is going to upset you," he said. "Are you prepared to be shocked?"

"I think I am," said she. "Is it something about you?"

"It's about you, and your own affairs," said he. "I've wanted to keep these things to myself. But I can't. I have to have more authority in this house to act as I think fit, or else I'm not worth a pinch of salt to you."

"Do you want me to change doctors?" said she anxiously. "Is that it?"

"I want you to send Aunt Maggie away."

She looked at him with childish wonder.

"But how could I ever live without Aunt Maggie?" said she.

25. Questions and Answers

Weldon stopped to reconsider. He had come full of a sort of stern purposefulness to tell her his mind, but seated in the chair opposite her, he hesitated, and looked more closely beneath the shadow which her broad-brimmed hat cast. He could not help remembering, at that moment, the scornful remark which Wilbur had made, that no woman could be beautiful unless there was a certain amount of the glow of strength in her.

So it seemed now with Helen O'Mallock; for there was doubtless the glow in her face. A strange glow, contrasted with the pallor of her hands, and their slender feebleness. But he wished that he could banish the sun which shone upon her, for it was difficult to decide what portion was the actual radiance of Helen O'Mallock, and what part was

126

due to the reflection of the light of the strong sun, filtered through the translucent brim of the straw hat.

Her very smile, in these conditions, seemed rather different. It was not altogether the childishly innocent thing which he always had thought it before. It had a suggestion of cynical amusement, as she lay there, watching him.

So strongly did this thought grow upon him that he scowled violently at the floor to banish the illusion.

She had been waiting all this time for him to speak but, at his frown, she leaned forward a little.

"You're angry about something. You're not pleased with me," she said.

He glanced up again. Her lips were parted, and he could see that they were trembling a little with anxiety as she watched him. All the doubts of Weldon flew away.

"I was only thinking where I could make the best start," he said.

She nodded and smiled a little, to encourage him, and he could not help thinking what a strangely pathetic smile it was. She, young, beautiful, wealthy, fitted to have the world of strong men at her feet; but robbed of her wealth by scoundrels, and soon to be robbed of all her beauty by cold death—and so reduced to him!

Dark passages out of his life rushed back upon his mind. Bitterly he despised himself, and what he had felt for her before this moment—gentle affection, pity, kindly devotion—now was transferred at a stroke and changed to worship, to self-immolating sacrifice, to boundless passion for service.

"Then I'll begin with a name, Francesca Laguarda," he said. "What do you know about her?"

"Francesca Laguarda?" she said. "Francesca Laguarda? But I know her very well, of course! Why, she went to my school! She was in my year. Why, I know all about her!"

It stirred his heart to hear her speak so. He leaned forward a little and planted his elbows on his knees.

"You know all about her?"

"Oh, yes."

"What was she, then?"

"Was she?" cried the girl, her soft, husky voice raised a little. "Is Francesca—"

127

"Ah, no, not dead!" he said in haste. "I didn't mean that. But what I wanted to know was—well—who are her parents?"

"Ah, poor Francesca!" said Helen O'Mallock. "They died when she was quite young, I think. She never knew them. She grew up rather by herself. I mean to say—other people raised her. Strangers, almost."

He nodded. That description of her early life fitted perfectly into what he could imagine about her past. He felt, with a hot rush of championship, that if she had had the proper opportunities, if she had been surrounded by the right environment for a young girl, surely she would have been able to grow into a pure and perfect maidenhood—even like this of Helen O'Mallock!

The comparison was fatal. He bowed his head again. No, this strange night flower, this beautiful and wild girl never could have been like Helen O'Mallock!

"Does that make you sad also?" asked Helen.

"No, no!" said he. "No, no!"

But his eye wandered wildly.

"Do *you* know Francesca?" she asked with eagerness.

"I don't know her," said he. "I was almost beginning to think that nobody knew her, but you say you did?"

"Oh, yes," said she. "I was her roommate, you know!"

"Ah, yes. And that made you know her?"

He added, as she stared a little: "I mean to say, that there are some people one could live with for ten years, side by side, and still one wouldn't know them really!"

"Are there such people?" she asked innocently. "I've never happened to meet any like that!"

He bit his lip. He would not have changed her, of course. No, she was perfect as she was, and not a line nor a color of her character should be altered. Nevertheless, it would have been very useful to him in this moment if he could have learned a little more about Francesca from a companion of a more worldly nature.

"No doubt you never have," he said, as gently as possible. "But I have. But tell me, Helen, what would you say about Francesca?"

She looked at him and then above and beyond him. "I don't know," she answered. "It's hard to put people into words."

"Why, we could go stage by stage. Was she beautiful or plain, for instance?"

"Ah, most people said that she was beautiful. Very beautiful, most people said."

"But what did you thi.ik, Helen?"

"I don't know. I never thought a great deal about her looks."

"And why not? I mean to say, one generally has a pretty strong impression about the looks of a person one is constantly with. How long were you with her?"

"Two years."

"As a roommate?"

"Yes. Always. We never would have any other."

"And yet you never had an opinion about her looks?"

"Yes. I thought she was handsome, of course. One could see that. She had regular features, you know."

"Regular features!" breathed Weldon. "Regular features! Didn't you see that she was a most heavenly and sky-towering beauty?"

"Such a beauty as all that?" gasped Helen O'Mallock. "No. I never thought that. It seems that you know her very well?"

"No, no!" said Weldon.

But suddenly he was so stirred, remembering the loveliness of that face, and the fragrance of her, and the dangerous elegance, and strength, and swiftness of her body that he had to leave his chair and take a pace or two about the room, for otherwise he would not have been able to keep his countenance at all before the sick girl.

She was watching him all the time.

"Ah," she said slowly, judicially, "but I think that you *do* know her rather well, after all!"

He made a brief, fierce gesture.

"I don't want to talk about myself and her," he said. "Beautiful, heaven knows she is. But now, tell me what else you thought about her. Was she—in short—a good girl?"

"I have an idea," said Helen O'Mallock, "that you have found her a very good girl."

He looked sharply at her, started. There could be no doubt that she was smiling at him. Yes, and smiling

129

openly, a little. As though she began to read him, and keep the knowledge to herself.

At that, he went to her and leaned a little above her.

"You can read my very shallow secret," he said. "I haven't kept it well at all. But I tell you, and I swear to you, that what I think of her has nothing to do with what I ask you. I want your honest opinion. Was she honest?"

Helen O'Mallock slightly turned her head. The smile was still on her lips, a little thoughtful and a little sad.

"I don't think that I could say she was honest," she admitted at last.

"Not honest? Did she, for instance, ever deceive you?"

A sort of anger came into the face and the voice of the girl as she answered: "Yes, yes, yes! Sometimes I used to think that her chief delight in the world was in deceiving me!"

He drew in a great breath. It was a very damaging thing that he had heard. He could not stay still under it, but again he walked the room. It was well enough for such a girl as Francesca Laguarda to deceive others—strong spirits—men. But to deceive this angel, this not-yet-risen spirit—that marked her very blackly indeed!

"She deceived you?"

"Yes."

"Almost as if she enjoyed deceiving you?"

"Yes. I don't want to hurt your feelings—"

"Forget me!" said Weldon, his great voice reduced to softness, but with a vibration that made the whole room tremble with its violence. "I want you to speak as if I never had laid eyes upon her!"

"Yes," said Helen O'Mallock obediently. But she seemed to be frightened and, lying back in her chair, she watched her guardian with awe-stricken eyes.

"How did she deceive you?" said he, his voice rough again.

"Why—I hardly know how to put it. Yes, I do. She liked to pretend that she was nothing but good. That there was no evil in her. She even liked to pretend that men made no difference to her. But all the while, that wasn't true. I used to believe her for a long time. And then, gradually, I began to see that she couldn't live unless she

130

had the admiration of men. I saw it by degrees, you know!"

"But isn't that hardly more than natural for a girl?" he answered. "Isn't it—"

He checked himself with an effort. He had come here to find out what truth he could about this wild woman he loved, and now he was shielding himself from the knowledge of the facts and trying to prove not that she was bad, but that at any rate, she was good enough for him!

26. To No Purpose

He was thoroughly ashamed, when he saw this. And particularly when he asked the next question:

"What else did you have against her?"

"I haven't anything against her," said Helen O'Mallock faintly. "And I hope that I'm not displeasing you!"

"Displeasing me? Nonsense!" said Weldon.

He spoke the last word under his breath, but he was very afraid that she had heard it.

"What has my pleasure to do with the matter? I'm asking you for the facts."

She raised her handkerchief to her lips. Above the handkerchief, he could see that her eyes were very big, and rather hurt.

"Tell me," he said suddenly, "this woman—"

"Do you mean Francesca?" she asked gently.

"Yes, yes. I mean her. What was she to you?"

"I don't know how I should answer that."

"You say she was your friend?"

"Oh, yes."

"A good friend?"

"Yes."

"Your best friend, perhaps?"

Helen turned her eyes away and then nodded, almost reluctantly, as he thought.

"I suppose that she was."

"And did she steal your affection, Helen?"

"I don't mean to say that!"

"I'm not asking you to defend yourself," he assured her. "I want you to take this easily, to speak only the truth, to care for nothing except to tell the truth exactly as you see it. Are you afraid?"

"Yes," she whispered.

"Of me?"

"Yes!"

"Confound it," said Weldon, half through his teeth, "don't you see that I'm not here to torment you, and that I'm only asking you these questions because I have to? Can't you see that, Helen?"

She paused. He saw her swallow.

"Yes!" she said.

He gripped his hands hard and turned away from her. He was enormously moved. In part because he felt that the naked, terrible truth about the girl he loved was being revealed to him—yes, and standing more dark and awful as compared with the bright and angelic clearness of this child's nature.

He could hardly look upon her as more than a child. And, like a child, she was rebelling against this torment that he imposed upon her.

"Then answer me without any trembling. I see that you're trembling, Helen."

"I can't help it," said she. "I don't want to tremble. I want to be very brave."

"Then what unnerves you?"

"It's you," said the poor girl. "You look so terribly upset and—and scourged by everything that I say!"

"I'm not," said Weldon, fuming at his lack of ability to play a part. "I'm not at all. As a matter of fact, I'm—"

He paused and looked miserably at her.

"I've thrown away the thought of her, except as a curi-

132

osity, and because I have to find out about her for other reasons!"

There was a little intaken breath; Helen O'Mallock looked on him almost with horror.

"But I don't want to make her out too bad!" she said.

"Of course you don't! But she lived with you all those years and still she took her pleasure in deceiving you!"

She folded her hands together, tried to answer, and failed. She could only look at him with great eyes of remorse.

"I haven't wanted to hurt you," she said.

"Helen!" he cried at her. "How could you hurt me? What strength is there in you to hurt a huge hulk like me? Now be reasonable and don't talk foolishly. This Francesca Laguarda, you agree with me—she's bad."

"I haven't said so!"

"Ah, you haven't said so!"

"I've told you, instead, that she was my best friend. But I admitted that she had a few faults, because you wanted to know!"

"I wanted to know," said he sadly. "I hoped against hope that perhaps you could wash her clean. But I see that you can't. Don't argue about it. Let's be simple, clear, and frank with one another. Now I'm going to tell you what I know: That Francesca Laguarda has been at this house, or near it, trying to do you some injury."

"Francesca?"

"Yes."

"But not Francesca!"

"Yes, yes. Beautiful, beautiful Francesca!"

"But how could she be here, when she's in Italy?"

"Are you sure of that?"

"Ah, yes. She wrote to me less than six months ago!"

"Where was she then?"

"In Verona."

"Perhaps she was there. Perhaps it's a good idea of hers to keep moving rather briskly about the world. But now, Helen, I'm going to speak to you frankly. Will you try to believe that what I say is true?"

"Yes, yes!"

She was pale with excitement, her hands knotted. He could see her breast rising and falling with her emotion.

133

"Then I have to tell you this—that Francesca Laguarda is the most thoroughly dangerous woman on the face of the earth!"

"How could she be, and be so—"

"Beautiful, do you mean?"

"I—"

"Well, yes. Beautiful she is. So beautiful that the thought of her makes my head swim, and that when I stand here, Helen, there is a darkness shooting before my eyes, and I want with all my heart to cry out: 'It's not possible or true. She's not wrong. She's right, and in the end I can prove that she's a good woman!' "

And the girl answered him with a sudden ring of warmth in her voice:

"Ah, and you've said it, and I believe that you can!"

He shook his head in disbelief at her statement.

"There's no hope in this world for her. I assure you of that. But now, Helen, I want you to know that this girl is trying hard to injure you—that she has been here—that she was here last night!"

"Ah!" gasped Helen O'Mallock.

He answered the incredulity of her voice: "I've seen her, I've touched her. I've carried her into this house. And then—"

He paused, overwhelmed by what seemed to him his incredible folly: "And then I left her for a few minutes under the care of Aunt Maggie—and, of course, in those few moments the wily creature beguiled the Negress and was able to escape!"

Still Helen O'Mallock could not answer.

"And as for the Negress, she acted in such a way that I was sure she had had her own shady experience in life. She carried off the part too well. Like a professional. And I've seen enough of the criminal world to recognize the criminal professional touch!"

He paused and immediately went on: "You have to get away from Aunt Maggie!"

"But how?" said Helen O'Mallock. "How could I drive her out of the house?"

"You don't have to drive her out of the house. You have to leave the house yourself."

He continued, as she gaped at him: "The doctor will

134

take you away. Thank goodness for an honest man in the world, even if he's not the strongest. Honesty is better than a regiment of soldiers!"

"Ah, it is, it is!" she agreed with a broken voice.

"You have to leave here and go away with the doctor. And I'll stay behind and watch the place."

"I can't let you do that?"

"And why not, then?"

"Because, what would I have to say to myself afterward, when I knew that you were in danger here?"

"I shall be in no danger. How could I be?"

"If Francesca came here to threaten me—then there are others. A woman would not try to do such a thing alone."

He saw that she was reasoning closely to the point, and he was anxious to close the argument. He tried sheer force.

"Helen, here is a case where you must stop trying to work out what is right and wrong. You must do what you are told to do. You must leave this house!"

He added gently:

"You must go away to some much brighter place where there will be a chance for you to find real happiness—where there are no shadows under the sun; a dry climate that will be good for you, with the doctor to take care of you—and let me stay behind here to try to untangle this snarl in your affairs. I'd ask nothing better than that!"

She watched him with eyes which, as he knew at once, hardly saw him. They were looking at ideas behind him —the great ideas, perhaps, which overmastered Weldon himself.

"I never could leave," she said finally. "I never could say good-by to Aunt Maggie. I never could doubt Francesca. You never will understand. No doubt you are right, and no doubt I am wrong. I admit that I'm weak. But I haven't the strength to start doubting now—the few people who have been true to me. That's why I can't talk any more. I want to stay here. I want—to die here—in this house—believing in things, you know——"

Her voice trailed away. The weakness of which she spoke came over her. And he thought that the color was brushed from her face. It was the sun going behind a cloud, stealing the glow from her features.

He knew that there was no purpose in arguing or commanding. He had done his utmost, and she had given him her confession of faith. He simply backed from the room. He was crushed.

27. Puzzled

This much he could put down in black and white: Francesca was a thoroughly bad one. Helen was a sainted spirit from heaven. And the battle must be fought out with the poor girl on the battleground.

In the library he found the doctor biting his mustache nervously.

"Well, well?" he asked.

"I failed," said Weldon.

"Ah, of course you failed! I knew that you'd fail. But I mean: how is she? Is she well? Did you upset her too much?"

"I don't know," answered Weldon, and sank into a chair with a sign of despair, while the doctor trotted hastily away.

He came back in due time, looking even more grave than usual.

"You'll have to mend your methods while you're in this house," said he, and shook his head at Weldon.

"How is she?"

"Stretched out in bed. Very weak. Heart hammering at a high rate. Another touch or two like that——"

He glowered at Weldon from the corner of his eyes and

went to the window, where he stood rocking back and forth from heel to toe, and flipping out the tails of his coat in his indignation.

Weldon smiled. Indignation in the little old fellow was something like fury in a poodle! Then he stood up from his chair.

"At any rate, I'm no good without a bit of sleep," said he. "You can go in and watch beside her. I'm going to have a few winks."

The doctor agreed with his usual amiability to this, and Weldon fell down on the couch in the library and closed his eyes. He was instantly asleep and remained so until the softest of touches fell upon his ankles and then upon his throat. He looked up and saw the retreating back of Aunt Maggie, waddling softly from the room. She had covered him with a downy blanket.

He mused upon this, very startled. For there was assuredly a state of war existing between them, and yet she had chosen to do him good in secret, and that was not the way that he had expected from her. The thought led him onto other broodings. Nothing ever would explain women to him, really. Nothing, for instance, would have prepared him for that last speech from Helen O'Mallock. Unless, indeed, there is a strength of passivity in even the weakest of creatures.

That last speech had told him something which even Doctor Watts did not know about her—that she expected death, and expected it so soon that she hardly cared what became of her so long as she could cling to the old actualities of her poor, starved life until the finish came.

These thoughts so thoroughly upset him that he could not close his eyes again.

For a time he sat up on the couch, turning vague thoughts through his mind, but reaching no conclusion. At last his restlessness drove him out of the house. He wandered for a time up the hillside, past the desecrated tomb of the general, and as he passed it, he paused and wondered if of right he should have told Helen O'Mallock what had happened in this instance. That might, perhaps, have been the incident which would have turned her definitely against the house and decided her on leaving the place for happier surroundings. Yet he felt sure, on second

137

thought, that not even this would have moved her. She had made up her mind resolutely, and nothing could disturb her inward conviction.

He turned down the hills through the pines.

It was the rich prime of the day. The sun burned like the flare from the opened door of an electric furnace when he passed into the full blast of it; the very shadows beneath the trees were warm and drowsy and brought back his lack of sleep to him. He began to look about him for a place where he could find a pleasant couch and so sleep away an hour or two before he returned to that grim vigil within the house of the O'Mallocks.

Here the ground was too rough. And there pine needles had not fallen thickly enough. And so he went casually on, his senses quite asleep, until he had come to a little distance beneath the house. How easy it is to wander, when one walks downhill!

So thought Weldon, and turned for a moment to regard the towering eastern face of the house, ranging far above the tallest treetops. He had been a moment in this manner, standing fast, when a stir among the lower brush beneath him made him jerk his head around in time to see a man glide out from the shadows.

He stepped softly within the shelter of a broad trunk. There was a stumble and a snarl at the same instant, and then the sound of two men in dialogue.

"The ground is slippery as ice, with the needles! I'm gunna break my neck to-day!"

"Keep your head up, and stop talking," said an answering voice.

"There ain't anybody near us."

"How d'you know?"

"Listen for yourself, you poor sap. D'you hear anything but that squirrel crackin' a nut up yonder?"

"I tell you," said the other, in a voice so guarded that Weldon hardly could make out the words, "there might be somebody right behind that broken-backed pine this minute."

"Well, let's have a look!"

And Weldon, looking up, saw that the tree behind which he had sheltered himself swerved sharply to the side from the straight line, and thus must have filled the description which had been applied.

He slipped a gun into his hand and waited with straining eyes and ears.

"You poor fool," said the other speaker, "I don't mean that tree in particular. I mean, he's likely to be anywhere!"

"Who?"

"Who have we got to watch for in this here job?"

"Aw, I dunno. You mean Weldon?"

"Who else *would* I mean?"

"Dang Weldon! I ain't afraid of any man!"

"You darn near turned yaller the other night, though!"

"Oh, that? That ain't the kind of work that I'm cut out for. I don't like it!"

"A job of shootin' in the back would please you more."

"Look here, 'Slim,' I ain't on the job to take side talk from you!" said he who had been accused of showing the white feather. "What's more, I ain't gunna have it!"

"Have it or be danged," said the companion. "I say that you welched on me!"

"I ain't a gravedigger, and I never set out to be!"

Weldon started so violently that he was afraid he had made a noise.

"What in heck *do* you set out to be?"

"I'll leave that for my boss to decide."

"You've come along with me pretty pronto today to claim your share of the coin."

"I was on the job," said the other stubbornly, "and I get my full split or I'll raise a row."

"We'll talk about that later."

"What's the way in?"

"I'll show you. Come along. You've talked enough to tell the squirrels. Now, mind you, walk soft and talk soft. Better still, don't talk at all. This Weldon is everywhere. And he's poison. The big boss says so, and she ought to know."

"She!" How vastly much that word spelled to Weldon under the circumstances, for to his mind it could mean none other than beautiful Francesca Laguarda!

He ventured a glance around the corner of the tree and saw the pair walking carefully on toward the eastern face of the house.

"She!"

There was no better time than now to stop them!

His mind was made up immediately. "Halt!" said Weldon, and stepped from behind his shelter.

The one was a tall, powerfully built man. The other was a slender, thin-shouldered fellow. And yet he had been the one who had talked the more boldly of the pair and had spoken of his comrade's "welching."

Now, as they heard his voice, he expected them to whirl about, gun in hand, since they were that breed.

Instead, the short one yipped like a frightened rabbit: "It's him!"

And they leaped away for shelter, the tall fellow turning to the left and the other to the right, diving for the shade of the brush.

Their swinging to two sides threw Weldon a little off balance. He fired instinctively at the taller of the pair.

Both disappeared at the same instant. There was only a stifled curse in the air to tell Weldon that he had struck his man or had, at least, come perilously close to the mark.

He leaped on, regardless of their chance to turn, in shelter, and riddle him with bullets as he advanced. But no gun sounded. He burst through the screen of brush and the house was before him, with no man in sight.

He turned to the right, thinking that he had heard a sound like the grinding of a pebble under foot in that direction. Sprinting hard, they might have reached and turned the corner of the house in that way. He in turn ran as fast as he could, his gun always ready, and so turned the corner, teeth set for action—and saw nothing whatever!

He went on, still sprinting hard, and turned the second corner to the rear, with the long stretch of the patio wall before him. But still there was no sight of any fugitive.

He stopped to a walk, and began to retrace his steps. It was very odd, indeed!

He made a swift detour, then through the brush beneath the house thinking that they might have managed in some way, to dodge back. But there was no sign of them. Then, taking slower and surer measures, he began to examine the ground. It was fairly soft in patches, and following it with care, he finally distinguished their footmarks. He saw where they had dodged behind the brush. He followed and discovered that their footmarks converged and finally came together right under the wall of the house.

He examined the ground to either side most carefully. It was rock or hard gravel, but it did not seem that two hard-running men could have passed over it so recently without making a mark upon it. And yet there was not a token on either side!

At last he raised his puzzled eyes to the wall itself. What secret did it inclose?

28. "Do It at Once"

He took up a good-sized stone and with this he tapped a number of times against the wall, holding his ear close to it, in the hope that he would be able to detect a hollow sound, significant of a passage within, for it began to seem to him that the pair must, really, have disappeared through the solid masonry. However, that was a bit too fanciful to suit him; it savored a great deal too much of "Arabian Nights" and fairy tales. Therefore, he shook his head over the puzzle and went on back to the house.

It was the second mysterious disappearance.

Pausing under the window of the library, he scanned carefully the greenery of the vines that climbed up the wall, but he was unable to see any place where they had been bruised, as by hand or foot. How else could that wild girl, Francesca Laguarda, have managed to escape from that room?

He gritted his teeth over the renewed problem which was brought up by the disappearance of the two he had overheard approaching the house.

Unless they were most miraculously quick of foot, into the wall they must have faded. Or else, with wonderful courage and adroitness, they had managed to slip silently into the brush, and so avoid him.

He was doubtful about their ability to accomplish such a feat. The brush was dry. There were plenty of twigs and fallen leaves upon the ground, and altogether that pair did not seem of the kind who would possess woodcraft. They had to Weldon all the earmarks of common or garden city crooks, such as he had known by the gross. "The rank and file," as Wilbur was used to say with his sneer.

Deep in those reflections, he climbed the stairs and reentered the library which he had left such a short time before. The doctor was there, and looked up from a newspaper with a cheerful, dim-eyed smile.

"She's sleeping, dear child!" said he.

Weldon grunted.

With the burden of these problems upon him, the doctor was a most unwelcome presence to him. Weldon merely nodded and went on from the library toward his own room.

"I thought I heard a shot," said the doctor with unusual calmness.

"I took a pop at a squirrel," said Weldon, and went on.

He sat down on the edge of his bed, his face between his hands, his brain whirling. In every way he had been checkmated. He had arrived at the desperate measure of having the body of the general exhumed and an autopsy performed; and the body had been stolen away the very night, as it seemed, that he was to do the work.

Then there was good proof of this, circumstantially, in the appearance of those two rascals in the woods—they who were coming to be paid.

By whom? By Francesca, of course! And that meant

142

either that she had not left the place at all, or else that she would return to it.

This deduction reduced Weldon to actual despair. If ever he had his hands upon her again, it would go very hard if she should escape from him the second time. He would keep her and use means to wring her secrets from her!

In all that he had done, he felt that he had acted as wisely as possible except, perhaps, in revealing his suspicions to Helen O'Mallock. But surely he had meant that for the best, and how could he have dreamed that she would be so sadly set on taking whatever fate offered to her?

Staring moodily at the floor, his gaze finally centered on a little round spot of red, as big as a man's finger nail. Very red it was, standing out against the darker surface of the varnish. It made him so curious that he reached down, half absent-mindedly, and touched it with the tip of a finger.

When he looked again, half the spot was gone, and the finger-tip was brightest crimson, blood-red, indeed.

Weldon was startled from his dream. Blood-red? Why, it was blood in very fact! And who had been dripping blood on the floor of his bedroom?

He went to the library door.

"Doctor Watts?"

"Well, well, well, my boy!" said that worthy old gentleman, blinking his glasses off the bridge of his nose so that they slid halfway down to the tip of it. "You startled me! I was just reading a very interesting account of a new discovery they've made at Capua—"

"Darn Capua!" said the impolite Weldon. "How long have you been sitting there?"

"Only a few moments. Half an hour, perhaps."

"In fact, you stayed only a moment in her room?"

"She was sleepy. Sleep is the best medicine, you know, and I always feel that if we could learn true relaxation, true sleep, there never would be the slightest need for—"

Weldon, more impolite than ever, slammed the door in the doctor's face and went back to his study of the blood. He went crouching here and there across the chamber, spying at every inch of the boards and making a special scrutiny of the rugs, for one of these, to be sure, might have received a similar drop. If he could find no more than a single one, it would show much—it would show in what direction the wounded man had gone.

For he had not the slightest doubt that this blood came from the wound which he had inflicted upon one of the previous pair among the pines beneath the house.

At last he found what he wanted—an even larger splotch, and it lay upon the floor just opposite the room of Helen O'Mallock. Exactly in front of her door it had fallen!

It fairly stopped the heart of Weldon to find such a proof! But how had it come there? Had the fugitive fled into the room where the girl was lying? Had he, perhaps, stifled her before she could make an outcry, while the doctor sat in the library, his ears stuffed with the recent discovery at Capua?

Where was Capua, anyway?

He listened for an instant at the crack of the door. Then he opened it softly—and, more amazed then ever, he found himself looking into the wide eyes of Helen O'Mallock.

She was badly frightened, apparently, though the fear in her eyes changed at once to a smile of recognition and pleasure.

"Helen, have you seen something here in your room?" he asked, looking eagerly around him.

"I saw the door open stealthily, just now," said the girl. "It frightened me almost to death!"

"How long have you been awake?"

"Half a minute, perhaps, before that door began to open. I woke up with my heart racing. I—I'm so glad it was only you!"

"Tell me—who did you think it might have been?"

"Well, you see, if there are people who want to get rid of me from this house—they might not wait until—"

Here she paused—and dropped her head so that the broad shadow of the hat screened her face.

"I beg your pardon," said she, faintly. "I shouldn't speak of that!"

The heart of Weldon was softened within him. He went

144

to her and took her hand in his, and the coldness and the smallness of it struck a chill through him.

"You should speak to me of anything that comes into your mind," he told her. "You should speak to me of anything and of everything. I am part of you, like an extra hand, say, and you must use me. I know what you meant to say. Ah, well—if I could take you away from this place—"

"But what would you do with me?"

"I thought that I would stay behind and watch the house—but I've changed my mind. There's nothing in this house that really matters except you. I tell you, Helen, I'd bring you to a place where no enemy could follow you. I'd sleep like a dog outside your door. I'd be living in your shadow. I'd keep you safe and, by heaven, I'd find a way of pouring some of my strength into you and making you strong again, also!"

She looked at him with the oddest of smiles, and the most gentle. Partly as if she were amused, a little, by this boyish enthusiasm, this boyish surety, promising miracles where science had failed to help her. And partly she smiled like one already beyond this world and passed into the dim verge of shadows.

He withdrew to the doorway, and there he thought of suggesting to her that he should be allowed to search her room. But a sort of holy awe came over him, such as he had felt before, when he was in her presence.

He turned away, and then he went back to the library to find the doctor sitting bolt upright and shaking his beard over some article which greatly excited him.

When he became aware of Weldon, he cried out: "They have it. They really have it at last!"

"They have what?" asked Weldon grimly.

"The missing arm, of course."

"Of what?"

"She wasn't holding a baby at all," said the doctor, wagging his head, and at last looking up to Weldon with the broadest of grins. "She wasn't holding a baby at all. She was holding a mirror!"

He laughed with great pleasure.

"It wasn't a Latona at all! Not a bit of it. I always knew that it wasn't a Latona! As a matter of fact, it was a

145

Venus. The idiot might have known that long ago, if they had paid attention to a little article which I published as long as eight years ago in the—"

"Doctor Watts!" said Weldon.

"Dear me!" exclaimed Doctor Watts. "You shock me —like an electric current—half a dozen times a day. I wish that you could manage to speak to me without taking my breath away!"

"I want to wake you up, if I can," said Weldon.

"Ah, true, true," said the doctor. "As the years advance, I often feel a somnolence which increases in the—"

"Watts, there's blood on the floor of my bedroom!"

"Good heavens!" said the doctor. "I assure you I didn't put it there!"

Weldon gritted his teeth.

"Someone who came out of the door of her room let that blood fall in passing through mine. Do you understand?"

"Upon my soul!" breathed Doctor Watts. "I don't understand at all!"

"Try to, then. You heard a gun pop a little time ago?"

"Yes, yes!"

"I told you I was shooting at a squirrel. I wasn't, however."

"Ah, at a bird, perhaps? There is an old crow which often perches on the—"

"This bird was a man," said Weldon. "I shot at him as he dodged, and I heard him cry out. Apparently I wounded him. Perhaps in an arm as he jumped to the side. He and the man with him disappeared between the edge of the trees and the wall of the house—the eastern wall, you understand?"

"Upon my soul!" cried the doctor. "Disappeared? My dear lad, there are certain laws of nature and of science which really must be—"

"Be quiet," said Weldon wearily, "and listen to what I have to say. There is a passage from the lower part of that wall to the room of Helen O'Mallock, and every moment that she spends in that room—which we have been guarding so carefully!—is a moment spent in the hands of her enemies! Now will you do what I want you to do?"

"I!" gasped the doctor. "I? Weldon, you overwhelm me. I simply don't—"

"You don't have to. All you have to do is what I tell you to do, and I'll make that as simple as possible. Go to Helen O'Mallock and persuade her out of her room. Get her out and keep her out. I want to examine the walls and the floor of that place!"

"Do you want me to use force?" asked the doctor faintly.

"Tell her that the room has a draft—that the floor is too damp—do something. That's all I say. Do something and do it at once. We can't waste any more time!"

29. A Crude Little Trap

The doctor went toward the door, feeling his way from chair to chair, so overwhelmed was he by this announcement. Weldon overtook him and shook him roughly by the shoulder.

"Look here," said he, "are you going to go in to her with a face like a death mask? Brace up—cheer yourself a little. She's had enough nerve strain today. Put it all gently. We must get her moved out at once!"

He went over by the window of the library and half closed his eyes. He could almost have smiled, now, for since he had a definite thread to follow, he swore to himself that he would follow that thread until it led to a hempen rope large enough to hang a thief and murderer!

He waited for long moments, and then the doctor came in, shaking his head.

"Wait one moment," said Weldon. "I think you're going to tell me that you haven't persuaded her? If that's the case, turn on your heel and go back to her room again!"

The doctor drew himself up stiff and straight. It added actual inches to his height, and his old, filmed-over eyes gleamed with real fire.

"Young man," said he, "I like you, I even esteem you. You have strength, courage, and devotion to a good cause. But I want to remind you that there are some things in life which all the stampings and bellowings of a bull are powerless to effect! I shall not return to the room of that weary, tormented child to persuade her. She has consented to move from her room tomorrow. Isn't that enough for you?"

Weldon smiled, his teeth set hard.

"And leave her another night in that danger? A door open to the world?"

"What chance is there that she will be disturbed by them tonight? How many nights has she lain there without being troubled?"

There was point to this, and the doctor spoke the words so sharply that Weldon felt himself subdued a little, particularly when Henry Watts continued: "She has been under a great strain today. Who placed that strain upon her? You did, Weldon! Heaven forgive you for it, but another day like that might be the end of—"

He paused, caught his breath, and said deliberately, with unspeakable emotion: "Another day like this might be the end of Helen O'Mallock. Do you want *that* on your head?"

And Weldon submitted, though writhing with impatience.

To make the best of that bad day, he lay down on the couch in the library, and the turning of the newspaper, crinkling softly under the touch of the doctor, soothed him to sleep.

When he awakened, he was astonished to find that it was late afternoon. The room was filled with dim, golden light, with a flush of rose in it. Before him stood Aunt Maggie.

"You been needin' just this sleep," she told him kindly. "Ain't you missin' your lunch?"

"Is that for me?" he asked her, pointing to a paper in her hand.

She nodded, and taking the envelope he tore it open and read:

I am in desperate need. Can you help me?
F. L.

Francesca Laguarda!

In desperate need—could he help her?

He slipped the paper into his pocket and stood up.

"Who brought this?" he asked.

"Is it poison?" she asked him, her eyes popping.

"I think it may be," he answered. "Who brought it? Or was it slipped under the door?"

He thought that much more likely, but she answered at once: "A city man, by the look of him. He's sitting down in a right fine automobile, downstairs."

In half a minute, Weldon was down the stairs also, only making sure that both his guns were loaded and in place beneath his armpits. He stepped outdoors at the rear of the house, cautiously, and there he saw beyond the patio gate a powerful looking, green roadster, and in the front seat, lolling with a cigarette, his former acquaintance, Cunningham.

He went out to the man with wonder in his heart. Cunningham, seeing him, reached out a cordial hand.

"Well?" said he, without preliminaries.

"Do you know what was in this letter?" asked Weldon.

"Not a word," answered Cunningham.

There are ways and ways of deceiving, and the best of all is a blunt affection of indifference; but Weldon thought now that he was hearing golden truth indeed.

"Cunningham, if you don't know what's in the letter, how do you happen to have brought it?"

"I had a letter," said Cunningham with perfectly obvious caution. "This note was inclosed and I was asked to deliver it to you."

"You don't often run about the country delivering notes, do you?"

"Look here," said Cunningham, in the tone of one who wishes to be conciliatory but will not be pressed too far, "I want to talk to you as a friend, Weldon. I won't be treated like a sneak thief."

"I don't mean to put it that way," said Weldon, "but I really have to find out who gave you this note for me?"

"A man in whom you'd have no interest. A Mexican, in fact. Confound it, I don't know that I should have told you even this!"

"Cunningham," said Weldon, "I want to believe you, but isn't it a fact that Francesca Laguarda gave you this note?"

Cunningham opened his eyes a little.

"Francesca?"

Then he shut up and sat in his car, saying not a word.

The latter was quick to appreciate the difficulty. He brought the note from his pocket and passed it to the other. "That's what you delivered," he pointed out.

Cunningham read it slowly, aloud, but with his voice hushed.

" 'I am in desperate need. Can you help me?' "

Then he added, lowering the paper and frowning at Weldon: "But why in heaven's name should she send to *you* for help?"

"I wanted to ask you that."

Cunningham bit his lip and flushed.

"I have an idea," said Weldon curiously, "that you'd as soon that she asked you?"

"Nonsense!" scoffed Cunningham. But the cloud remained on his brow. He seemed to be trying to puzzle out a vast problem.

"Will you tell me this," said Weldon. "Is she in trouble? I mean, is she under the control of any person who could—"

"Under the control of the demon!" said Cunningham with bitterness. "Who else *could* control her?" He added: "No, she's all right. She's stronger than ever, so far as I know."

"Then I think you can take back word to her that I'm engaged here."

150

Cunningham nodded, but he surveyed Weldon with interest.

"You really won't go?" said he.

"Certainly not."

"You're even a rarer sort than I thought," said Cunningham. "Tell me how you manage it? How can you keep away when she asks for you?"

"Because you gave me an excellent warning in the first place," replied Weldon. "Because you told me what a hellcat she is, Cunningham. I've taken her, as one might say, with a grain of salt."

"I told you about her?" said Cunningham, laughing rather bitterly. "Well—I suppose I did!"

That small sentence told Weldon a great deal. The prophet who told of the fire had not been able to save himself from the flames.

"You really are not going?" asked Cunningham.

"I've told you before. As a matter of fact, this is the crudest little trap that I've had sprung beneath my nose!"

"Trap?" cried Cunningham. "Why, man, do you think she'd try to harm you after appealing to you?"

"Do you think she's above that?"

"Man, man," cried Cunningham, like one bewildered, "don't you know her any better than that?"

30. The Song the Sirens Sang

By small strokes and by small touches the portrait is finished. Now these last words of Cunningham's were like the sweep of a master, running the bold line which gives new life to the sketch. And Weldon stared at him like one who sees a ghost of glory.

"I want to believe you when you say that," he warned Cunningham.

"And what if you do believe me?"

"I step into that car and go with you."

"Where?"

"To her."

"I have no authority to take you there," said Cunningham.

"You will, however."

"Are you sure of that?"

"You won't be an ass, Cunningham."

"Lord knows what I am. I don't know myself! Get into this car. I'll vouch for nothing about her except that she's not a sneak."

And Weldon paused for a moment, then turned on his heel and went back to the house. He returned at once and climbed into the vacant seat.

"You'd better bring an overcoat. It gets cold at night," warned Cunningham. Weldon did not seem to hear.

"I've done it, then," he merely murmured.

"Done what?" asked the other.

"Told them that I wouldn't be there tonight."

"Is that a great deal?" asked Cunningham, pressing the starter.

The telltale hum of a straight eight answered as Weldon murmured: "I've stepped beyond my limit, I think. Heaven help me!"

Cunningham made no remark. He was busy in sending the car down the first rough stages of the trail, handling her with masterly efficiency, clipping the curves straighter, and burning up the open road.

Then he said: "You know that, do you?"

"Know what?" asked Weldon, for his thoughts had moved far since his last speech.

"That Francesca's beyond your depth? Beyond any man's depth?"

"Is she? Beyond every one's?"

"Perhaps not," said Cunningham. "Somewhere there is probably a skinny slip of a smart-tongued whelp whom she'll begin to mother one day, and who'll get her money, and treat her like a dog, and leave her like a dog in the end!"

He snarled the words.

"Ah," said Cunningham, "she has no flaw in her armor. It's only where her heart takes her that she could be weak. If she has a heart! If she has a heart!"

"You've come to know Francesca better since I last saw you," said Weldon. "How long have you known her altogether?"

"I? How long? Weeks—centuries—I don't know—there's no time where Francesca is!"

He shot the car from under the shadows of the pines. They dropped rapidly toward the desert valley, with all its waves of creosote bush and cactus now softened with the sunset rose.

Then, reaching the level floor, he turned to the left.

"Is this for Francesca?" asked Weldon.

"It is," said the other, and accelerated until the exhaust hissed like a snake behind them and the desert rose in an endless wave against their faces. However, the surface was firm. Only at sharp corners the rear wheels shot sickeningly to the side. But Cunningham like an expert, met every swerve with the wheel, and straightened the heavy car again. It was as though he were trying to run away from his thoughts, so darkened was his face.

"Know her?" he burst out suddenly. "I don't know anything about her! Why, I don't even know where she keeps her cars! Nobody knows the whole story of her. She gives you a glimpse. She gives me another. She's twenty things to twenty men. And all of them dangerous—dangerous. You know the old riddle? Ah, but she solved it. She knows the song the sirens sang!"

They drove out of the dusk into the darkness. The stars flew up like sparks behind the mountains.

"There's a shorter way," said Cunningham, half apologetically. "There's a way about a quarter the length of this. But I want her to wait a little. It will do her good! It will do her good!"

But presently he was settling anxiously over the wheel, his lights darting over the waving surface of the sands, his spotlight focused on the side. It was plain that he no longer

153

drove in passion and pique, but because he was terribly anxious to reach the girl.

"Cunningham!" said Weldon suddenly.

"Ah?"

"I don't know you very well, but I can guess that you're a little upset. You think that she might have sent to you for help. Is that it? In fact—let's be open about it—you're a bit jealous of me, old fellow?"

"No more than I am of any one else she looks at, I suppose," said Cunningham frankly.

"Have you a claim on her?"

"No more than I am of any one yonder!"

For that blazing star was rising like a planet in the east.

They turned again to the left. It was plain that they were driving in a partial circle, and now they went up a shallow valley, with low hills on either side that sent back the song of the motor in a softer moan.

Out of that valley they shot into a dark and narrow chasm which opened again a little, and before them were the lights of a small house.

"That's the place Jorram has, just now," said Cunningham. "She's expected there, tonight."

He shut off the motor. They coasted through a fringe of tall shrubs into an opening which had been cleared of underbrush. Half a dozen cars were already there. Cunningham looked about at them with a careful eye and shifted the spotlight from one radiator hood to another.

"She's expected, right enough," he said bitterly.

Then he led the way back through the shrubbery, and they came out at the side of the house. A music of twanging strings came floating through the open window, and the voice of a man singing.

"That's Loomis," said Cunningham. "Poor Jack Loomis! Wait a moment. Wait for the chorus. If she's there why—"

The chorus came in a moment, and into the rhythm of the singing struck the voice of a girl, not very powerful, not very well trained, but rich and filled with the joy of the music, the rhythm.

"She's here," said Cunningham, "and so Heaven help your soul, Lew!"

Weldon followed his guide to the front door, and

through it down a small hall. A heap of coats were thrown on a couple of rough kitchen chairs. Hats were hung here and there or lay on the floor. Under foot was a decaying flooring. It was plain that the old shack had been recently resurrected from near ruin to serve some purpose. And no legal purpose was apt to bring the owner to this secluded bit of wilderness!

Another door stood open at the end of the hall and as they approached it, someone looked out, saw them, and advanced on them. He was big, rosy-faced, smiling. But his shifty eyes were as bright and quick as the eyes of a ferret.

"She's here, I see," said Cunningham.

"She's here. Just came five minutes ago."

The song ended. There was an outburst of hearty applause and the big man turned and clapped.

"Jorram, this is Weldon."

Jorram acknowledged the introduction with a nod, and finished his clapping before he extended his hand and shook that of Weldon heartily.

"Come in," said he. "We're short on lights but not on drinks. What d'you take?"

"Water," said Weldon.

"Ah," murmured Jorram. "Working, eh? Do I know you?"

"No."

"You will," put in Cunningham, in what Weldon felt was rather a sarcastic voice.

Their host led them into the next room. It was very small. On overturned boxes, on rickety chairs, tied together with wire, were seven or eight men whom Weldon surveyed with an expert eye. Take them one by one and they never would have been noticed in a crowd, or singly. But the group had certain characteristics in mass which he did not miss. They were, above all, manly men. In the second place, they were men of "experience," in several senses of that word. They ranged in years from gray-headed Jorram to a blond-haired youth as pink-cheeked as an English debutante. But, young or old, every one of them carried definite hall-marks. One could not have said that they were all criminals. But one could have said that every one of them was a fellow to be reckoned with by a most close account.

And yonder was she, Francesca Laguarda. She was dressed in a khaki blouse and a riding skirt and wore riding boots that looked battered and scarred as though they had seen much hard work through brush of the thorny kind. But the rougher her costume, the more delicately feminine appeared Francesca. He thought, when his glance first crossed hers, that she looked a little startled, a little frightened. If that were true, it was only a flash; and then she was smiling at him.

Big Jorram introduced him around the circle. There were curt nods; strong, quick pressures of his hand, and keen glances that searched him through and through. The heart of Weldon grew lighter. On him, like a great, dark burden, lay the knowledge that he was leaving Helen O'Mallock unguarded in the house on the hill. It might well be that Francesca had drawn him away for the very purpose of rendering the other girl helpless. And yet he began to forget these doubts and fears. With such men as these, he felt as though he could tear down mountains. And, after all, his hands had been empty of employment for many days. Only his wits had had to work. She would not want him for that. Not Francesca! She had her own subtle brain to work with. She wanted the weight of his hand!

In that circle of introductions he came to her. She did not sparkle or laugh with pleasure. She merely took his hand and looked long and gravely into his eyes.

31. Who Listens Is Lost

Jorram came up to them.

"Is this your man, Francesca?" he asked her.

"I want to talk to him for two minutes," she said. "Where can we go?"

"Here!"

Jorram showed them into an adjoining room. It had not been furnished. There was a dusty dirt floor, a broken chair lay on its side in a corner, and the moonlight streamed pale and steady through the window, where a shutter hung by one hinge.

Francesca went to the window; he stood before her. They remained quiet for an instant, she studying his face, and he bracing himself.

"I hoped—" she said suddenly. "I didn't think you'd come. What made you feel that it wasn't a trap?"

"Cunningham."

She shook her head.

"Not Cunningham," she said.

"No, not entirely."

She neither flushed nor smiled at the implication. She was as steady as a rock, and, he felt, almost as hard.

"I told you that I was desperate," she said. "Because I have a thing to do that requires help that only you can give me. I have to cross the river and bring back with me a man who's closely guarded by people I have to get him away from."

He gestured toward the door.

"You have plenty of men in there," he said. "And,

mind you—I'm not a genius at driving a car or using a rifle."

"I know you're not," she replied. "There are men in there who could shoot out the whites of your eyes, I suppose. At least, with rifles. But if there's any shooting to be done—and there will be—it will be with revolvers."

She waited again, to see how he would take this, and he responded with perfect silence. If there was need for revolvers it meant desperate, hand-to-hand work of some sort.

"I'll tell you exactly what it is," she went on. "Then you can withdraw and simply say that you're not interested. Or else—"

She hesitated, and as she paused a smile quivered on her lips—very much as though she said in silence to herself: If he accomplishes this thing for me, he will be one man in the world!

And the heart of Weldon beat faster than ever.

"His name is Jim Dickinson. Did you ever hear of him?"

"Yes. Somewhere. I don't know. I have the name in my mind."

"Of course you have! Everyone's heard of him, at some time. Jim Dickinson is held across the river in San Trinidad by Miguel Cabrero. Cabrero is holding him for a ransom so high that it can't be paid."

"Holding him in the gambling house?"

"No, in his café. Letting him have a perfectly free life, but every minute of the day and night he's surrounded by half a dozen fighting Mexicans. Do you know Mexicans?"

"I do."

"And you know they can be fighters?"

"I know that."

"But sometimes they need leading?"

"Yes. That's true."

"He has a white man to lead them. The name of that man is Benjamin Wilbur."

"Wilbur!"

"You see why I had to have you," she said simply.

She had laid the facts before him in a straight line. Nothing could have been simpler than her declaration, and he

158

was aware that it must have been the truth or very close to the truth.

She continued: "Every evening they sit late in front of the café and drink beer and smoke cigarettes and watch Jim Dickinson. We have to go there and try to get him away—a desperate undertaking, you'll admit."

"You must give me time to get in touch with Wilbur. I might be able to influence him."

"Of course you could, but there's no time."

"Must it be done tonight?"

"It must. The Mexican police want Jim Dickinson. Every police force in the world wants him, I suppose."

She smiled a little as she said it.

"And they know where he is, now?"

"They begin to suspect. It was very clever of Cabrero to keep Dickinson so openly. That fooled the Mexican police like hiding a hat on a hatrack. But now they're on the trail of Jim. They'll have him before morning, probably. That leaves us tonight, and we have to work."

"You leave one thing out of the count. Cabrero and Cabrero's men know me and they would be after me like foxes after a goose."

"Of course they would, but they won't have a chance to recognize you after Jorram is done with you. Unless you begin to sing: 'Eyes like the evening, throat like the dawn.'"

And she smiled again.

He recapitulated carefully: "We are to go to San Trinidad to the café. There I'm to try to speak a word to Wilbur in a disguise and try to bring him over to our side. After that he and you and I are to try to handle six fighting Mexicans and get this unarmed Dickinson away from them."

"Not the six only," she said frankly. "One yell from them and the whole street will rise up against us."

He half closed his eyes, thinking hard.

"Dickinson pays high for this, I suppose?" said he.

"And you want to know what your share would be, of course?" she asked.

"I don't do this for money," said Weldon. "But—"

She would not aid him. He had to say: "I don't think that you're doing this for money, either."

Her eyes flashed to one side and then to the other. He

159

could tell that a lie was forming in her throat, but then she gave her head a little shake.

"I'm not doing this for money," she admitted.

He set his teeth and drew a breath. Not money—love! But it was always true of these women of the Francesca type. A thousand men could become fools about them and their beauty; they, in turn, were sure to be weak-minded about one man, and usually a worthless one. He could not help adding: "Dickinson—will he be a help?"

"Jim Dickinson is a tiger," she answered. "He's as strong as you are, I suppose. And he'll be fighting for his life, as soon as we can throw him a weapon!"

Not so worthless, then, after all! And she had chosen a man, even *if* he were a criminal! It was a grim satisfaction to Weldon. And yet he could have laughed aloud at the irony of this trap in which he was caught. He, with all his strength, at the peril of his life, was to rescue the lover of Francesca and give him back safely to her. He was to do it not for money but for love of the girl. And she knew it was love of her that forced him on!

How had she been able to tell? Certainly not by any gentleness in his treatment of her at the O'Mallock house! But, brazenly, fiercely, she intended to use him!

Scorn of her rose hot in his heart; scorn of himself to be the Samson to such a Delilah.

"I suppose I'll go," said he.

And then he saw a sudden relaxation in her. Her lips parted in a sigh of relief. Surely she never had doubted from the first that he would do what she wanted, or else she would never have sent for him. Relief then, because of what? Because this interview was ended!

Even Francesca Laguarda, in the deeps of her soul, possessed some vanishing relics of shame, it appeared! And Weldon smiled to himself again. Something in him was turning to iron, and he knew that if he fought this night, he would fight to kill.

"So Jorram can start on you?" asked Francesca.

"Yes. As soon as you please."

"We're late already," said the girl. "Horribly late!"

He followed her to the door of the room, but she turned back to him.

"I'll send Jorram to you here. He'll have everything."

"Very well."

Still she lingered, and stepping closer to him she touched his hand.

"Everything that you think is wrong," said Francesca. And she vanished through the doorway.

32. True or False?

He sat on the window sill and waited. The moon glittered in the tops of the young poplars; the ground was dappled with shadows that stirred slightly to and fro like the shifting footfalls of unseen dancers. And a thousand things rushed through the brain of Weldon.

All his thoughts were wrong, she had told him. All of what thoughts? That she was saving Jim Dickinson because she loved him? What other solution, indeed, could there be? Had she spoken the truth, or merely told him a lie at the last moment for the sake of enlisting him more completely in the cause of the night's adventure?

Leaving the window, he walked gloomily back and forth.

Jorram did not come. That troubled him not a little. At the last moment, of course, they might decide that it was better to get rid of Weldon than to use him, and he told himself that nothing was beneath Francesca—perhaps nothing was above her, either!

At last the door opened. A big man stood on the threshold carrying a bundle of clothes over his arm and a lantern in his hand. That lantern light flared up on a brown face glistening with moisture, on beetling, black brows, and a short mustache hardly thicker than the mustache of a Chinaman.

"The time's come for you," said the voice of Jorram, speaking from the throat of this apparent Mexican, "and if I can't make as good a job of you as I can of myself, still, I'll pass you at night in a crowd."

He set to work at once. Weldon had to throw off his clothes, and then he was liberally stained with walnut juice to a nut-brown color. Some red was worked into his cheeks, his eyebrows made black as jet, and over his head was pulled a rough wig of which the hair seemed as stiff as bristles, standing up wildly, or falling low down over his eyes. All that was rough and brutal in the face of Weldon was now apparent, and Jorram chuckled as he stood back and looked at his victim.

"They'll jump ten feet to give you room, Weldon," he said. "You look like a Yaqui, and they give those fellows passageway every time, you can be sure!"

The clothes to complete the disguise consisted of a wide-brimmed sombrero of ragged straw, a battered, time-stained coat, and trousers which had once been white and now were gray—or worse. They were in such tatters below the knees that they had to be furled. As for shoes, there were rude sandals bound tight to the foot, with thongs which wound round and round the leg and tied above the calf. As if this were not enough, the shirt he was given was of flaming-red silk, also so worn that the skin peeped through it.

"Can you play any instrument?" asked Jorram.

"The guitar a little."

"No good?"

"I'm fair at it. Pretty good, in fact."

"Let's hear you."

He left the room and returned at once with a perfectly tuned guitar. Weldon seized it, laughed aloud, and from his throat burst a tremendous baritone voice that rang and shook through the room:

"Eyes like the evening, throat like the dawn!"

"Good!" said Jorram, stuffing his fingers into his ears. "Don't deafen me! That will do very well! We'll have to start. Have you your guns?"

"I have to arrange those."

They were arranged oddly enough, in cleverly devised holsters, the straps of which fitted about the shoulders, and the revolvers were suspended beneath the pits of the arms. They were spring holsters, and the weapons came away at a sweep of the hands, which could reach up easily under the loose coat.

Jorram eyed this contrivance with much interest.

"But does it work?" said he. "Can you get out a Colt that way?"

"It works fairly well," said Weldon, and to prove his point, he conjured a weapon out of the naked air and made it vanish again, smiling.

The other blinked.

"Wonderful!" said he. "And I'm going to school to you, one of these days!"

He led the way out of the house. They found Cunningham standing mournfully beside the long, gray car.

"I thought so," said he, as he saw the pair approach. "And I'm left out of the party?"

"She'll kindly accept your head another night," said Jorram. "But I'm not sure of all the plan. Perhaps she'll take it now!"

He had hardly ended his speech when a strange young barbarian came through the night. Around her head was twisted a red scarf of silk which floated down her back. In her ears were big, green-glass earrings. Around her throat was a gilded necklace of great beads. She wore a short jacket, set off with a border of flashing gilt braid, and her short skirt flared like that of a ballet dancer. Her footgear was like that of Weldon, the thongs lashed over the calf of the bare, brown leg. To give an impossible touch of modesty, she carried, however, a long web of black lawn as a mantilla. And yet in this dark-skinned, shameless creature, Weldon was sure of Francesca Laguarda.

She laughed at him beneath the moon.

"See the señor!" she said to Cunningham. *"Muy diablo,* no?"

Cunningham answered gravely: "I ought to be in this party, Francesca. I've been in school long enough, and you ought to let me go with you."

"Of course you're coming," said Francesca pleasantly. "We couldn't get on without you. You have one of the most important parts! Get in. Jorram, you drive. I'll save myself for the return trip!"

163

So taking for granted, apparently, that she was the premier chauffeur of the party! She waved Cunningham into the front seat beside Jorram.

"I have to sit behind with Lew," she said cheerfully. "Throw me a blanket; I don't want to freeze!"

She sprang into the automobile and when Weldon climbed in, she wrapped herself in the blanket which Cunningham passed to her and curled up on the seat, her feet tucked skillfully beneath her, her head against Weldon's shoulder.

Cunningham surveyed this scene from the front seat.

"If you're going to play baby doll," he said with disgust, "I'll stay home."

"Keep your eyes on the road and help the driver," said Francesca. "I'm lonely and need comforting."

"You're a wildcat in the wilderness," said Cunningham in half-serious retort, "and you'll have all our throats cut before morning. Go on, Jorram, and while you drive, tell me what this is all about."

Weldon, stiff and uncomfortable, looked down at the head against his shoulder. The car moved, grated in first, hummed in second, and then went into top speed with a hiss of sand beneath the spinning wheels, and a mutter of the exhaust.

They shot through the brush and tore up a slight incline. It did not seem a road, but the sand was level and compacted. They flew up the slope and ducked at the top into a long, easy ravine. With the lurch of the turning, Francesca tipped far to the side.

"You'll have to hold me in," she said in the ear of Weldon.

He laughed and put his arm around her.

"This is a very old song for such an artist as you, Francesca," he said. "I suppose they've all held you like this and looked in your eyes?"

"Who?" she asked, watching him, and stirring to make herself comfortable.

"The lot of them!"

With a jerk of his head he indicated the men who were behind in the shack of Jorram.

"Nobody in the world," said Francesca.

164

The car leaped down a sharp incline with a speed that took the breath of Weldon.

"No one in the world!" she said.

She explained slowly: "Roger is a silly fellow. He doesn't understand!"

"He's rather sad about you, Francesca."

"This month. Yes. But he never has more than a thirty-day fever. I don't want to talk about him."

"What is this for?" he asked her.

She looked ahead of her for a moment. Already they were leaving the hills. Two long, sloping arms of silver retired on either side and the pungent scent of the desert was in their nostrils; the sand purred against the mud guards.

"Well," she said, "what do you think?"

"Because you feel that I'm not quite safe," said Weldon. "A little more devoted to you, and I'll fight a little harder. So I'm to sit here and grow foolish under the moon. Isn't that it?"

She let her head fall back on his shoulder. It was not coquetry. Angry as he was, and more than half scornful, he could tell that. The car, reeling along the road at great speed, made her head sway a little from side to side.

"We may all be dead in another hour or two," said she. "Have you thought of that?"

"No."

"Does it make no difference to you?" asked Francesca.

"None whatever."

"Do you mean that?"

He said gravely: "I've been a good deal of a scoundrel in my time, Francesca. I've taken life as I found it, and one finds it in need of a good deal of sifting, as a rule. That made no difference to me. But recently I've found a chance to do one good thing; no money in it, no reward of any kind except a sort of satisfaction and a duty done. Well—you sent for me, and I gave up that work, tonight."

"That's the girl on the hill. That's Helen," said she.

He was silent.

"But do you really think she is such an angel?" asked Francesca. "Is she so pure and perfect?"

"We'd better talk of something else," said Weldon.

"You can be a snob, I see," said Francesca. "Well, most men can be. But I'm glad to talk of something else. Only I want you to know what I meant when I said that we may be dead before the morning."

"And suppose we live through it?"

"Ah, then we can be happy forever!"

"Running guns and Chinamen across the border?"

"Doing whatever you want. From clerking in a store to wrecking trains. I don't care," said she.

He laughed ironically.

"You'd come with me, then?" said he. "Do I understand that that is what you mean?"

"Yes. Don't be sarcastic and hard-minded. I'm talking like one about to die."

He looked away from her, trying to think logically, with a straight mind. The moon was well up. The thin, desert foliage swept past them like silver mist in low cloud on cloud. And his thoughts tangled and fell into confusion. He began to be aware of the racing of his heart, fast as the racing of the motor, it seemed.

Cunningham looked back at them, shrugged his shoulders, and then resolutely squared himself to watch the road.

"He thinks that I'm talking to you like a chorus girl," said Francesca.

"And what are you saying instead, Francesca?"

"I'm trying to make you understand that for more than a year I've schemed and worked and prayed and fought for tonight. If I win—I can't tell you what!—but if I win, there's happiness before us. And if I die—"

He waited, and then suggested, more gently: "And if you die, Francesca?"

"Then, before the end, I want you to know that I loved you."

He stared at her, sick with unbelief.

"Tell me the cold, naked truth," he begged. "I'd like it better than this bare-faced lying."

"Are you sure of that?" she asked him.

She settled herself a little closer to him, looking up with the wide, empty eyes of a child.

"I'm sure of that, of course."

"Will you tell me why?"

"Then, instead of going on this foolish chase across the river to find a criminal named Dickinson, we'd leave all these people and—"

166

"And then?"

"Go up to the house on the hill and take care of poor Helen O'Mallock until she dies!"

She said patiently: "You spoke of duty. I want you to know that it's duty that takes me over the river tonight. I can't turn back, even for you. And if you knew why, you wouldn't wonder at me. You'd simple take it for granted, and believe me, utterly."

"Believe that you care for me?"

"Believe that I love you—I love you!" whispered Francesca.

He, all ice with cold wonder, looked before him and tried to see the truth, and then he glanced down at her. She was still waiting for an answer. And then belief grew up in him and unfolded like a strange flower, poisoned with the very unbelief from which it had come, and all the more beautiful because of it.

"I do believe," said Weldon.

Now, if it was a cunning lie she had acted, what would she do? What would she say?

She merely closed her eyes.

"You've made it terribly hard work for me," said Francesca. "Hold me safe. I want to sleep!"

33. Over the River

And sleep she did, while the desert flew behind them, and the lights of the towns grew brighter to the left, and the black brow of Bull Mountain rose to the right. At last, the face of the water was before them.

They turned straight down the bank and the jolting

jerked the head of the girl far forward. Carefully he made her comfortable. She opened her eyes and smiled sleepily; an instant later she was slumbering again.

Then he saw that there was a flat-decked barge before them, with a man standing on either side of it. The front tires pressed upon a gangway which ground against the pebbles underneath. Then the deck jarred hollow as they lurched out on it. The brakes groaned; the car was still.

At once the two boatmen loosed the barge. A motor began to cough, sending its voice far off through the night, and they headed well up into the current.

Still Francesca slept, and Jorram turned and regarded her gravely; changed his studious glance to Weldon, and then touched the shoulder of Cunningham.

"Is it real?" he asked, making little effort to keep his voice low.

"When conversation is hard, it's the easiest way, isn't it?" said Cunningham with contempt.

Perhaps he was very right. Certainly there was much in the heart of Weldon which said that it was sheerest acting. All except the sleep; that was real enough. And as for the rest—well, a great actress may command her audience, of course!

Besides, there was a certain sting in the voice of Cunningham, as if he disbelieved his own words.

They met the center of the current, the force of it sending them downstream. The motor increased its beat. And as though released from a strong hand, they swept in suddenly toward the farther shore.

"No border patrol, thank goodness!" said Jorram. "You can't buy off those fellows!"

The motor was shut off. The barge grounded, the two boatmen, who had not spoken, now ran the gangway on shore, and the heavy car trundled cautiously off.

With the rear wheels still on the boards, Jorram turned in the driver's seat.

"Can you buck up against the current?" he asked.

"If we can keep in the shallows—and not run aground."

"If you ground her," said Jorram savagely, "I'll make the rest of your lives short and hot. You hear?"

There was a sullen muttering, and Jorram continued: "Get her up there above the bend, and run her in under

168

the branches of those willows. Stick some other branches along her side and the stern. We've got to take no chances. Make her look like a part of the shore. Remember, boys. There's a cold thousand if we get back across."

"Loaded or empty?" asked one of the boatmen in a sharply nasal voice.

"Loaded or empty," agreed Jorram. "I'm talking about the car, not about what's in it."

"I'll do my bit," said the bargekeeper. "Only I want you to know that they're looking sharp lately. They've got two launches that cut the water like a pair of fish. Machine guns, too."

"The border patrol!" said Jorram, swearing beneath his breath. "They're too alive here. We'll have to shift headquarters. Hang hard onto the job tonight, Jerry. That's all. And so long!"

"So long," said Jerry.

He waved a long arm, the car rumbled off the gangplank, and went up the bank with a snort of effort, like a lunging horse. Part of the bank crumpled. Still the big tires caught hold and shoved the weight upward until the level of the plain was before them.

Francesca sat erect.

"I'll take the wheel," she said. "I know the lay of this land!"

Jorram changed places with her, and she drove the car steadily ahead, swinging in and out through mesquite and past the reaching, low-spread arms of creosote bushes.

"Watch her," said Jorram. "Beauty, ain't she? Makes the car work out like a good pointer. Not a whisper out of it!"

Silently indeed they stole forward, circling slightly with the town to the left until they were well in the rear of San Trinidad. Then she brought it to a stop and blew the hand horn twice—long, soft notes.

They waited. No one spoke. A hoot owl sounded in the distance, a long and mournful cry, and then shadows appeared in the brush. They developed into what seemed a ragged peon, leading three mules. They bore on their backs high Mexican saddles, with the leather peeling from the pommels. Behind the saddles appeared small packs.

"It's Joe," said Francesca, springing down from the car. "Joe, have you been working them?"

"I've given them twenty miles across country," said Joe. "They're hot enough and dusty enough to look as if they'd been traveling."

"Where did you get them?"

"Here and there."

"You bought them, of course?"

"Pay when you have to, take when you can," said Joe with the air of a philosopher. "Why should you pay for things that you can pick up anywhere in Mexico?"

"You idiot!" broke in Jorram. "Suppose somebody spots these mules tonight? You've jumbled it, you junk head!"

"Leave them be, leave them be!" said Joe, still perfectly calm. "You can't tell one mule from another, not if you was the mother of one of 'em. Don't look a gift mule in the mouth, old son. I got 'em trimmed to a fare-thee-well. Packs and everything!"

Jorram and the girl examined the appearance of the three with care and at last pronounced that they would do.

"Go back for the river," Jorram commanded the muleteer who believed in accepting the gifts of Providence. "Work up the bank until you find the boys and the first barge. Hang out with them. Have you got a gun?"

"Nothing but!" said Joe, indicating a rifle which was slung at his back.

"Tonight is an exception to the rules. Shoot first and ask your questions afterward. Pass that word on to the boys, too."

"They'll be sorry to hear it. But I'm not! So long, chief!"

He turned on his heel and went off with a long stride.

"Good man," said Jorram, looking after him.

"Too good for his job," said Francesca, with some irritation. "You shouldn't use a general for a corporal's work, Jorram! He's stolen those animals, and that may mean trouble for us all!"

"It's too late to cry about it," said Jorram. "Too good? Perhaps he is! It's time to start, Francesca. Isn't it about the right time?"

It seemed odd to Weldon to see grown men, certainly with experience, deferring to a mere slip of a girl at a time of such apparent importance.

"We're almost half an hour later than we should be," said she. "Perhaps they've gone to bed by this time."

"Not on a night like this," said Jorram. "Perfect night, Francesca."

"Perfect for them when they start hunting us," she snapped.

She swung into the saddle lightly, unassisted, and sat sidewise in it. Onto her hands she slipped a pair of castanets.

"Are you ready?"

Weldon and Jorram mounted.

"You, Roger!" she said to Cunningham. "You have a lone hand to play. Is that all right?"

"I suppose so," he answered, not too enthusiastically.

"Start about a half hour after we leave. Drive slowly down the street and sound your horn a time or two to let us know that you're coming."

"I understand."

"When you come to the café—you know the place?"

"Yes."

"Be prepared for a good deal of life, Roger. We'll probably be making a running fight of it. You'd better have a gun on the seat beside you."

"Are you going to be in the gunfire?" he asked her sharply.

For answer, she snatched from her dress a glittering little nickel-plated revolver. It flashed in the moonlight, and she laughed as she put it away again.

"You fool!" cried Cunningham.

"Today I brew, tomorrow I bake!" said she, and led the way toward the town.

34. On with the Dance

All positions which meant excitement and profit were agreeable to Benjamin Wilbur. Medicine could have contented him if, twice every day, he had had to perform an operation on which life or death depended. But since he could not reach that happy condition; and since, moreover, he was apt to be a trifle rash in his medical experiments, he had left that honorable profession and roamed the world as he found it. And much he found in it, to be sure!

Yet never was he more perfectly at home then when he sat in the café of Miguel Cabrero in the town of San Trinidad. The café was not a money-maker, like the gaming house of Cabrero, but it was a substantial business, and even more to the mind of Cabrero than the risks of the gambling place. Good food one always can afford to give one's patrons; good luck, one cannot! He had a thread of the honest man in him, this Mexican. He and his brown, fat-faced wife loved the café and did much to make it attractive. The inside room flared with reds and yellows and flashed with gilding. Pictures of lovely girls smiled or laughed from the walls, and big mirrors enabled the patrons to see their own contented faces. But the majority of the business, except in the few cold winter months, was done outdoors.

The second story of the building projected well over the ground floor, supported on a row of arches. Within the arches, Cabrero had laid down a pavement of large, red flags and there he set out small, round tables. Larger tables could be set out at mealtimes, and always those tables were crowded. The food was good. The mescal was excellent. The white brandy would have burned the throat of a tiger. There was fresh pulque for those who preferred that strange liquor. And Miguel had several brands of wine which tickled the palates of his customers on great occasions.

On this night the proprietor himself strolled among the tables as usual, bowing and smiling right and left. He was known to be rich. Therefore his bowing and smiling flattered everyone. The ladies smiled and grew pinker. The men swelled their chests and sat deeper in their chairs, full of importance when the rich man passed.

Cabrero understood exactly what passed in their minds, but he did not feel humiliated. He had, in fact, the instinct of a servant. He liked to see people happy so long as it was putting money in his pocket. He would have made a good tyrant of the patriarchal type, or a good first minister of such a tyrant. He knew that he was a clever man; now as he walked among the tables of his café he almost felt that he was an honest man, too.

He was giving special care to the café in these days, because since the night that the fiend of an American had broken up one of his roulette wheels and torn the brake out of it, his gaming hall was not patronized so heavily. It was all very well for him to explain that the brake was never used—except against a dog of a gringo. It was well enough, also, to say that all the rest of his machines could be examined in turn—for he had made them honest for the moment! Nevertheless, the fact remained that he had been exposed. He had not been shamed, really. It would have taken a monstrous lot to shame Miguel Cabrero. But he had been checked. Now he gave his mind to the café and waited for time to heal the wound which his gambling house had received.

He checked the guests off on the tips of his mental fingers. The prosperous rancher received one sort of bow and word of greeting; the poorer but more constant visitor another. Cabrero knew exactly how much of himself he needed to give to each of his guests until he came to Benjamin Wilbur, who, as usual, occupied the rear table in the corner of the arcade at the rear, watching everything with his keen eyes, and particularly watching the tall, powerful man who sat opposite him, his back to the crowd.

That was Dickinson—who was a pocket of gold to Cabrero. Before long, he should turn it into current coin of Mexico. He could not help but halt and rub his hands together until they glowed.

He leaned for an instant above the table. His face was fatherly as he glanced from one to another. Eight men in all. Dickinson the guarded. Wilbur the keen chief of the guard. And six good men and true who were the body of the guard itself!

He had a taste in scoundrels, had Cabrero, and these were hand-picked men culled from a long list of his acquaintance. There was not one of them that did not have at least a single murder to his credit. Most of them had more. They demanded high pay, but he was willing that they should have it. He hoped to squeeze from Jim Dickinson enough to refill his pockets and to even more than make up for the blow which had been dealt to his gaming hall.

So he beamed upon them, one by one, a caress in his eyes.

And: "You are comfortable, señor?" said he to Dickinson.

That big man turned his lean face slowly toward his host.

"I couldn't be more happy, señor," he replied.

"And your dinner tonight?"

"That was perfect," said Dickinson. "Did your wife cook it?"

So bland was his smile that Cabrero almost let the thing slip by as a casual mistake. But then he flushed and bit his lip.

"Manners of an American—" he began hotly.

Then he stopped. The cold, bright eyes of Benjamin Wilbur were watching him, and the soul of Cabrero shook within him like a winter leaf on a twig.

"Go on," said Wilbur, smiling. "I won't hear you!"

But Cabrero already had said enough. He turned his back on the table and went to the musicians, who were a little apart. They could make more noise than any other four musicians in the world. They could play a piece with more hysterical liveliness; they could play a piece with more drawling sentiment; in short, he was sure that they were the finest in the great Republic of Mexico. He called for a

174

lively piece, now. Lively music pays. It makes people talk faster. It makes them forget the state of their pocketbooks. It makes their drinks disappear more rapidly.

A tall-wheeled cart went by, spinning a dust cloud into the air from its revolving tires. The wind blew that dust into the café and spread it in a thin layer over the surface of every drink. But it was unregarded. Cabrero looked with anxious eyes. No one complained. People tapped on the tables in time with the stirring air, swallowed their drinks and called for more. The panting waiters began to scurry here and there, and Cabrero smiled.

"A business needs the touch of the master's hand!" said he to himself.

The music died away. Down the street he heard the sound of a guitar, and the faint rattle of castanets, and then the voice of a girl singing. Cabrero leaned a considerate ear in the direction of that song. No woman in San Trinidad could sing like that. It was not a strong voice, not a trained voice, but rich, and the song came off with a swing.

Also, there was a foreign taste in the accent. From the South, no doubt. What women they had there!

He worked his way to the front row of his tables. They extended out under the stars and blocked half the street, and more, but the city did not mind. The chief officials were all his friends. When they stood before his bar they knew that they did not have to pay!

He never walked out there under the open heavens, in fact, without having the sense of his own powers brought more strongly home to him. He was a master mind. He did what he would. Cabrero was full of complacence.

Down the street a small crowd was approaching. It was recruiting every moment. Little boys and girls ran out from doorways and entered the throngs. Above their heads, Miguel Cabrero saw the ears of three mules.

The procession came closer.

It resolved itself into a girl who walked alone before the rest. She entered the fringe of the circle of light cast by Cabrero's big gasoline lamp. It fell on her sandaled feet, it glistened on her bare legs, twisted about by her sandal thongs, it touched her green earrings, the gilded beads around her throat, the red scarf which flowed down behind her shoulders, or fluttered behind her as she walked. Light as the wind she came, still singing, and in the pauses of the song making a dancing step or two, with the rhythmic jangling of the castanets.

Cabrero knew dancing. This girl would fill his café every night of the year. She was a treasure.

She drew still closer. The nearer she came, the higher rose the heart of Cabrero. She was very, very brown. But that only pleased him the more, because he liked the rich Indian blood. There was plenty of it rushing riotously in his own veins!

In fact, she was a rose among women, and her great dark eyes were flooded with the joy of living.

She stood before the café and sang the last verse of her song. Behind her stood the big, swarthy muleteer, holding the heads of the three mules. Closer to her was the guitar player. He was a Hercules. A great brute of a man. Those shoulders of his could have battered down a wall. His face was lowering, scowling. A shag of black hair, like the mane of a horse, poured over his eyes.

A beast of a man!

Something about his shoulders reminded Miguel Cabrero of another place, another scene, and a quiet-voiced American asking for money—thousands of good dollars, honest dollars, from his safe!

But he shrugged that thought away. He was not displeased by this monster. He made a perfect background, as a matter of fact, for the slender grace of the girl.

Her song ended. Applause broke from the tables. Men were standing up and throwing coins, shouting, clapping. Cabrero was delighted, for he knew that pocketbooks are like hearts: Once opened, they never cease to pour forth!

The muleteer left the mules to some admiring boys to hold and went about on hands and knees, picking up coins with a feverish eagerness.

How base can men be! thought Cabrero, thinking of his shining safe of steel and the treasure within it. Thinking of his strong, clever brain, where still more treasure was buried.

Ah, life, world, how sweet it is to breathe and be!

But while the muleteer picked up the coins, the girl held up her hand. Cabrero saw a golden snake clasped about the round upper arm. The crowd fell silent at that commanding gesture.

Then the guitar was struck. She began to dance. Lightly, and strongly, too. Nothing of that feathery smoothness which swims effortless through a maze of motions, but a power that struck off every high point. She whirled with spinning skirts. Her sandaled feet smote the ground as she stopped and whirled again. Her arms, her hands, her tilting head all swayed in the drunken joy of that dancing. She seemed to be dancing for no one but the god of dance; she seemed to be dancing for every leering pair of bright eyes in the café.

In the middle of a bar the music ended.

The dancer stopped. She was panting hard, her lips parted, her eyes starry.

There was no applause; they were drinking up her beauty to the last drop in the glass. Then she leaned back and threw her arm around the neck of the burly brute, the guitar player. She kissed him. He merely scowled and shrugged her arm away. It was as though she had bestowed a caress on a surly lion, born to frown.

"Goddess! Goddess!" cried Miguel Cabrero, and struck his heart.

The applause roared like rain. Like rain the coins showered glistening. They struck the ground. They struck the dancer's body. She stood still and laughed and held out her arms while the gold and the silver beat about her.

35. Treason!

Benjamin Wilbur and James Dickinson were the only people in the café who were not overwhelmed with excitement. They sat like statues, looking at their excited companions, smiling faintly and critically at one another. They had been sympathetic from the instant that Wilbur took charge of the guard party. There was no malice felt by Dickinson because of the work which Wilbur had undertaken. Rather, he seemed to feel an especial kindliness for the other. They chatted familiarly, always. And yet they never misunderstood. Each was ready to tear out the throat of the other at the slightest real provocation. They made an interesting contrast—Wilbur, more smooth, polished, talkative; Dickinson, huge, swift, and grim. But six men stood beside Wilbur. Therefore Dickinson remained quietly in place, waiting as a tiger waits, with the patient ferocity of a cat.

"What is it?" said Dickinson as one disdaining to turn in his chair.

"A singing, dancing girl," said Wilbur. "Greaser," he added carelessly.

Dickinson poured himself another glass of beer. His eyes grew blank again. But then Wilbur was leaning forward.

"What is it?" asked Dickinson again.

"She's one in a million," said Wilbur critically. "I wish she'd come closer."

"She'll come closer to collect," Dickinson assured him.

In fact, the guitar began to be strummed again, not with

any great art, but with powerful strokes that beat into the blood. The girl, singing, passed weaving among the tables, her extended arms swaying through graceful gestures, the golden serpent flashing. Behind her walked the abysmal brute, glaring fiercely about him beneath his shag of tumbling hair. Behind him went the bulky fat man, holding out a hat, into which silver coins tinkled. Everyone gave.

An excited vaquero caught the hand of the dancer and kissed it.

"They won't bother with us," said Wilbur. "They're going the other way."

"They leave the best for the last," said Dickinson, dry as always.

He would not give a glance, and Wilbur shook his head.

"You're missing something worth while," he said. "Because she has the spark!"

Dickinson yawned.

Presently the singer came closer, pausing by the tables, bowing to generous donors. Someone had thrown flowers to her. She slipped a crimson blossom into the gray hair of an old, iron-faced rancher. The people laughed and shouted. It was becoming a festival. The sweetness and the passion of spring stirred again in their blood, and they leaned from their chairs to follow her with their eyes.

She came again to the table where sat the two Americans. And there, as her song ended, she paused with arms lifted and stilled the applause. The guitar worked in muffled strings, humming an expectant air. And in the pause the girl swayed a little, like a bird on a wind-touched branch, a brilliant bird with music swelling in its throat, about to take wing and whirl and soar and dip in the glory of the sun. So she stood, poised, and full of the joy of motion to be.

The guitar struck a piercing note. She swept into movement. Around the table of the guarded man she went. The guitar player took post behind the chair of Wilbur, stooping a little, murmuring with the words of the song. Even his brute nature seemed to be touched. He was excited in his turn, and a terrible excitement it was, for his eyes flashed through the fallen hair, as fireflies shine through brush.

And then Wilbur heard a cautious voice saying at his

179

ear: "Look straight before you. Don't turn. It's Lew Weldon. And we've come for Dickinson!"

Weldon—Dickinson!

Never had Wilbur showed the strength of his nerves more perfectly than at this moment. He merely lifted the glass of beer to his lips. Then he began to wave a hand in time with the beat of the music. The Mexicans of the guard around him were open-mouthed, agape. They looked like starved creatures drinking nectar. They reeled in their chairs and swayed their heads. They looked at one another with mad, unseeing eyes.

And again the voice at Wilbur's ear:

"If you're with us, take up that glass and drink again. If you're against us—Heaven help you!"

Wilbur closed his eyes. He liked a fight as well as any man in the world. But he thought, as he sat with closed eyes, of the brutal face of the guitar player. Weldon! Aye, and he could be brutal and terrible, too, as Wilbur very well knew.

Then he opened his eyes and looked straight before him, and it happened by the sheerest chance that at that moment he saw Cabrero standing with legs braced, eyes almost shut and twinkling with pleasure, and hands that were rubbing softly, plumply together.

Wilbur raised the glass to his lips.

Said the voice behind him:

"Good boy, Ben! Now tell Dickinson and, if you can, pass him a gun."

Wilbur pointed to the girl and leaned across the table, nodding to Dickinson.

"Weldon is behind me," said Wilbur. "They've come to take you. I'll help. Reach under the table in a moment. I'm going to let a gun slide down my legs."

He leaned far back in his chair, settled down in it, began to wave his hands again in rhythm with the dance. The girl had spun away among more distant tables, but the abysmal brute with the guitar remained where he was, behind Wilbur's chair, as though he expected that the dancer would return in that direction again.

So, beating time with one hand, with the other Wilbur slipped out a gun and placed it on his lap. By depressing his knees the heavy Colt was made to slide down in the trough of his legs until it came to rest across his insteps.

Dickinson coughed, dropped a box of matches with which he was about to light a cigarette, and stooped to pick it up again. He seemed to fumble at it twice, as a careless man will do. Then he straightened slowly. One hand fumbled at the match box. The other placed the gun in his own lap, between his knees. There it could remain.

An excited man now ran out of the crowd before the café. He approached Cabrero. He caught the arm of that gentleman.

"What do you want?" asked the rich man, and struck the detaining, grimy hand away.

"Those three mules were stolen from my farm!" said the excited fellow. "Those—there in the street. I know them as well as my children."

"You are a fool!" said Cabrero.

What was the price of three mules compared with the good which this singing girl was doing for his café? He would have paid the bill out of his own pocket. Of course they were three rogues! Only rogues wander through the country like that.

"An accursed gringo was seen driving them off! I ran all day down the road. My heart broke. I was ruined if I lost them. Kind señor, help me to take them back!"

"Gringo? Gringo?" said Cabrero.

"My little son saw him."

"Your little son is a little fool!"

But Cabrero began to stare at the three strangers. He looked at the dancing girl. Her accent, when she sang, was strange—not altogether of the South, either! And yonder, he saw the brute of the shaggy hair leaning close to Wilbur and his lips were moving. A hand of ice seized upon the heart of Cabrero.

But he was in his own city, and Heaven be praised for it, the kind Heaven that watches over the thrifty and the sharp-witted!

"When I drop the guitar, that's the signal!" Weldon was saying.

Wilbur leaned across the table.

"When he drops his guitar, that's the signal," he repeated.

And Cabrero saw Wilbur lean, saw him speak!

For answer, Dickinson picked up a bottle of brandy, and poured out a tumblerful. It was Mexican brandy—terrible as white fire. And here was enough to strike down a mule! But he filled the tumbler to the brim, and raised it toward his lips.

The Mexicans of the guard saw and pointed. They began to laugh hugely, their heads straining back in their mirth. Even this sullen American, this vast and terrible man, had been caught in the flames of the song and the dance, it seemed!

They grinned at him with a sort of horrible fellowship.

Cabrero turned to the door of his café. Two waiters stood there.

"Call the men from the inside. Get everybody. Guns, guns! Knives! Weapons! Move quickly! Quickly!"

The pair vanished. They scurried like frightened rats to do as they were bidden.

The dancer was turning back toward the table of the Americans and the armed guard. How Cabrero hated their gaping, mirth-ridden faces—those practiced warriors, now helpless with joy in the dance, in the beauty of the girl.

She seemed to Cabrero no longer beautiful. She was like the spirit of evil, plague in her touch, in her very presence.

But now his men were coming. Praise Heaven again, who gave to him such legions of the faithful!

A sudden discord crashed on his ear. The guitar had fallen from the hands of the player—and in its place appeared the flash of two long revolvers, swiftly conjured into being like a terrible stroke of magic from a fairy tale.

"Treason!" shouted Cabrero.

The glass of brandy had been at the lips of Dickinson. Now he whipped it away with a gesture that flung the contents in a swift semicircle into the faces of four of the guard. The pale fire filled their eyes. They fell back from their chairs, yelling, clawing at weapons, blinded.

"Treason!" shouted Cabrero again.

The whole café was in a swirl; through the street, jamming amid the crowd, came the long hood of a big gray automobile.

36. "Thorough" Is Their Motto

Four of that worthy guard had been incapacitated by a gesture and the devilish cunning of Dickinson. There remained two, however. A split second wiped the joy from their faces. Then, their courage returning, they brought out their guns.

But Fate stood behind them in the form of Weldon. The long barrel of a revolver dropped on the head of one and he pitched forward onto the table. The second was clubbed across the back of the neck and he swerved to the side with a single gasp and lay writhing on the floor.

Like the vortex of a whirlpool, a gap appeared around that table, all dashing from the point of danger. And behind them went Weldon, rushing like a bull, splitting them apart like the point of a wedge. There were two shoulders to that wedge. One was great Dickinson, silent, gun poised; he struck with it with cool precision and trampled the fallen under foot. The other was Jorram, older, less springy of nerve and muscle, but now exerting a really great strength and nobly bearing up his share of the labor.

In the cup behind this wedge followed the graceful dancer. Cabrero saw her go. She ran half turned, and as hands reached at her, they shrank as from the touch of fire, for she carried a weapon, also. It glittered like silver in her slender hand!

So they split through the crowd and came to the automobile and were in it, instantly.

The girl sprang into the driver's seat and jammed the gear-shift lever home in first. The engine roared. She sat erect in her place. And in the car were four armed men. The noses of their guns looked over the sides.

"Kill them!" shouted Cabrero. "Kill them! Tear them to pieces! Guns! Where are my men? I go mad! Help!"

His men were there, fighting through the crowd, keen enough for battle. But their path was littered with a crowd of struggling humanity. A hundred armed hands ready, but all helpless with confusion. Two calm riflemen could have stopped the car, shot the woman from her place, riddled the machine with bullets.

Here were a hundred, shouting, shooting blindly. Men who had ben knocked down cried out profanely as they were trampled. The cheerful café was a storm center from the inferno itself.

And yonder the car moved down the street, and the crowd swayed out and around it again. The horn honked steadily; the guns roared.

The car began to gather speed.

Weldon sat beside Francesca, crouched a little, his armed hands ready, his head turned back.

Only he gave her a glance now and again, curious in the midst of this battle, and saw that her lips were set hard, and that her nostrils quivered a little. A very tigress, not a woman.

A wild yell—they had bumped a slow-moving man into a wall from their path. He lay groaning, a bone broken, doubtless. They swerved to the left into a narrow lane as a bullet struck the front windshield and sent out the glass with a single crash.

The confusion was ending. Hot pursuit was rushing after them. Weldon could hear the squealing of horses as they felt the spurs driven home. He heard the frightened yelling of women and children, scattering from beneath the plunging hoofs.

They shot about a corner of the lane—and before them arose a squat shadow—a hand cart squarely blocking the path.

No time to back up from that alley into the street behind! The savage crowd would have them and tear them to pieces. No time to pause, even, and heave the cart to one side.

She did not hesitate, this cool, erect, slender figure at

184

the wheel. She thrust the lever into second and gave the car gas. So, like a living thing, it sprang forward and smote the cart.

There was a screeching, a crashing, a groaning. The big machine staggered, swerved heavily to the right. They bumped with a second crash. An open door, caught by the right fender, was ripped neatly from its hinges.

And then they were shooting through.

Shooting through a chamber of blackness, a smooth flume of dark with only the powder of the white stars scattered carelessly high above their heads.

Suddenly the darkness opened in a wide, pale fan. They were through the town and in the open country. They were among the mesquite, dipping and swerving through it under the clever guidance of the girl.

Ah, heart of steel!

But still the pursuit had come swiftly behind them. Riders like shadowy spears flung themselves out from the streets of the town, firing as they came, and with a good aim.

A dozen times bullets hissed above them, or thudded against the rear of the machine.

"It's all right," said the girl, calm as ever. "We have a sheet of steel down the back seat. This part of the game is over."

With a purr like that of a contented cat they slid over the sands, dipping easily in and out among the obstacles. It was like the weaving flight of a bird, so effortless and sure. She was an uncanny master at the wheel.

Jorram stood up in the rear.

"Cut to the left. Semicircle. Bear in, then, toward the point. You'll tell it by two big trees. That's the place I told them to take the barge."

She swung obediently to the left. The brush flew past. She neared the river trees, at last, and safety.

A lantern flashed before them.

"Halt!" The command came in good American, a little through the nose. "Halt or I'll blow you to—"

They darted past that light. A gun began to fire rapidly, and every bullet struck the rear of the machine. Only the steel plate was keeping those slugs from boring through the body from end to end?

185

"Border patrol!" said the girl through her teeth.

"But this is Mexico!"

"What's that to them?"

A pair of lights gleamed suddenly just before them, and between the lights stretched a glimmering chain.

"Halt!" came a roaring chorus before them, and a pair of guns barked into the air in warning.

Almost too late for that! She could not check the car before it struck that heavy chain, and to strike it would be to tip it over end for end and smash those within.

So she jammed the brakes and swerved to the left. Sickeningly the big automobile skidded. The brakes were off; the power was shot on again, and staggering between the two impulses the machine lurched ahead.

Dust had billowed before them high and far. It seemed to shut the shouting voices away like a blanket of silence. Guns were barking, however, and hornet-sounds thrust through the veil at them.

Then, before them, a spreading shadow. Mesquite, and they were lost. Creosote, and they might smash through.

Creosote it was. Like a shadow it had risen. Like a shadow it was gone, and the big machine, heeling over with dizzy suddenness, sped away, exhaust opened, roaring triumphantly.

Guns still clanged in a steady uproar. There must be a dozen men in that ambush, but now they were safely out of sight in the desert brush again, and with the cut-out thrown in, they were whispering forward over the sands.

The moon was high. Weldon could not help turning and looking behind at Dickinson, and he saw that he was comfortable in a corner of the seat, his hands folded in his lap, a smile on his lips.

It was as though he had seen something in the distance, not as though he had been in the center of a typhoon. And, for the first time in his life, cold awe of another mortal descended upon Weldon!

Jorram was on his feet again, clinging to the rear-seat windshield.

"Francesca, you're a knock-out, you're a wonder!" he cried. "All gold, and a yard wide! Now, head straight upstream. There's a second chance. If they've blocked us

186

there—it's back into the Mexican mountains, and Heaven help us!"

She nodded, and gave the car more gas, so that the sand, upflung from the spinning wheels, rushed like water through a flume against the mud guards. The girl's confidence was amazing.

They followed a long bend of the river to another knot of trees, and there, from the bank, they looked down on the comfortable bosom of a big barge. A shadow stood up in the moonlight.

"We're here! Charlie!" yelled Jorram.

"Aye, aye!"

Another form joined Charlie. Down the bank they slid with grinding brakes, over the gangplank, and onto the barge. The motor was shut down to the faintest of whispers.

"Look the old car over," said Francesca to Weldon. "I think there may be a flat in the rear."

There was—flat and in ribbons!

So while the noisy motor of the barge was started, the men jacked up the car and changed tires.

When Weldon had finished the work and put the tools away, he found Dickinson standing beside the driver's seat. He was holding out his hand, and Francesca barely touched it.

"Thanks," she said, "but you'd better save that for Jorram. I'm simply a hired hand!"

The central current was forming around them, now, when she called: "Jorram!"

"Aye?"

"Look down there! I thought I saw a pair of headlights for a second."

They all stared. And, for an instant, the lights gleamed again, though even in that brief moment it could be seen that they were rushing close at a great speed.

"Border patrol again," said Francesca. " 'Thorough' is the motto!"

37. The Man Without a Soul

Nerves which had gradually been relaxing were wire drawn once again. Automobiles were not casually driven over roadless desert at such a rate of speed; and the flashing of the lights seemed to show that they were turned on in glimpses only to illumine some special difficulty of the path.

The motor of the boat was now driven at full speed ahead. The barge tore loose from the central current and sagged swiftly in for the shore line with unquenched effort. The result was a grinding crunch—the barge slid far up, in safety, but with prow pointing upward at a sharp angle.

"Dumb!" said Francesca Laguarda, standing up at the wheel and looking at the result of this work.

"Dumb? Dash their stupidity," said Jorram. "I'll ride them for this!"

But the gangway was manned by everyone, except the girl. It held down at a sharp angle. And before it was a high bank at what seemed to Weldon an impossible inclination for any automobile.

"You can't do it," he told her. "Why try to kill yourself? You never can get a car up that bank!"

"Sooner that than prison," snapped Francesca Laguarda. And she sent the car onto the gangway.

The heavy boards sagged and groaned, down dipped the gray monster, its hide ripped now, and torn by the impact of many bullets, but its heart still pulsing and filled with vital energy.

Taking full advantage of the down-drop, Francesca sent

the engine humming with the clutch in second speed and hurled it at the bank—not straight up its face, but sideways, at a slight angle.

The spinning wheels cut and dug at the face of the bank. Still the car skidded dangerously, swayed, gained the very top, and there staggered and toppled—

Weldon closed his eyes. A sharp slap came on his shoulder. It was Wilbur.

"She's over," said he. "Wonderful girl, by George! Wonderful! Wonderful!"

They scrambled up the bank and piled helter-skelter into the car, Weldon again in the front seat beside that dauntless driver, while across the plain, through the brush, came the pursuer—if such it were.

It had unhooded its lights now. Fiercely they flared through the brush, and a mighty searchlight, poised above, swung this way and that. They had heard the roar of Francesca's car; now they were searching for it like a hawk for quarry!

"One moment!" said big Dickinson. "I'll blacken their eyes for them!"

He was seen standing, a rifle glued to his shoulder, and then he fired three times. The first snuffed the searchlight. The next two put out the headlamps of the car.

"Now let him follow if he can," said Dickinson.

And follow he would, headlights or none.

For as the car lunged ahead, soon screaming through second and dropping into the whine of third speed, behind them they saw the shadow of the other swerve to the side and follow like a flung javelin across the desert.

Jorram stood up in his place and leaned over the rear-seat windshield.

"Seven men in that car, honey," he said to Francesca without excitement. "And she's holding us even—and it's the border patrol, my dear, as you may guess for yourself!"

Weldon looked back in turn.

It seemed impossible that any other machine in the world could be rivaling the rate at which they were traveling now, but certainly the monster to the rear was succeeding. A monster it was, even longer and lower than the gray beauty, and fully holding its own—yes, gaining a little and a little!

Wilbur snatched up a rifle and began a steady, dropping fire, until Weldon heard Jorram say:

"It's no good, lad. I know that car. She's got a set of steel shutters in front, and she's got a bullet-proof windshield. You can't dint her!"

"Worse luck!" said Wilbur, lowering the gun unwillingly.

"I know her like a book," said Jorram, calm as ever, but his big voice rolling up in spite of the rush of the engine. "A hundred horsepower, specially built. Goodness knows what she develops. But you can see for yourself—with seven men aboard her. Duck, boys. They're opening up!"

That was true. It was like the rattle of a machine gun as at least three repeating rifles began to pour a dropping fire on the gray car from the distance.

They were shooting past the lower feet of Bull Mountain with all the moonlit features of the landscape turned fluid and flying off behind them.

Then Francesca dipped the gray machine into a narrow valley.

The voice of Jorram came again over their heads, a shout of excitement now.

"Francesca! Francesca! Are you crazy? There's the ditch here ahead of us."

She did not seem to hear. Her face was like steel. She sat erect, immobile, hands merely twitching up and down to meet the lurching of the front wheels as they tore through soft and hard in the sand. Sometimes the upflung pebbles whipped through the shattered windshield and stung the face of Weldon. They must sting her face, too, but she remained unperturbed.

"Francesca! Do you hear?"

They were on a down grade. Adjusting the mixture, she swung an extra ten miles an hour from the laboring motor. The air whistled past, tearing at their eyes, at their hair, with soft, strong hands.

"Francesca!" yelled Jorram. "You'll smash us to a pulp! The ditch! The ditch! You fool! Weldon, Weldon—for Heaven's sake, take the wheel away from her."

Weldon, instinctively, put his big hand on the wheel.

She did not turn her head, but cried so that he could

hear above the wind, above the motor—"I know what I'm doing!"

He removed his hand.

"Sit down!" he shouted back to Jorram. "She won't make a mistake."

Jorram collapsed onto the rear seat and covered his face with his hands.

In the glance that saw him fall, Weldon saw more—he saw the pursuing car leap the crest of the rise behind them like a wild beast and then lunge forward down the near slope. Gaining—gaining fast! Nothing could keep them from overtaking their quarry, and confident of the victory, they had ceased firing, though almost at a point-blank range.

Weldon, under the silver white of the moon, could make out the barrels of long rifles, and the darkly masked face of the driver. Well did he deserve from his country for this headlong pursuit of which he was the soul!

Then, looking ahead, Weldon saw a dark line drawn across their path. It widened instantly into a deep ditch. From the back seat the voice of Jorram shouted something. The ditch turned into a little chasm, with ragged sides of rock showing. Then they went at it with all the speed of the motor, with all the speed of that long, breathless drop down the hill.

For the highest point of the nearer lip of the gorge she aimed.

Life or death in a breathing space now! Then they flung forward. The darkness was hurled behind them with a white flash of water at the bottom. They struck the sandy top of the farther bank with a shock and a crash that soaked the speed out of them in a moment, and then lunged slowly forward—safe!

Safe unless that speeding demon behind them took the same chance!

They looked back. The girl, throwing in the clutch, sent the car forward again—ah, wonder of strength that wheels had held under that shock!—and now they saw the long machine of the pursuit shooting straight down for the mark.

As it came, Francesca, with the gray car sliding swiftly and smoothly over the sands, threw out the clutch and shut down the motor. Like a whisper they drifted, and then from behind came a wild cry from many throats—a terrible, ringing, tearing cry that Weldon knew would be lodged in his heart forever!

He saw the big machine beyond the gorge stagger, then swerve, then spin rapidly round and round, lunge ahead, and come to a halt with its front part sagging.

On the very lip of destruction the driver had halted his car.

Weldon looked back, with a gasp of relief. Francesca lay buckled over the wheel, her arms hanging down.

He drew home the emergency, then, and lifted her out of the car. Dickinson leaned above her, and pressed his ear to her heart.

"I thought it had killed her. She went down when she heard that yell, as though it was a bullet through her. But it's only a faint!"

"Take the wheel!" Jorram barked at Cunningham. *"Only* a faint," he said, as they rearranged themselves in the car, Weldon in the rear, holding Francesca's limp body. *"Only* a faint! I tell you, it's the finish of her. She'll never be no good, no more. She's burned herself out. Women are that way. They can last up to the burning point. That's all. A man—you can have him on fire a hundred times, and he'll still come back. Her—she's through! She was worth half a million to me this morning. She ain't worth a cent over her carfare home now. Wherever her home may be!"

His anger was plainly manifest.

"There," said Dickinson with a grim smile, jerking his thumb at Weldon. "He'll be the junk receiver!"

There was an utterly heartless scorn and amusement in those words that Weldon did not, at first, comprehend. Then he realized slowly, as a man realizes any prodigy, that here was what the world produces not once in a century—a man without a soul!

He did not look at Dickinson. He did not even feel anger against him. He felt as one who looks over the side of a ship and sees the white horror of a cuttlefish rise to the surface and sink again.

38. Deep in the Sand

She recovered almost as quickly as she had been struck down. She turned her face to Weldon and clung to him.

"They were all killed!" she exclaimed wildly.

"Not one! Not one!" said Weldon. "All safe. You hear me? Not one hurt. They stopped their car on the edge of the rock, the front wheels dipping, but safe. Do you hear, Francesca?"

He had to say it over and over. She was like one whose brain has been dimmed with ether, gradually fumbling back to understanding and clear mind.

"Not one?" She could understand at last.

"All saved."

Still she clung for a moment. He felt the shudder of relief that ran through her.

"I'm well enough now," she said, and slipped from his arms into the seat between him and Dickinson, who looked straight before him, smiling a little, his face blackened by the shadow of the moon. Nothing but disdain for this softness, this weakness, was in his expression. The girl looked up to him only once, and then shrank closer to Weldon.

Jorram was right, he felt. She had thrown her soul into that one great adventure, and the heart in her was burned out. The demon in her, might he not say? All that remained might be true womanly and gentle! And the very soul of Weldon took wings at the thought. Yet he fought back all sense of surety.

One could not tell. On the journey out, she had surrendered to exhaustion and slept beside him like a child. And

193

after that, she had been a spring of steel on which all the venture depended, and which had supported them all through terrible peril. She might recuperate again. There was something in her, at least, which a thousand years of study never could explain to Jorram or any of his kind. So perhaps she would once more be a bird of prey—all wings, and cruel talons, and beak—to soar and strike and live a man's life, in a man's world.

In the hands of Cunningham, the car was a different thing. It had lost throbbing power and dizzy speed, it seemed. Softly and gently it pulsed across the sands, swerved up through the hills, and there was the house of Jorram again.

Jorram himself took Francesca into the house. He talked to her like a father. She was to go to bed and sleep. She was not to move from the place. He would take care of her, himself. To this she said nothing.

The other cars were gone. The place was silent and dull, and the white moon shone over all, revealing its tawdriness in every detail.

So Weldon went to the room where he had left his clothes. He had hot water brought in. Slowly and painfully he removed the dye from his body, dressed, and went out into the hall.

Jorram, Dickinson, and Cunningham sat with Wilbur in the little front room, drinking whiskey from large tumblers as though it were water. None of them spoke a word.

"Where is she?" asked Weldon. "What room?"

"The outside room," said Dickinson.

And he grinned, his evil grin of too much knowledge.

"What room is that?" asked Weldon.

"She's gone," said Jorram gently. "Come in here, Lew, and share the split. Jimmie has paid up. You get your whack."

He took from his pocket a stack of bills.

"You wonder where Jimmie carried this?" smiled Jorram. "He didn't carry it. He's paid me in something else. I pay you in cash! It was fifty thousand for this job, son. Thirty per cent for overhead. Cut the rest four ways, that gives you—"

"Nothing," said Weldon briefly. "I'm not in the game. I want to know where she's gone!"

He came to the edge of the table. He waited.

Said Jorram, with a gesture, palm up: "I don't know, Lew. I'd tell you if I did. She goes her own way. She's never with us, except for business. You'll find a bunk in the back room. Turn in and sleep, old son, and in the morning you can change your mind about the split of the coin."

"I'll walk back," said Weldon. "I want to leave a message with you—for her."

"He'll never see her again," said Dickinson.

Weldon turned on him with a sudden fury.

"Do you know her?" he asked savagely.

"Do you?" sneered Dickinson.

"Yes!"

"Like fun you do!" said Dickinson.

Weldon tapped the other on the shoulder. That shoulder was ridged with rubber-hard muscle.

"I don't like the way you say it," said he.

"There ain't much about me that you *do* like," said Dickinson. "You don't like my face, for instance?"

"I don't," said Weldon, and waited.

"Look here," said Jorram, "don't talk like that. Wilbur, take Weldon off. Dickinson—"

Dickinson remained at ease, lounging in his chair, amused as he looked Weldon up and down.

"What do you want?" he asked. "Hands—guns—knives?"

"Anything that you ask for," said Weldon. "On foot or horseback, day or night, gun or knife, or bare hands. I don't like you, Dickinson. And, if you take her name in your mouth again, do you know what I will do? I'll throttle you where you sit!"

"I won't have you—" began Jorram.

But Dickinson cut him off coolly.

"I'm not that kind of a fool, Jorram," said he. "I thought you worked with real men. I see that you have to fall back on this!"

Total disgust and contempt were in his voice as he indicated Weldon.

"I'll attend to you in due time," said he.

Weldon turned on his heel and left the room. Only at

195

the door he paused and turned back again for an instant. They were all watching him, curiously keen of eye.

Then he went on down the hall. Nature had given him a soft step and a keen ear, and as he neared the front door of the little shack, he heard Wilbur saying quietly to the others: "Some of us grow old; some of us grow young. Weldon, for instance!"

"Yes," said Dickinson's hard voice, "he'll hang in his swaddling clothes one of these days."

Then Weldon went out under the open sky.

He was glad of the great space—none too large for him to breathe in. And, with a long, swift stride, he went over the hill and toward the O'Mallock house in the far distance. It would not be long until the dawn would come.

Coming to the last of the taller hills—for he was cutting across on an airline, as nearly as he could plot his course—he was aware of a small house in a hollow. The house of the doctor, no doubt. It seemed odd that he never had been there before. It seemed odd that the little house should be sleeping there under the white of the moon, its front patterned in black by the trailing of climbing vines.

So, he felt, lived the good old doctor, placid and gentle and true to all that was best in life, in the midst of the turmoil, and the intrigues, and the bloodshed that were sweeping across these mountains and turning the border red.

He found that the house lay not far from his course, and, therefore, he dipped a little to the right and came up before it. Its very face, even at night, spoke of the good man within. All was trim, well-clipped, and the whole place breathed forth peace. And so it was that Weldon stood for a long moment, staring, and wondering to himself if, in time, he could school himself until in his nature there would be found some shadow of the virtues which appeared so bright in Henry Watts.

With strength, with patience, with endless love, he might in that manner redeem even wild Francesca Laguarda and—

He turned away, as if to shut that sad thought from his mind and, turning, he saw the trail of wheels leading to the doctor's garage, which was a shed attached to his house.

The doctor's car! He could remember it—the little old man sitting bunched at the wheel, holding its course as

196

well as he could with uncertain hands. All that he did was fumbling and vague, like his large, mild, dim eyes!

And Weldon smiled, his heart growing soft.

He paused at the side of the tracks again.

Large tracks for so small a car, they were. And many and many a time the doctor must have run it back and forth in the same line to wear the trenches in the sand so deep.

Odd, too, that he should have been so accurate!

Here, in one spot, a streak of darkness showed where the water from the watering of the climbing vines that clothed all the place and trailed fingers across the windows had seeped into one of the ruts.

Weldon leaned over it, and saw in the wet of the sand, faintly illumined by the moon, the pattern of great oversized tires whose new tread had marked the place.

The doctor's car! Ten of his cars side by side hardly could have made such an impression in the ground!

And Weldon stood still, desperately combing his wits, and arriving at no conclusion.

The doctor!

He went to the door of the garage. It was fastened tight. He went to the window. It was covered with thick dust, like white milk beneath the moon.

But that he rubbed aside, and so made a peephole through which he could look, and the moon with him.

Then he saw the doctor's car, indeed. And, beside it, long, and low, and apparently unmarred by all its labor, the great gray car in which Francesca Laguarda had driven and dared so much that night of nights.

He leaned against the edge of the wall, his breath gone, his wits whirling.

All seemed a great machine, and all the wheels were interlocking and grinding together, but what that machine was accomplishing he, Weldon, could not guess. Francesca —the doctor—Dickinson—Jorram—the O'Mallock house —poor Helen O'Mallock.

What could it all mean?

39. Mystification

Dawn began as he neared the O'Mallock house. There was a wintry cold in the air and a sharp breeze driving the cold through him. He was glad of that. Physical discomfort kept his mind in play, kept it from turning back to the strange jumble of his thoughts, like a great, unsifted junk heap where all things were wrong. The doctor, Francesca—Francesca, Dickinson—Dickinson, Jorram—Helen, the doctor—the robbed grave, the blood on the floor—

So he faced that wind gladly, and coming to a little eminence within sight of the high roof of the O'Mallock house, he even stood still, letting that sharp wind like icy water drench him, blowing freely through his clothes.

Now that he had left his post, perhaps they would not want him back. He would have to meet the sad eyes of Helen, conscious of death, conscious of the terror of this world—so he welcomed the cold and miserably set his teeth. For he would have given all his soul to be able to reduce this problem to one of physical force, with which he could use his strength and grapple. He understood, now, why Hercules was enslaved, even to a woman, for might of hand goes in service, always, to the keener brains. So he, Weldon, was enslaved also, and bitterly he resented it.

Through the dim pink of the growing dawn, he saw a rider come down out of the blackness of the pines, jogging a cow pony without haste, like a weary man who has journeyed all the night.

Leaning against a poplar in the little nest of trees which sheltered him, Weldon watched the man with interest. The horse picked its own way, while the rider sat with bowed head, that jogged with the loose jogging of the pony. Winding back and forth, never hunting for short cuts, the pony came down the hill as though it were following the twistings of a trail, but there was no trail to follow.

Very hungry and weary this man must be. He had been far away, dancing all night, perhaps, drinking moonshine whiskey, being very gay. Now he returned to pick up his work, and go yawning and groaning through another day of labor. Ah, how much Weldon envied him, who had ridden so closely past the O'Mallock house without any thought, doubtless, of the tragedy which endured in that unhappy place!

The rider drew nearer. He seemed asleep in the saddle. But as he came past, the stumble of the cow pony made the man throw up his head a little, and Weldon saw the familiar face of that worthy young man who had been addressed as "Slim" on the day when the two of them had disappeared into the wall of the O'Mallock house.

He snapped out a revolver and fired inches before the face of the sleepy rider. Slim shouted in bewilderment. The pony shied, throwing his rider off balance, and before he could right himself, Weldon was stalking down from the trees with a leveled gun.

Slim thrust his hands lazily into the air. He appeared rather disgusted than afraid.

"You're a kind of standing crop around here, it looks to me," said Weldon. "What are you doing here now?"

"Ridin' herd," said the other, yawning. "What are *you* doing?"

"Watching the coyotes and the wolves," said Weldon, "and I think that I have one now. Get off your horse and stand with your hands over your head, and your face to his shoulder."

Slim sighed.

"You're gunna fan me for my gun," he said. "All right. It's a little one in my right coat pocket. There's a pocketknife in the left trousers pocket. That's all."

He slid down from his horse and stood obediently in the required position, yawning again.

Quickly Weldon found the indicated weapons. He patted the body of the other from head to foot. There were no more guns. But a fat wallet came presently into his hand.

"Leave that be, will you?" sighed Slim. "I worked fair and honest for that."

"What did you do for it?" asked Weldon.

"What business is that of yours?" asked Slim, anger mastering his weariness.

He made as if to turn, and Weldon took him by the nape of the neck.

"Listen to me, old son," said Weldon, "I never was a patient man, and what little patience I had is all used up now. All gone, in fact! I want you to pay attention to me. Whatever you have on your mind about the O'Mallock house, out with it and tell me a straight story."

"That's a fine idea," said the other with a sardonic chuckle. "You want me to give evidence against myself, eh? Look here, Weldon, I'm not such a fool."

"Don't say no to me," answered Weldon gently. "Think this thing over for ten seconds and change your mind about talking, or I'll break you up fine. Break you up so small, my boy, that people will be able to pass you in bright daylight and not know that you're a man."

He whirled the other around as he spoke, and let Slim have a look at his face. It was worth seeing, at this moment. Slim nodded.

"All right," he said with wonderful coolness and cheerfulness. "I'll talk turkey. Where do I begin? And how does it come that you're double crossing the little girl in the house, yonder!"

That remark, with all it suggested, brought a bull-like bellow from Weldon.

And Slim went on: "Well, well, I'll talk. Only, where do I begin?"

"With the beginning!"

"All right, all right. Keep yourself from falling apart, will you, and I'll talk, fast enough. The Negro woman got me."

"Aunt Maggie!"

"That's her. She said that her lady wanted a couple of good men. She came to me."

"How did she hear of you?" asked Weldon.

"I ain't unknown," said Slim, and nodded with some satisfaction.

"Go on, then."

"I went up to the house with a pal. A weak sister he turned out! Anyway, Aunt Maggie showed us into the house."

"How?"

"Through a neat little door in the wall of the place."

"Ah!" murmured Weldon, satisfied that he was hearing the truth. "And then?"

"We went up and seen Miss Helen. She wanted us—" He paused and frowned.

"Go on," urged Weldon.

"To do a job of body snatching!"

Weldon, stunned, said not a word.

"I felt the same way," said the other, "particular when I found out that it was the body of her old man that she wanted moved. But, anyway, the pay was good that she offered, and we took the body away."

"What did you do with it?"

"Put it in a buckboard and carted it clean across the hills to Busby."

"And there?"

"Turned it over to Doctor Marten."

"Go on! What next?"

"Came back to get paid, with Marten's note, saying that he'd received the body, and when we got to the house, you was waiting. I thought at first that you had been posted by the girl to beat us out of the payment, but afterward I remembered that she'd warned us particular not to be seen by you, or trouble would pop! She don't like you much, does she?" suggested Slim with a malicious grin.

Weldon turned a dark red.

"And after that," went on Slim, "we got away, my partner with his hand cut by your bullet. A pretty neat snap shot, I called that! Anyway, we faded through the wall and got up to her room. There she paid on the nail. We wouldn't go back the way that we came, because I had an idea that you'd be watching on the trail. So we went out through another room, and right out the rear door of the house, through the patio. Before I went, though, she promised me another hundred if I'd go back to Marten and bring her a note that Marten would have ready for her. I done that. I got the note—"

"What was in it?"

"I dunno. It was sealed."

Weldon hesitated.

"What were you paid?"

"A thousand cold for the first job. I got five hundred out of it. A hundred for this ride. And I'm dead fagged. There's the money. Count it for yourself!"

But Weldon did not count; he stared at the face of Slim and told himself that the man was honest. He had told the truth.

"Here's the wallet. Climb on your horse, and get out of this," advised Weldon.

He tossed back the wallet. He even threw the gun at the feet of Slim and watched the latter put away the weapon and climb into the saddle.

"They must pay you pretty big," said Slim, "to make you hang around to spy on a poor girl like her. What's she ever done to you, Weldon?"

With this parting comment, he jogged the tired pony again.

Helen O'Mallock! Helen the tender and the fair, to whom he had not dared reveal that the body was missing—it was she who had done the thing!

He went up the hill in grim silence. The sun rose as he came to the patio entrance and he saw Aunt Maggie crossing the court with a bucket of milk.

"Back again, are you?" she called to him. "Now, I never thought to see *your* face again!"

He passed her in grim silence and entered the house.

40. Almost!

The little brown-faced cat of Aunt Maggie met him on the stairs. It was a playful bit of a creature, not much more than a kitten, and because Weldon had given it some notice before, it now raced up the stairs with him, pretending to hide at every corner they passed.

So he came to the library and through it to his own room. There he paused, nerving himself. And he had to stare at the places on the floor where he had seen the spots of blood before he could compel himself onward. The little cat went before him and scratched at the door of the girl's room.

He remembered then that some people feel sure that a cat can sense coming evil, and it gave him a slight shudder, as he went to the door in turn and tapped against it.

He heard the low, husky voice of Helen O'Mallock answer, and he opened at once.

Aunt Maggie had built a cheerful fire on the hearth at the side of the chamber. But since there was little light from the sun, Helen lay with her head toward the windows and a book in her hands. Always a book in those thin hands, so fragile and bluish white!

He went to the side of the bed, and her pathetic smile was turned up to him.

"I knew you'd come back, in spite of the doctor!" she said.

"The doctor had his doubts, did he?" asked Weldon grimly.

She opened her eyes a little wider, observing his tone

203

rather than his words, and it seemed to Weldon that she turned paler still as she watched him, frightened and expectant.

"Helen," said he, "when I came here I expected we would play with the cards on the table, you and I. It seems that you haven't been doing that. Mind you, I don't want to be brutal or harsh. But I have an idea that I ought to know what was in the letter that you received from Marten!"

He watched like a hawk, to see the effect of shock; but apparently there was none whatever! She simply reached under her pillow and brought out a stiff white envelope.

"After you read it, will you please put it in the fire?"

He took out the fold of paper and read rapidly, then over again to make sure of everything:

My Dear Miss O'Mallock: It was some time before I allowed my scruples to be overcome by your persuasion. There is a legal penalty for such a thing as you proposed to me, and while I did not doubt that you had sincere reasons for the suggestion, still I delayed, as you know, for what may have seemed to you an unreasonable length of time.

However, the body was duly received from your two emissaries and I made the examination which you suggested, trying to free my mind from every preconception which you had given me. It was impossible, however, to doubt. The very slightest examination convinced me. The internal organs were wonderfully preserved. That alone would have been almost enough proof. But then I made a chemical analysis which finally convinced me and I have retained the specimens.

There is no question that your unfortunate father died of arsenic poisoning!

I am prepared to take the stand in any court and swear to that.

Further details would be unpleasant for you to hear and unnecessary for me to relate at present. I retain the body. You will tell me how it must be disposed of. In the meantime, you will realize that I am troubled by the possession of it, and trust that you will plan its removal quickly.

Faithfully yours,

O. H. Marten.

Weldon dropped the paper into the fire and watched it flame and die to a black cinder, and then to a white fluff which finally blew up the chimney with the draft.

"You suspected it for a long time?" he asked finally.

She nodded.

"And you couldn't tell me?"

"No."

"You suspected also who had given the poison?"

"I knew who had given it!"

"Who, then?"

She shook her head.

"I can't tell you that."

"Is it someone I have met since I came here?"

"Yes."

He bit his lip. There were many possibilities, of course. Before he could ask another question, there was a knock at the door, and Aunt Maggie came in with a steaming cup of milk.

"This'll rest you and quiet you," she told the girl. "Lemme see you drink it now before I leave!"

Helen O'Mallock took the cup and saucer and touched the cup to her lips.

"It's too hot, Aunt Maggie. I'll drink it when it cools."

"And what about this Mister Man?" said Aunt Maggie. "He gunna stay here with us again?"

"This is your busy time of day, Aunt Maggie," said the girl quietly. "You mustn't stay here to gossip. Of course Mr. Weldon stays with us!"

She looked at him with a question, however, as Aunt Maggie left the room.

"I don't know," muttered Weldon. "I stay if I'm needed. But you work without me. You leave me in the dark. And you seem perfectly able to get on without my help!"

She was perfectly calm, the husky voice barely audible as she answered:

"I haven't dared to tell a soul what was in my mind. I don't dare to tell everything, still. I can only beg you to stay with me this last day. It's life or death for me. It's life or death for the murderer of my father. And I'm helpless to do anything unless you stay. Could you stay? Blindly, still, doing what I beg you to do?"

205

The answer was past his lips without his own volition.

"I'll stay to the end," he said gravely. "This day is the last?"

She closed her eyes with a shudder, stroking the little brown-faced cat of Aunt Maggie, which had climbed onto the bed and now lay curled beside her, purring contentedly.

"They won't wait," said Helen O'Mallock. "They are clever, but they won't wait, I'm sure. There's too much at stake for them, and they'll strike quickly."

"At you?"

She did not answer him directly. "Look," she said. "It's starving, poor thing!"

For the kitten was sniffing eagerly at the milk in the cup.

Helen poured some into the saucer and the cat drank it greedily. Still more, and still the kitten lapped.

It sat back, at last, curling its tail around its forepaws, licking the white from its whiskers, and half closing its eyes in content.

Helen O'Mallock poised the cup at her lips.

"Is that all you have for breakfast?" asked Weldon, scowling.

"It's all I need and—"

The cat bounded down from the bed and ran across the floor to the door.

"It wants to get back to Aunt Maggie," said Helen. "Will you open the door for it?"

Weldon went at once to the door, but the kitten, with arched back and standing fur, struck and spat at him.

"What's wrong with it?" asked Weldon.

There was an almost human cry of pain from the cat. It pressed close against the door, its back arched high, its belly drawn up.

Helen O'Mallock turned in the bed.

"The milk!" she cried suddenly. "It's the milk she drank here!"

And Weldon, drops standing cold on his forehead, realized that that was true.

As for the brown-faced cat, its agony was not long. It whirled, as though seeking a place of escape. Then it leaped up to the nearest window sill, scratched at the

206

iron bars, and finally fell limp to the floor and remained still.

It was dead, with a slight white froth at its lips.

"The Negress!" said Weldon. "I warned you about her before, and now she—"

"No, no!" answered the girl in a voice suddenly harsh and ringing. "She has nothing to do with it. Aunt Maggie? She's the one honest soul in the entire world! But the others—they— Call Aunt Maggie immediately!" she went on.

Weldon went to the head of the stairs and called. Aunt Maggie's cheerful voice answered, and presently she came waddling up the stairs, heaving and panting.

"Up and down, up and down all day!" she complained. "I ain't one woman; I'm three in this here house, Mr. Weldon. Three women's work and one woman's pay! It ain't fair. I'm gunna stop it!"

And she went past him as he told her that her mistress wanted her at once.

Weldon himself followed and reached the door in time to hear the cry of Aunt Maggie.

The limp little body was in her big strong hands as he came into the room.

"I gave it some of the milk," said Helen simply.

"The milk!" cried Aunt Maggie, "Oh, Heaven forgive 'em!"

"Go to Doctor Watts," said Helen O'Mallock. "Go as fast as you can. Tell him that you gave me my morning milk, and that afterward I fell into a spasm and died, frothing at the mouth!"

Aunt Maggie stood at the door, stricken with wonder.

"And tell Doctor Watts that Mr. Weldon came back this morning early, and I sent him away again because I was angry that he left the house last night!"

41. The Yawning Gap

Aunt Maggie heard these strange directions with bulging eyes, and at the door, clinging to the jamb with both hands, she cried: "And if you is dead, what—"

"You saw me die, Aunt Maggie. I was in terrible convulsions. I sprang out of bed. I ran to the window and beat at the window bars. Then I dropped back and struggled once on the floor and was gone!"

"Oh, Heaven forgive me!" moaned Aunt Maggie, pressing a hand across her eyes.

"But I'm not dead, after all, Aunt Maggie," said Helen O'Mallock, smiling a little.

"No, no, honey, praise Heaven!" said the woman, somewhere between tears and laughter.

"You carried my dead body back to the bed and you stretched it out here, and folded my hands across my breast—and closed my eyes, Aunt Maggie. Do you hear?"

"I hear you, honey," said the Negress, blinking rapidly.

"And you've run all the way to the doctor's house. And you're barely able to talk. And when you talk you scream. And when you scream, you weep. Do you hear me, Aunt Maggie?"

Gradually a smile dawned upon the broad face of the Negress, and spread across it. It widened and grew richer. It shone like a light, and the bulging cheeks reduced her eyes to glittering points of light.

"I'm gone!" she said, and hurried from the room, and they heard her rapid footsteps pattering down the stairs, as though she really were prepared to run all the way to the house of good Doctor Watts.

Helen O'Mallock, in the meantime, looked after her with keen eyes, like the eyes of a man. Her face was tense, but resolute, and her head was carried high.

Weldon, almost past surprise, watched her carefully. He could hardly recognize in her the prostrate, relaxed invalid. Then she looked at him in turn, half frightened and half expectant.

He merely shook his head.

"You're an O'Mallock," he said quietly. "Now what am I to do?"

She half-closed her eyes. He could see one hand. It was tightly clenched.

"Within an hour," she said, "there will be a door opened in that wall."

She pointed to the space between the two windows.

"Men are coming in. One man surely; probably two; perhaps more. They are going to see that I am lying in this bed, with a sheet drawn over my head. The windows will be darkened so that they won't see any too clearly. But there will be enough light for them to do what they have come to do, I think.

"You will be standing within the curtain that hangs over the closed door to my father's room. Can you stand there now without being seen?"

Without a word, he went to the curtain and passed behind it. It touched the floor, securely covering his feet.

"There's not a bulge," said the girl. "And your feet are covered completely. Now, with your knife cut two or three small slits in the cloth so that you can look out and see everything that happens in the room.

He obeyed again, without pausing for questions.

"Can you see the wall, and the bed?" she asked.

"I can see practically everything in the room."

"Come out again, then."

"Very well."

He stood before her once more. He felt rather a fool, so completely in her hands, so utterly blindfolded as to the meaning of these maneuvers.

"You have your guns with you?"

"Yes."

"Let me see them."

Instantly they were in his hands.

And then she nodded. Her lips were compressed, and yet there was something like a stern smile fighting for control of them.

"Those who come will be utterly desperate men, ready to kill without warning," she said. "Shoot them down as you would shoot down so many dogs!"

"Without warning?"

"What warning did they give to me?" she asked. "They would have killed me this morning without more mercy than they would show to a beast!"

Weldon dropped his head in thought.

"I'll do what I can," he said calmly. "But I can't strike them without a warning. Even a rattler does that much. However, bullets will come fast on the heels of the first word! Will you trust me?"

"You're right, and I'm brutal and wrong!" said the girl. "Do as you wish."

Then she added:

"When did you last eat?"

"Yesterday. I forget when."

"Go down to the kitchen and make yourself a cup of coffee."

"I'd rather stay here."

"Do as I say. There's time for that. Drink a cup of coffee and eat some bread. Your hand will have to be steady afterward!"

He knew that she was right, and in the silence which he had clung to, he obeyed, leaving the room and going straight down to the kitchen.

There he found the fire humming, as Aunt Maggie had left it. He put on the coffeepot with a liberal supply of ground coffee and a small amount of water.

It boiled quickly, and sitting on the kitchen table, he looked out at the brightness of the day. For the sun was high now, the mountains gleamed with cheerful warmth. In the patio the bees were at work among the flowers, flying heavily from blossom to blossom, burdening themselves with pollen.

He munched the heel of a loaf and drank a first and a second cup of coffee, unhurried.

An hour, she had said. It did not occur to him that she could be wrong.

Then he lighted a cigarette, smoked it, and finally went up to her room.

As he opened the door, the dimness of the room perplexed him. She had drawn the shutters; there was only a twilight in the place. Good for many purposes, perhaps, but very bad for straight shooting.

Then he saw the girl half sitting up in the bed, the covers flung over the foot of it, and only a white sheet drawn up to her shoulders. Her eyes were dark and great with fear and excitement, and as he would have spoken, she put a finger upon her lips and made a flashing gesture of her arm toward his place of concealment.

He went to it with a gliding step, realizing that she must have heard some alarm in his absence.

Ensconced behind the curtain, he looked out. The peep-holes which he had cut and which had seemed all-sufficient while the room was flooded with the broad daylight now gave him only dim glimpses, but by the first glance he saw that the girl had lain down and drawn the sheet up over her head, and was now gradually working her hand down to her breast without disturbing the cloth.

That movement barely had ceased when he heard a faint sound like the clicking of a well-oiled lock, and into the room yawned a whole wide section of the wall between the windows, swinging open without a whisper of noise.

Weldon, guns in hand, set his teeth hard and cursed because his heart thundered.

A very tall fellow stood in the dark mouth of the entrance. There was something familiar about his look in spite of the dimness of the light, and even though over his face a black mask was fitted.

Like an executioner he came to the chamber!

Presently, beside him, came a smaller man, masked also. But his beard was freely seen; and he panted audibly with effort.

It was Doctor Henry Watts! The curve of his back, and his whole build, plainly identified him to Weldon!

Watts, the good, the gentle, the wise! Watts, the friend

of Francesca! Watts, the friend of delicate Helen O'Mallock as well!

It was a shock against which Weldon had to steady himself resolutely.

"Go take a look at her and pronounce her dead," said the big man in a very quiet voice.

"There's no need," said Watts. "A quarter of what she took this morning would have killed three people."

"I tell you," said the other, "I want to make sure of her before we move."

"Do it yourself, then," said Watts with a touch of irritation. "Examine her, if you wish. But, Heaven forgive me if I can look at her face again."

"The clever little panther," said the big man. "She had even you half under her thumb—you old fool!"

"Perhaps I'm a fool. She trusted me, as you know."

"Trusted you? Why did she have the body dug up, then?"

"That? I don't know. An idea that Weldon, darn his meddling, must have put into her head! Ah, man, it's his luck that we haven't him here today."

"The fool left, eh? She had tangled his brain in a fog yesterday. Too clever, after all! A little too clever! But what a woman! I'm going to have one glance at her!"

He crossed to the bed, and behind the curtain, Weldon raised his hand and leveled the revolver. He saw the big fellow draw back the sheet. Almost instantly he replaced it.

"I thought I was past shudders, Watts," said he. "But she's like a white statue of a child! So cold, poor girl! Tush! I'll be sentimental! But there was a woman!"

"To what room do we go?" asked Watts anxiously.

"Are you funking it?"

"No, no. Only I want a little haste. I—I can't hold out forever. What if Weldon should make up his mind to come back?"

"As for Weldon, I'll handle that young man when I meet him. As for the room—this is the place."

"This place?"

"This is it."

The big fellow turned as he spoke to a spot on the wall opposite the foot of the bed.

"Are you sure?" asked the doctor.

"Didn't I help the old general to hide his money in the two places?"

"Ah, yes," said Henry Watts. "And how could he have trusted you so implicitly?"

"He had his weak places. He was growing old. He liked to feel that he had the ability to pick out men and make them faithful."

"He knew you were wanted for murder even at the time."

"That was what pleased him all the more. That he could trust me, even though I had murdered others. And he was right, after all. I had no share in the killing."

"You?" stammered Henry Watts in anger. "It was you who put the first thought in my mind—"

"You would have had the same thought before long, however. Once a poisoner, always a poisoner. Ah—here we are!"

There was an audible creaking, and a stone fell out from the wall, and sagged on a hinge. The big man reached into the aperture and drew out a considerable bundle, wrapped in cloth.

He opened the cloth. The doctor crowded near.

"Is it right?" gasped Henry Watts. "Is it right?"

"Of course it's right," said the big man. "There's more than four hundred thousand in this little parcel. Do you wonder that I was willing to pay fifty thousand to get back across the border! And she's so keen to help me across! I must give you the credit for that, though. Fifty for four hundred. Good odds, I'd call that!"

Dickinson, then! Aye, no other man had quite such shoulders, such a look of the tiger about him!

"Not quite eight to one," said the doctor in an ugly voice, his breath drawn in with a sort of gasp of greed and hunger. "I suppose half of that goes to me, as before?"

"To my little Henry? To my dear old friend, who has stayed so close to the nest to hatch this egg for us?" said Dickinson. "Of course you have to have a share! As great a share as any man could have of anything. And here it is for you, Henry, with all my heart behind it!"

His movement was so sudden and so totally unexpected that Weldon saw only a flash.

The doctor stepped back against the wall, his hands clutching his breast. The flash gleamed again, and Weldon distinctly heard the thud of the hand driven home as the blade of the knife was buried deep in the body of Doctor Henry Watts.

The doctor sagged to his knees, pawed oddly at the air as though he were drowning and trying to get to the surface of water. Then he collapsed on his face.

He had not made a sound.

Dickinson turned the body on its back, the while wiping his knife on the doctor's coat, and then fumbled at the heart of the fallen man.

And at that moment Weldon pushed the curtain aside and walked stealthily forward across the room, past the yawning gap of the open door in the wall.

42. Fairly Beaten

"So!" said Dickinson, and rose to his feet. "And there's the end of a very wise man. He also was bound to have a little share of trust!"

And he laughed. An incredible sound in the ears of Weldon. That laughter had not yet ended on Dickinson's lips when he whirled as a dancer spins. The least creak on the floor had reached his ears—or the slightest whisper of moving cloth. He whirled, and as he whirled, he cast his knife at Weldon. It was a ponderous bowie, and the loaded handle struck Weldon fairly between the eyes.

He fired with both guns at the same instant, but even

as he fired, he knew that he had missed. Then a human avalanche struck him and crushed him to the floor.

They spun over and over, stars shooting and blossoming like red flowers before the eyes of Weldon, as he vaguely fumbled at the other.

From lumber camps to range fires, he had closed man to man with the strongest, but never had he felt such a body as this, supple and incredibly hard like steel cable.

The guns were gone from his hands. They had fallen as he fell. Now, in their rolling course, the two men crashed against the wall, Weldon on the inside, receiving the full shock.

And yet he was not stunned by it. He felt blood spring hot from the back of his head. Blood, too, ran down across his eyes, but his head was clear once more and his strength was his own.

A strangle hold was clamped across his throat. He reached up and broke it as if it had been a straw. Bending his head into the hollow of Dickinson's shoulder, he laid his arms about the other and exerted all his might. Aye, almost for the first time he used his full power, and felt the back of the big man arch out against the restraint. Dickinson himself was fumbling to gain that strangle hold again, and the tips of his fingers tore at the throat of Weldon like iron hooks.

But a shudder was beginning in the body of the criminal. There was a gasping curse, and he collapsed against Weldon. Another twist, and Weldon was on top. A fist of iron struck at him; like iron it glanced across his head, half stunning him. What had been the black mask of Dickinson became a large blur, and for the center of that blur Weldon struck once, and felt his knuckles grind against flesh, and through flesh to the bone. He struck again with terrific power. Dickinson lay limp as a weed.

So, his head clearing again, Weldon turned that great sack of a body upon its face and gathered the wrists in the small of the back. And wiping the blood from his face, he looked up.

She stood beside him, a ghostly form in white, with the glitter of a poised revolver in her hand. She had been there how long? Ready to strike if there were a need, but coldly judicial as a man.

215

She whirled away now and came again with a length of curtain cord. With that Weldon secured his man—hand and foot. He lifted the burden of Dickinson into a chair. Helen O'Mallock had opened the shutters of the room and the bright daylight flooded in, as Dickinson opened his eyes.

Weldon tore the mask from the face. A gash beneath the eye and a bruise along the jaw told where the two blows had gone home.

But, in spite of those stunning strokes, Dickinson's mind was clear again.

"The best man fights once too often," he said calmly. "You win, my dear girl. That fool of a Watts—I should have known that his mixture couldn't be trusted."

"Not this time," said the girl quietly. "It took a life, but by the grace of chance, it was not my life." She added: "But still you would have lost. He was still here, waiting for you!"

Dickinson turned a blazing eye on Weldon. Gradually the fire died away from his glance.

"Fairly beaten!" he said at last. "And I'll fairly hang. But it took a man to break me down—and a woman. The first two of either breed that I've met in my trip around the world!"

43. If Ever You Grow Tired

Dogget brought up the sheriff.

Weldon, his face swollen and bandaged, watched big Jim Dickinson led away. Aunt Maggie had done that for him, muttering and mumbling with horror and excitement.

The body of Henry Watts was gone likewise. And Weldon sent the Negress to her mistress.

"I want to see her for five minutes," said Weldon.

So Aunt Maggie left him and Helen O'Mallock came in hastily.

There was color in her face. Her eyes were clear and bright. She stood at the door, hesitant, expectant, and smiled at him.

But Weldon looked at her vaguely.

"Still you don't see?" said she.

He shook his head.

"I'm not thinking very clearly," he said. "But I wanted to tell you that as soon as you can conveniently let me go, I have another thing to do."

"As hard a thing as what you've done here?"

"As hard? A thousand times harder!"

He thought of Francesca Laguarda and laughed bitterly.

"A thousand times harder," he repeated. "I have to find a woman's body. I have to find her soul, too—if there is one."

"There is a reward waiting for you," said Helen O'Mallock.

His mind wandered.

"All the time you weren't an invalid?" he said. "It was only play acting?"

"Only play acting. And now the reward—"

He made an impatient gesture.

"I've had my monthly pay. I want nothing else. Only to be free as soon as you can let me go. I don't want to be rude," he added heavily. "I'll stay here as long as you're afraid to be in the house without a man—"

"No, no," said Helen O'Mallock. "I think I understand what you mean. And you're free as the wind, only—only—"

She looked helplessly at him.

"I want you to take a note with you, if you will," said she.

"I? Gladly, of course."

Then, he added, with an effort at lightness:

"Is it a testimonial?"

"Ah, no," said she. "It's an appeal!"

He saw her sit down before him at the library table.

217

She thought for an instant, and then her pen traced rapidly across the paper:

I am in desperate need—

She could write no more.

Then a great cry came rushing from the throat of Weldon. He caught the paper away and stared at it.

The girl stood up, very white indeed, and faced him.

"I'm trying to think," said Weldon thickly. "I'm trying to think how I—"

"See!" said Helen O'Mallock.

She raised her hands to her head, and fumbled a moment. Then the great mass of shining, golden hair came away and left her head short-cropped. She looked suddenly younger, like a boy, of a wonderful and delicate beauty.

"And then a black wig," she said.

He put out his big hands and laid them on her shoulders; and she, in turn, laid her hands upon his.

"And the voice, too!" said Weldon.

"Oh, that was a shameful sham. There are things you eat that irritate the throat a little and make a horrible-sounding, dry cough—"

He drew her to the window.

With the palm of his hand he covered the short-cropped soft hair—and there was the face of dark Francesca Laguarda, beautiful and wild.

"Francesca!" said Weldon.

"Helen," she corrected.

"Never," said Weldon, "to me!"

Even knowing what he knew now, it still was hard for Weldon to follow the course of events, until she took him through the whole strange history, step by step.

There had been the death of her father, not terribly sudden, but odd in many circumstances, so that it haunted her. And there had been the original suggestion made by Doctor Henry Watts that perhaps the absence of money from the house indicated a theft. That, and the open wall pocket in the cellar.

The disappearance of Dickinson had been a most suspicious circumstance, in a way, though explainable in many lights. For the hounds of the law had been hard on his traces, and he had perhaps been driven away by the fear of them, and the danger that not even the house of the general might be a secure retreat for him.

As for the doctor, his conduct was easily explained. It was truly for his health that he had come from the East to the West. Fear of throat trouble had driven him. Throat trouble consisting of a hempen noose around the neck! For he had his record in another State! So he had come here and found a haven with the open-handed general and put up a cottage on the general's land.

But, as the years drifted, the old passion had come back on him. Not for nothing had he made to Weldon his speech in admiration of the old poisoners! Then, Dickinson came, and put the thought strongly in his mind. Dickinson himself had intimate knowledge of every architectural secret in the house. He knew the two wall pockets. He could guess that when the general sold the majority of his property, he would be placing the cash in those hiding places, forgetful that a secret known to two has no value.

So the worthy doctor had poisoned his friend and benefactor, and the same night of the death, he and Dickinson had visited the cellar. There they looted one portion of the general's wealth. But the other portion was in the girl's own room. They would wait till the morrow for that. Before the morrow, Dickinson had fled South for his life, only promising the doctor that he would return when he could to get the remainder of the spoil.

The worthy doctor then, after a year, received a covert message from Dickinson that he was held for high ransom—held openly!—by the arch scoundrel of San Trinidad—Cabrero.

The doctor was in a dreadful quandary.

He thought at once of appealing to Jorram, the smuggler, of whom he knew by chance. But then the doctor was tormented, apparently, by doubts. He went to Helen O'Mallock and confided in her. The thief who had rifled the wealth of her father was in San Trinidad. His name was Dickinson. He was trying to get to this side of the border. Once here, he would of course come back to the house to complete its plundering.

How could they keep tab upon his movements?

The girl herself made the answering suggestion: She had done more than her share in school theatricals. Her veins were full of the wild O'Mallock blood. What if she stepped into a new rôle, joined the ranks of the smugglers, became aware of all their plans?

Jorram surely would sooner or later attempt to rescue Dickinson. When he did it, she would know. And then she and the doctor would strive to arrange a trap in which to catch the thief on his return!

That was all her motive as she entered the affair. She had spent her savings on one great venture—the long, gray car, which she stored at the house of the doctor. Then, from that place it was easy to return to her house, take off the black wig, remove the darkening from her brows, place on her head the wig made of her own hair.

Only one person need be let into the secret partially— that was Aunt Maggie.

But then the tale became more dangerous and complicated. Twice, men were found in the house. The later explanation of this was simple. Cabrero had learned some hint from Dickinson, and he had sent on a pair of his rogues at odd times to examine the house. The girl, frightened, wanted a fighting man to protect her. The doctor, baffled, agreed. And so Weldon was hired. And his coming brought the place security. Too much security to suit the doctor.

But still he was hounded by the fear that when Dickinson returned, he would not play fair, but would make a private visit to the house. In fact, all that finally drove Dickinson directly to him was the belief of the master criminal that it would be necessary to murder the girl before looting her room. And therefore the doctor had given the cook a tablet to drop into the hot milk of the morning's drink.

So that story was told. Not all at once, but in many installments, of which the last ended when Weldon and his wife stood on the prow of a liner, listening to the crashing of the bow wave, roaring, dying away, and roaring again.

"But why was it necessary for you to be an invalid?" he asked her.

220

"How else was I to stay awake all night on smuggling raids, and then stay in bed most of the day?" she asked him. "Particularly after you came to mount guard!"

"And every day you slept there, knowing that there was a hole in the wall through which they might come?"

"I had a bell which would bring you; and if you came, I was not afraid of an army."

"And one more thing—"

"Yes?"

"Is Francesca really dead or will she come to life again?"

She was silent for a long time. He almost thought that she had not heard him.

Said she, at last: "If you ever grow tired of me. Then —perhaps—"

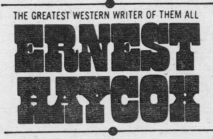